INTO VUSHAAR

ROBERT M. KERNS

KNIGHTSFALL PRESS

Published by Knightsfall Press
PO Box 280
Mineral Wells, WV 26150
https://www.knightsfallpress.com

ABOUT THIS BOOK

Help his friend go home.

Just because Gavin's goal is simple, doesn't mean it's easy!

His friend's home is Vushaar, the world's oldest monarchy and a land fractured by civil war. Slaver parties roam the countryside at will, claiming any they desire for their vile trade, and a great army lays siege to the capital.

Many question if Vushaar will survive, so what does that mean for Gavin and his friends?

Ties of friendship from two directions compel Gavin to enter this war-torn land, but will he succeed in returning his friend home safe and sound?

Read Now to find out!

CHAPTER 1

The Vischaene River rocked the ferry's hull against the algae- and moss-covered stones of the quay. The ferry's stop was so abrupt, a few travelers lost their footing. Gavin, however, flexed his legs and moved with the ferry's motion, catching Kiri before she could begin her own close-up inspection of the deck.

Down through the years, a small settlement grew up around the eastern ferry landing, but an inn with stables and a general store were the extent of its day-to-day highlights. The primary population for the settlement was the ferry-masters' families and the inn's staff, along with any travelers who arrived after the ferry shut down for the night.

The general store looked much like any storefront Gavin had seen in the city. Large windows allowed passers-by to examine the shop's goods, while the building's aura of Conjuration made Gavin suspect the merchant didn't rely on oil lamps. The shop's windows were clean enough for Gavin to see two small children at the shelves of candy jars, and he smiled as he watched the older merchant dole out some of the treasured goods. As Gavin watched the children receive their treasure, a memory of his daughter floated to the forefront of his mind, and he smiled. The memory brought with it an almost overwhelming urge to pull his daughter into a big hug and tell her how special she was, and Gavin took a deep breath, letting it out as a slow shuddering sigh and turning away from the store.

The inn was a three-story structure and looked to be in rather good repair, fresh tiles on the roof and well-tended flowers in planters on either side of the door. A plaque hung from an iron rod attached to the portico overhanging the door: The Travelers' Rest.

"Do we have any reason to stop?" Gavin asked, his eyes meeting each of his companions in turn.

"I don't think so," Declan said. "Hakamri did us proud. I doubt we need anything they'd have here."

"Then, let's press on," Gavin said.

* * *

NEAR THE RIVER, smooth grasslands abounded. As they traveled away from the river, though, the grasslands transitioned to the rolling fields and minor hills that would give way to the Godswall Mountains looming in the distance. It was a pleasant day for travel, with a slight breeze blowing inland from the Inner Sea, carrying with it a hint of the salty sea air.

Within minutes of leaving the small settlement surrounding the ferry landing, Declan handed his reins to Braden—who rode just ahead of him and to his left—and retrieved his lute. Soon thereafter, they traveled to the accompaniment of a pleasant melody Declan strummed and picked out of his instrument.

"Gavin," Mariana asked as she nudged her horse to ride to the left of Gavin's Jasmine, "I'd like to ask you something."

Gavin chuckled. "Mariana, ask away. You don't need to give me fair warning; we're all friends here."

"It strikes me as a little odd we're going to Vushaar overland. There's just a narrow strip of land that is Tel's territory to the Vushaari border, and it's almost hit-or-miss whether the dracons respect it. Besides, I'd think a ship would be faster."

"I considered a ship, Mariana, but out there on the ocean, we have nowhere to go. We have no way to maneuver if the need arises.

I feel safer—even with the threat of the dracons—having land where I can run, ambush, or whatever we need to do. I feel traveling by land gives us options, whereas sea travel takes away options."

"And you didn't want to force a ship on Kiri," Mariana said, her voice barely above a whisper as she leaned close to Gavin.

Gavin glanced over his shoulder to where Lillian and Kiri rode side by side, talking and laughing, and he smiled. Then, he turned back to Mariana and shook his head, saying, "No...I couldn't force that on her. I suppose I should've given her the choice, but I was afraid she'd say yes when she didn't want to, thinking it's what I wanted."

Just then, the group crested a small knoll, and the sight in the small valley below caused Gavin to rein in Jasmine to a halt, as he lifted his hand to signal the same. Five people on horses clustered around two others—also mounted. The two people who were the center of attention, though, appeared to have their hands tied behind their backs, and Gavin's eyes were just good enough to make out ropes running down from overhead branches to their necks.

"This doesn't look good," Gavin said.

"Look at their elbows," Mariana said. "Those strips of cloth fluttering in the wind are the king's colors. Those men feel they're acting with the full knowledge and consent of the King of Tel."

"Not today," Gavin said, his voice slipping into the slightly deeper, resolute tone those present associated with 'Kirloth.'

Gavin leaned forward and brushed the side of Jasmine's neck with his hand, saying, "Let's go, girl." He didn't even nudge Jasmine with his heels; the mare took off at a spirited trot that soon became a canter.

Mariana and Lillian looked at one another for a moment before they and Kiri nudged their mounts with their heels. Soon, they were cantering in Gavin's wake, with Braden, Wynn, and Declan close behind. The pack-mules could wait for them at the crest of the knoll, and it wasn't long before they were a bit off the path grazing in the untamed grass.

· · ·

"WHAT SEEMS to be the trouble here?" Gavin said as he arrived at the edge of the people gathered around the tree. He was now close enough to see the two in the center were elves, one male and one female.

"The only trouble here is you and yours coming in on our bounty," the man closest Gavin said, turning to face the new arrivals. "We caught these ourselves fair and square."

"Bounty?" Gavin asked. "What bounty?"

"What rock have you been under, boy? The king offers a bounty in gold for every elf ear found in Tel. Now, shove off; these two are ours."

"About that…" Gavin said, "…you see, I don't approve of the King's new idea for revenue. There'll be no bounty here, today."

"And just who do you think you are to tell us what to do? We have more fighters than you."

Gavin focused his mind on his intent and invoked a Word of Transmutation, "*Rhyskaal*."

The slight tightening around his eyes and the sudden tension in his jaw was the only indication of the pain he suppressed. The ropes around the elves' necks and wrists fell away as they turned to dust. Both elves' eyes widened just a bit as they gazed at Gavin.

"You've got yerself a pair, haven't you? We'll kill you for this," one man said, his voice almost a snarl. He and his fellows all rounded on Gavin and his people, who were now in a rough line stretching out behind Gavin.

"Oh…forgive me," Gavin said, reaching into the neck of his tunic. "It appears I failed to introduce myself."

Gavin grasped a silver chain and withdrew a wizard's medallion. He released the chain and allowed the medallion to fall against his sternum. The silver wizard's medallion, the Glyph of Kirloth in its recessed center, gleamed in the late afternoon sun.

The five men paled almost as one, their eyes locked on the glyph. Beads of sweat broke out on their foreheads, and they gripped their reins so tightly their knuckles turned white.

"Now, what of the King's bounty?" Gavin asked, looking the center man right in his eyes.

The man's jaw worked as if he were about to speak, but no sound came. At last, he took a deep, shuddering breath and said, "W-w-what b-b-bounty?"

"That's right," Gavin said, nodding his head in a soft approval. "Now, get out of here."

"Thank you, milord," the man said, his voice almost a whimper. He motioned to his fellows as he nudged his horse into motion. Soon, those five crested a knoll to the north and were gone.

Once the men were out of sight, Gavin lifted his medallion and returned it to its place inside his tunic once more, before looking to the elves. They wore traveling clothes much like those of Gavin and his friends, except the coloring of theirs more closely matched the colors of forested terrain. Both elves' eyes were a vibrant green, with the female's hair being the golden color of pure sunlight, and the male elf's hair a dark, earthy brown.

"Are you well? Do you need anything?" Gavin asked.

The elves looked to one another before the female said, "We are grateful for your intervention. They came upon us while we slept and had us bound before we could defend ourselves."

"It's not common for elves to travel this far south, given relations between our two peoples," Lillian said.

"We're not here by choice," the male elf said, his voice harsh.

"Sarres," the female elf said, her tone reproving, "you should be more respectful of Grandmother."

Gavin felt the situation was about to become awkward, so he bowed once from his saddle, saying, "I'm Gavin Cross. This is Kiri to my right, Declan deHavand to my left. Arrayed out behind me are my apprentices: Lillian, Mariana, Braden, and Wynn."

The female elf scanned the group with her eyes before returning her gaze to Gavin. "And so does history repeat itself. Kirloth and his Apprentices walk upon the earth once more."

Gavin heard the subtle emphasis she placed on 'Apprentices' and said, "I never-"

"Gavin, my brother is Kantar, Magister of Tutation, and I am Elayna, *T'Eleren* of Xanta. Kantar…mentioned…you and your fellows in a recent letter. My associate is Sarres; he is what you would call a Sentinel of Nature."

Gavin heard a slight gasp from his apprentices behind him, and it seemed apparent he once again had encountered something he should have known.

"From the reaction of my friends, I gather there is something surprising about a Sentinel of Nature being this far from home."

Elayna smiled. "Yes. The Sentinels defend the High Forest and maintain the border between Tel and our lands, but they are sworn to Xanta's service first above all. When Grandmother commands one to travel, he or she travels."

"Grandmother?" Gavin asked.

"Xanta was already a mother at the time the Godswar began, and my siblings and I are direct descendants of Her."

"I see. Are you permitted to discuss where Xanta has commanded you to travel?"

Elayna and Sarres looked to one another before Elayna turned back to Gavin, saying, "We head for the Vushaari capital. My sister is the ambassador to King Terris's court. May I ask if you are headed south as well?"

Gavin nodded. "We are. I too have business in the Vushaari capital."

"May we travel with you, at least as far as the Vushaari border?" Elayna asked. "I don't know how well-traveled these parts are, and I never thought we'd encounter partisans of the king so close to the dracon lands."

Gavin took a deep breath and released it as a sigh. "Very well. Welcome aboard. Braden, Wynn…would you mind retrieving our pack-mules? We're losing daylight."

* * *

IT WAS EARLY EVENING. The sun hadn't set yet, but at most, an hour or two of daylight remained.

"There's a copse of trees that looks like a good campsite," Gavin said, pointing off to the right of the direction they rode. "What does everyone think?"

Lillian, Kiri, Braden, and Wynn remained silent.

"It should be adequate," Sarres said.

Declan smiled, saying, "I've spent many a night in a cluster of trees like that."

A CLEARING MADE up the center of the copse, and at the center of the clearing, they found a firepit, buried in decaying leaves and pine needles.

Declan shifted his gaze from the long-unused firepit to the surrounding trees, his expression speculative as he said, "I'd say this is a waystation. It's the perfect spot, too. We're about a day's ride from the river, and before the dracons withdrew from the old alliance, that track we've been following was a major trade route."

"It will make a good camp for the night, but we should still post a watch," Sarres said. "I have no desire to be awoken by a blade to my neck again."

"Oh, I don't think we'll have to worry about that," Gavin said, looking up from where he sat on a nearby felled log with a tome in his hands. "Declan, can you find me enough stones the size of your fist to ring the firepit and…one, two, three…nine stones small enough to fit in the palm of Kiri's hand?"

Sarres frowned, confusion clear across his entire expression. He started to speak, but Declan forestalled that by clapping him on the shoulder.

"Come on," Declan said. "There's no guarantee he'd answer, and what's worse, he just might. We'll find out soon enough."

A short time later, Declan and Sarres returned with the stones Gavin requested.

Gavin looked up from where he was scratching something in the topsoil with a sharpened stick and smiled, saying, "Ah, excellent! Thank you both very much! Please, make a ring around the firepit with the big stones, and bring the smaller palm stones to me."

Gavin closed the tome he'd been referencing and grabbed a small pebble with just a hint of an edge from the ground. He stood and walked over to the firepit and, once the ring of stones was complete, flopped down on the ground. He used the pebble to scratch a marking into the stone in front of him before shifting to the stone to his right and scratching a different marking into it. Gavin proceeded around the ring of stones until he was back where he started. Then, he hopped to his feet and retrieved the nine palm stones Sarres had handed him.

"Okay…everyone, please, gather around," Gavin said, his voice raised just a bit. Soon, everyone was standing around Gavin. "Excellent. Now, I will stand in the firepit's center, and I want everyone to stand where I direct, please."

Gavin hopped inside the ring and steadied himself on the uneven surface of old coals, decaying leaves, and pine needles that made up the firepit.

"Now, Lillian, stand right there, please, and hold this stone in the palm of your right hand. Kiri, stand to her left and hold this stone." Gavin worked his way through the entire group until everyone stood around the firepit and held a stone. "Good…excellent. Okay. The traditional way to create a wardstone keyed to a specific person is to use some of that person's blood; Marcus did that when he created the key to our suite for Kiri. I've decided to try something a little different, mainly because I'd rather not ask everyone to prick their thumbs. The *slight* downside to this is that, whether or not it works, it will hurt a bit…and it'll hurt worse for us wizards. Does anyone want to back out and do this the old-fashioned way?"

Everyone looked at one another, but no one moved to back away.

"Very well," Gavin said. "Everyone, lean as close as you need to touch me with your left hands, but take care to keep your feet outside the ring of stones."

"What happens if we stand inside the ring of stones with you?" Sarres asked.

Gavin frowned and remained silent for several moments before saying, "Well…I don't really know but probably nothing good."

The elves shared a glance but reached out with their left hands all the same.

Once everyone was touching him, Gavin closed his eyes and pushed everything from his mind except a clear picture of the effect he desired to achieve. He took a deep breath and invoked a composite effect, blending Words of Tutation, Interation, and Evocation into one multi-syllable Word, "*Sykhurhos-Naekhos-Phaethys.*"

The resonance of Gavin's power slammed into his apprentices like the concussion of an intense thunderclap right above one's head...but magnified a thousand-fold. It drove the breath from their lungs, and they staggered but remained standing. For several moments, nothing seemed to happen, and everyone relaxed.

Kaleidoscopic light burst forth from each stone in the ring as bands of power as thick as a weightlifter's thigh arced from Gavin's torso to the new radiance. With the radiance came pain, as every wizard present felt like every nerve was dipped in boiling acid. The commoners present were not immune, though their pain was a minute fraction of the intensity the wizards endured.

All at once and with no warning whatsoever, the radiance vanished as if it never was. Gavin—and his apprentices—collapsed to their knees, gasping and soaked in sweat. Blood trickled out of Gavin's right nostril and his left ear.

"What by all that's holy did you do?" Sarres said, his voice a gasping snarl.

"I warded the camp," Gavin said. "You don't need to set a watch; only those possessing wardstones can pass through the ward's perimeter without dying. We're also protected from the elements and a few other things. Look at each stone in the ring; you'll be able to see the various protections by the runes on each rock."

"Are we going to go through that *every* time we make camp?" Sarres asked, still almost glaring at Gavin.

Gavin shook his head. "No. From here on, we make the ring of stones and speak a command word to activate the ward. What we just did was embed the protections into each stone and link the ring to draw power from the ambient magic. Well, that and establish your wardstones."

Gavin pushed himself to his feet and stepped outside the ring of stones. He ambled over to the felled tree that had served as his seat not too long ago, returned the tome he'd been reading to his satchel, and eased himself down to sit on the ground with his back resting against the tree trunk. Within moments, he was asleep.

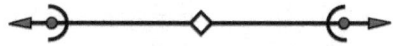

CHAPTER 2

The capital city of Vushaar lay nestled against the base of the Sarnath Hills. It started as a mining town that over decades grew into a city, the realm taking its name from that long-forgotten settlement. Little remained of the mining town, and unlike its structured counterpart to the north, Vushaar's capital expanded through organic growth. Out of historical significance, the original city walls—which were over seven thousand years old—remained and were well-maintained; the succeeding city walls were torn down as each new wall was built for the city.

The royal compound sat in the heart of the Old City, as residents referred to the portion of the city inside the original city walls. The compound consisted of a plaza just inside the gate, with a fountain to the east and a medium-sized park to the west. South of the plaza stood the royal palace. The royal palace served as both residence for the royal family, barracks for the Cavaliers assigned to security, and the offices and meeting rooms necessary for the government to function. A tower-like keep rising off the western side of the palace served as the actual royal residence, containing a private library, several studies and bedrooms, a dining hall for state functions, and a private dining room for the royal family.

. . .

TERRIS MURAN STOOD at the north-facing window of his preferred study, gazing out over the city below. A man of average height and medium build, Terris's deep brown—almost black—hair was shot with gray and white strands, as was his well-groomed beard and goatee. The window was his favorite place to look at the city his family had called home for millennia.

The view was marred by the large encampment north of the city, the primary siege camp of Sclaros Ivarson's army. Soldiers and slaves toiled long into twilight building fortifications, siege engines, and lines of both contravallation and circumvallation. Terris wasn't the military authority his remaining generals were, but he estimated it would be less than a month before the siege was established.

"Your Majesty, the serving staff informs me you haven't eaten since this morning," a voice worn with age said from over Terris's shoulder.

Terris recognized the voice and turned to face Q'Orval deBentak, his chief of staff. Q'Orval had served the Muran line since he was a boy, starting off in the royal stables and working his way up to be the King's right hand.

"Q'Orval, the siege is well and truly starting. How are the city's granaries? Did we get them topped off in time?"

Q'Orval nodded. "Yes, Your Majesty. The city is well supplied to survive a siege."

"Did Roth and his people get out of the city? I'm not about to pay for the return of my daughter, even if she's the only child I have left after losing Kiri."

"Yes, Your Majesty. Roth and his troublemakers left the city by the south gate earlier this morning. The Cavaliers are still investigating how Kaila was abducted from the palace; as you know, sire, they would've sworn it was secure. While we're discussing family, sire…"

"I know, Q'Orval; I know. The Privy Council wants me to name Kaila as the Crown Princess…or take another wife. I'm not ready to do either just yet, since we've no idea how this rebellion will end.

Ideally, I'll still have the throne, but we don't know that." Silence descended on the study for several moments before Terris sighed and looked away. "I'm not sure that Kiri ever forgave me for that indiscretion with Callie."

Q'Orval took the few steps necessary to bring him within arms' reach of the man he'd watched grow into being one of the finest kings of the Muran line. He placed his hands on Terris's shoulders and forced Terris to face him.

"Terris, it wasn't an indiscretion, and Kiri was too young at the time to understand."

"I miss her so much, Q'Orval," Terris said, his voice soft. "I should never have sent her away to Tel."

"We all miss Kiri, Terris. She was such a kind and happy soul; she enriched all those around her."

Silence descended once more and remained until it almost became awkward. Terris shook himself and took a deep breath, saying, "Have you eaten yet?"

"No, sire."

"Care to dine with me?"

Q'Orval smiled. "Of course, sire."

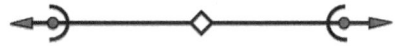

CHAPTER 3

They were eight days out of Tel Mivar, traveling along the old trade route between Tel and the dracons, and they reached the end of the road…literally. A placard stood in the center of where the road stopped.

"'Mivar Province ends here. Travel farther at thine own peril,'" Gavin said, reading the placard. "Well, now…that's encouraging, isn't it?"

"We are near the border between Tel and dracon territory," Lillian said. "In truth, the border is an hour or so farther on, given the speed we've maintained, but having logging parties and hunting camps any more eastward simply invites attacks. The last few dozen years, there hasn't been enough income from the area to warrant the risk of being even this close."

Gavin frowned. "From everything I've read, the dracons are members of the old alliance. Why would they attack?"

"When the royal line resumed civil authority over Tel," Mariana said, "the dracons withdrew from the world and closed their borders to everyone. They gave no explanation or even waved goodbye as they left. Since then, this region of Mivar Province has been something of a neutral no-man's-land, just to keep the peace."

. . .

Five hours later, the light was fading early, thanks to a stormfront blowing in off the Inner Sea to the west. Rather than try to push on in the coming storm, they chose a campsite on the bank of a small stream running out of the Godswall Mountains to feed a meager amount of water to the Inner Sea. By now, the ritual of setting up camp was second nature, and within no more than a half-hour, the camp was stocked, the wards up, and everyone was eating an early dinner. Once the dinner was over, the wizards moved off to one side to continue their nightly lessons while Elayna, Sarres, Kiri, and Declan conversed between themselves.

The study session lasted an hour at most, but that was more than sufficient for the four 'students.' Gavin had a way of packing more learning into an hour than most instructors at the College could manage in a month. After the session, they re-joined their comrades around the fire.

"What do you guys make of the light show off to the west?" Gavin asked as he sat on a felled log beside Declan.

Everyone turned to look that way, but the humans saw only dark storm clouds and lightning. The elves frowned.

"It looks like one of the Inner Sea's more vicious storms," Elayna said. "I can see the turbulent waves from here."

"What do we need to do to prepare for it reaching us?" Kiri asked, her manner tense and her expression worried.

Everyone turned to Gavin, who shrugged and said, "It would take a significant storm to get through the wards. We'll be dry throughout the night, and as long as we keep the fire fueled, we'll be warm as well."

Sounds of not so distant thunder reached the camp. Gavin could see Kiri tense with each rumble. Gavin sat watching the last rays of sunlight fade into twilight, but it was far from dark. Lightning strikes lit up the night almost bright as day.

Everyone else headed to their bedrolls and tents, but Kiri sat rigid on the felled log she had occupied all evening. Wherever she was in her mind, Kiri was not the woman Gavin had come to know. As Gavin looked at her, he saw only a woman grappling with a very basic fear...or at least something terrible that the storms brought to mind...and was vulnerable for it.

Gavin stood and walked across the camp to sit beside Kiri, barely a foot from her on the same log; she didn't seem to register his presence. He gave her a few moments, but when Kiri remained absorbed in whatever she was reliving, Gavin leaned close.

"You look like you could use a friend," Gavin said.

Gavin's voice pulled Kiri out of whatever dark place she was experiencing, and she turned her head toward him. Gavin knew in that instant she was vulnerable. In her eyes, he saw none of the strength, the poise, the resolve he had come to associate with Kiri. In that place, in that moment, Kiri was just a young woman.

"You're one of the very few people I'd term a friend, Gavin," Kiri said, and Gavin could hear her unease in her voice. A not-too-distant thunderclap echoed across the camp, and Kiri tensed.

"Do you want to talk about whatever's on your mind?"

"I don't like storms," Kiri said. "It sounds silly, I know, but I never have...not since I was very little."

Kiri took his right hand in both of hers. Gavin could feel how she almost clutched his hand, like she was afraid she might fall.

"My mother died when I was very young, and to the world at large, she died of a disease that was sweeping through the capital at the time. That wasn't the case; she was murdered. I don't think I will ever forget that night. Mother was reading to me, trying to help me sleep. We were in the nursery. Lightning flashed. There was a man in the room, and he had a blade. Mother set me down, told me to run, find my father. I ran, but I looked back when I got to the door. I wanted to be sure my mother was with me, but she wasn't. She was moving to block the man, fight him I guess. The man stabbed her twice with the blade—short, precise strikes—and my mother crumpled. Lightning flashed again. I saw blood dripping from the blade, and I screamed."

Kiri stared off into the night as she spoke. Tears filled her eyes.

"One of the nice guards who always followed me came into the room, and he put himself between me and the man. He told me to run, but I couldn't pull my eyes off my mother lying on the floor. I heard sounds of fighting. The guard was keeping the man at bay, shouting for me to run. He didn't survive long, but he fought long enough for my father to arrive with many guards. I was almost ten before I spoke again."

Kiri turned her head and looked up at Gavin.

"That's one of my earliest memories, and storms always take me back there. I can't help it. I try to fight it; I really do, but I always relive that night during the worst storms."

Gavin sat in silence for several moments while Kiri held his arm. He didn't miss her use of the words 'guard' and 'guards,' but he didn't think it was the right time to ask why she was surrounded by guards during her childhood. Finally, not knowing what else to do, Gavin nodded.

"Getting sleep will be tough for you tonight?" he asked.

Kiri flinched at a sudden, fierce crackle of thunder overhead. "I doubt I'll sleep at all tonight."

"Would it help you to move your bedroll beside mine? I'm not playing games, I promise."

Despite her frame of mind, Kiri smiled. It was a warm, heartfelt smile. "Gavin, you're such a good soul with a kind heart, I don't think you know how to play those types of games."

Gavin nodded his head toward the bedrolls. "Come on. Let's see if you get some sleep tonight after all."

While Kiri worked on moving her bedroll over beside Gavin's, Gavin walked over to the group. As he approached, everyone turned to him.

"Kiri's having a really bad time of it because of this storm. I know it looks bad, but she's going to lie down beside me."

Elayna was the first to speak. "Is there anything we can do for her?"

"I doubt it," Gavin said. "The source of her pain is an old wound, and I would explain, but I don't feel it's my place to talk about it."

Gavin waited for the others to speak up, but when they seemed content to keep their silence, he turned and walked back to his bedroll. Kiri already had hers laid out beside his, but she stood beside it with her arms folded across her midriff.

"Are you sure you want to do this?" she asked as she nibbled at her lower lip.

Gavin attempted a reassuring nod as he said, "I know I'm not going to try anything, and I doubt you will, either. Besides, if this is best chance you have of getting some sleep, I'll find some way to survive it."

Despite another rumble of thunder, Kiri grinned just a bit.

Gavin stretched a couple times before laying down on his bedroll, and he soon found Kiri beside him. At first, Gavin was going to lay with his fingers laced across his chest, but Kiri's determination to use his shoulder for a pillow convinced him otherwise.

Boy oh boy, Gavin thought as he lay there, *this is going to be a long night.*

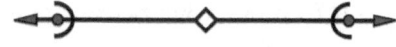

CHAPTER 4

Gavin felt himself being shaken, and he wondered why Kiri wasn't laying beside him anymore. He rolled over and pulled his blanket closer against his neck. Voices spoke, but Gavin didn't care. He was warm and comfortable and wanted to sleep more. Then, a voice cut through the mental fog of sleep.

"Gavin, I need you to wake up," Kiri said. "I'm afraid."

Gavin's eyes shot open, and he was on his feet faster than the others had seen him move. His right hand curled as if holding an apple, and a slight tension around his eyes indicated his concentration as a pin-prick of light appeared above his right palm and grew in size.

"What's wrong, Kiri? Why are you scared?"

Gavin then took in his surroundings, and he saw that everyone seemed tense and were looking at him. No. They were looking *to* him for guidance and leadership.

"Look over my right shoulder," Kiri said.

Gavin did so and saw three people standing at the edge of the wards closest the foothills. The smallest of them looked about Braden's height and build, wore a hooded cloak pulled close, and carried a quarterstaff. The two flanking the smallest wore half-plate

ROBERT M. KERNS

armor; they stood head and shoulders over the smallest between them, with powerfully massive builds to match, and they bore large swords strapped to their backs.

Their exposed flesh had no visible skin but were covered in scales, and the hands of the two taller individuals did not have fingernails. Each digit ended in a claw sized to match the digit from which it extended, and even as far away as Gavin was, those claws looked sharper than razors. They had snouts of varying lengths, and Gavin could see a pair of nostrils at the tip of their snouts and a thin line Gavin suspected opened to a mouth full of razor-sharp teeth.

Gavin then directed his attention to Mariana and lifted his left eyebrow in question.

"Yes, Gavin," Mariana said. "They're dracons."

Gavin scanned his apprentices and saw—like him—each hid their medallions inside their traveling clothes. He took a deep breath, releasing it as a slow sigh, and nodded. He squared his posture and rubbed the sleep from his eyes, then approached the trio.

"Greetings and well met," Gavin said as he neared the edge of the wards, making certain to remain inside. "We're traveling to Vushaar and stopped here for the night. May I offer you the hospitality of our morning meal?"

"We appreciate the invitation," the center dracon said, her voice sounding female to Gavin, "but we have broken our fast already today. We seek the creator of these wards."

"Is that so," Gavin said, making it a statement. "May I ask why?"

The two dracons carrying swords glanced to one another over their fellow's head.

"We seek that person's assistance," the center dracon said. "It is…a delicate matter."

Gavin reached for the silver chain around his neck, grasping it and withdrawing his medallion from inside his tunic. He dropped the chain so that his medallion rested atop his sternum and stood in silence.

The dracons' eyes moved to the medallion and widened. The tall dracon on Gavin's left let out a little gasp, and all three dropped to one knee without hesitation.

"Well, that's new," Gavin said, his voice soft. In his normal tone and volume, he said, "Please, stand. I don't want people kneeling to me."

"But you are of the Liberator's House," the shorter dracon said. "It is decreed throughout our people that those of your family are to be accorded our highest honors."

"Liberator?" Gavin asked, frowning in confusion before looking over his shoulder. "Mariana?"

Mariana walked to Gavin's side, saying, "Yes, Gavin?"

"Do you know anything about a Liberator? I've not come across that reference."

The dracons stood and, before Mariana could speak, the small dracon said, "I am Xask of Clan Qar'Kirloth. During the Godswar, He Who Dueled Milthas led the assault that freed my people from their slavery to Lornithar and his minions. We honor him in our histories as the Liberator."

"Xask, I'm Gavin Cross, Head of House Kirloth."

"I beg you, Scion of the Liberator, please return to Qar'Zhosk with us," Xask said. "We are in dire need of your help."

"First, let's clear up that 'Scion of the Liberator' business. I am not in Kirloth's direct line. My ultimate ancestor was Gerrus, his brother."

"Gerrus? You are of Gerrus's line? How did you come to be here, when he left with the refugees?"

Gavin shrugged. "I wish I knew. I woke up in the southwestern warrens of Tel Mivar a little over a year and a half ago. I know nothing of my past, beyond my name and that I have a daughter."

"You have my sympathy; it cannot be a comfortable situation," Xask said.

"I've grown used to it." Gavin turned and motioned for the others to approach. When they stood around him, he said, "The dracons have asked for my help. They want us to travel with them to Qar'Zhosk."

The wide eyes facing him and little gasps he heard informed Gavin something in what he said was notable.

"Okay...what am I missing?"

"Gavin," Mariana said, "Qar'Zhosk is the capital and largest city of the dracons. No outsiders have seen it since they withdrew from the world shortly after the death of Bellock Vanlon."

Gavin turned to face the dracons, saying, "Do we have your guarantee of safe passage? I understand your people have been... unforgiving, let us say...of trespassers in recent decades."

Xask's eyes widened just enough to notice before she said, "No dracon would *dare* raise a hand against you! It is part of our oldest traditions."

"Fair enough," Gavin said and gestured at his friends, "but my friends are not me. I would be *displeased* should anything befall them. Guys, show them."

Lillian, Mariana, Wynn, and Braden pulled their medallions from inside their clothes and let them fall to rest against their sternums.

"These are my apprentices, as was in the old ways. The female elf is Elayna, one of the *T'Eleren*, and the male elf is Sarres, a Sentinel of Nature. The last young lady is Kiri."

"Before my clansmen, I name these souls *Drak'Thir*," Xask said. "The closest meaning in your tongue is 'Friend of the People,' and it is a rare honor among us, even before our withdrawal. Any who raise arms against you may be struck down without concern for reprisal."

Gavin turned to his friends, saying, "I'm inclined to help them. You know me; I have a tough time refusing anyone who asks me for help."

The others nodded, Lillian and Braden smiling at Gavin's description of himself.

"We'd be the first outsiders to see Qar'Zhosk in centuries," Braden said.

Mariana grinned, saying, "I'd love to sit with one of their scholars and discuss their history."

Gavin turned back to the dracons and said, "We will help you.

If you give us a few moments to strike camp and collect our things, we can leave at once."

* * *

THE DRACONS SET the pace at what was an easy jog for them and a fast trot for the horses. The longer they traveled, the more Gavin felt both unsettled and amazed by what he was witnessing.

They traveled deeper into the foothills of the Godswall Mountains, and the overgrown path they'd been following turned into a wide road paved with smoothed stone.

"The road is radiating Transmutation and Tutation," Gavin said as he trotted along at Xask's side.

"Yes. The Clan Elders long ago saw no need to repave our few roads, so they requested the arcanists to build protections into the roads that would protect them from wear and decay because of the elements. Should a paving stone ever be damaged, the Transmutation you're feeling would draw some of the underlying strata deep underground to repair the paving stone," Xask said, the measured cadence of her speech the only sign of her exertions.

Just then, a mounted figure leaped into view over a small hillock to their left. The figure closed at a ferocious pace, and soon, Gavin could see the rider was a dracon in half-plate and carrying a vicious-looking halberd in his right hand. The rider's left hand held the reins of a creature unlike anything Gavin had ever seen.

The mount bore a *very* slight resemblance to a dog or a wolf, but it had no fur. Scales covered its body, and what would've been claws on a canine were talons that glinted like metal in the sun and tore small grooves in the rocky terrain as the creature closed the distance at a rate that would've foundered even the most tireless horse. A scaly tail weaved side to side, helping the creature keep its balance and maintain its great stride and pace.

When the mounted rider was just a few yards away, he leaned back in the saddle, squeezed the creature's sides with his legs, and pulled back on the reins. The creature responded by stopping its charging run and leaning back against all four legs locked at full extension. The talons dug into the rocky terrain better than a plow and tore furrows the width of the creature's feet as it skidded to a stop no more than five feet from Gavin's party. The creature's eyes had a faint red hue to them, and it didn't even look winded.

"What the hell is that?" Gavin said, staring at the new arrival's mount.

"It's a rock wolf," Xask said. "The dwarves use them as mounts and guard animals, and they gifted the original breeding pairs to us when we settled this region. It took several decades, but we soon bred our rock wolves to suit us as mounts…and their greater size and musculature improved their efficacy as guard animals."

At seeing Gavin's medallion, the rider's eyes widened just enough to notice, and he bowed so low his snout almost touched his mount's neck.

"Matron Xask, forgive me, but we have trespassers on the old trade road from Tel Mivar. They ride their horses hard and travel with remounts."

"Vossk is one of our finest scouts and border guards," Xask said, before turning back to the rider. "Were you able to identify them?"

Gavin heard a low rumble from Vossk's general direction, and he realized it was a growl when Vossk spoke in a harsh tone. "Yes, Matron. They are a deq of the Blighted Ones."

Xask pivoted on her heel to face her escorts. "Go with Vossk. See that none of the Blighted Ones live, and leave the corpses rotting in the sun. Let the carrion-eaters have them if any are that desperate."

"But why are they here?" Vossk said. "The Blighted Ones have not been seen since they murdered Bellock Vanlon."

"These Blighted Ones," Gavin said. "Do you mean they're Lornithrasa?"

The dracons hissed.

"We do not speak that word," Xask said. "Like all things connected to their master, it is an affront to all decency and goodness."

Gavin lifted his right arm and drew back the sleeve of his tunic, revealing the Void-scar and saying, "They hunt me."

Xask's eyes narrowed at seeing the Void-scar, and she said, "Not for much longer." She turned to her fellow dracons and gestured toward the northeast. "Go."

Xask's escorts took off at a sprint, little more than a fast jog for Vossk's rock wolf.

Gavin watched them go, saying, "I hope they kill the Lo—er, Blighted Ones—before any Void-blades are drawn. I'd rather none of your people die."

"It would not matter if they draw a Void-blade or even possess a Void-lance," Xask said. At Gavin's curious expression, she said, "Their master never conceived that we might choose a path other than His service and made us immune to his most potent weapons."

Gavin blinked as he processed Xask's explanation, saying, "Wait...what?"

Mariana nudged her horse up to Gavin's right side. She said, "Forgive me, Xask; I don't intend offense. Gavin, the dracons are not a natural race of this world. Lornithar created the dracons during the final years of the Godswar, because He was losing and thought powerful shock troops would turn the tide. Their heritage is draconic for the most part, obviously, but Lornithar also mixed portions of humans, elves, dwarves, and perhaps even minotaurs into their creation."

"Wow," Gavin said. "That's impressive."

"The females of my people were being held in a series of prisons, a closely guarded secret among His forces," Xask said. "The males serving as shock troops were told they existed only to win the Godswar for Him and that there were no others. When the Liberator informed them about the females, they recognized Him for the liar He is and rebelled. With the help of the Liberator and his people, those earliest males freed the females and chose freedom and to be a sovereign, self-determining people. We owe the Liberator much."

Gavin smiled, saying, "Xask, I only had a short time with my mentor, but I feel as though I came to know him to a certain extent. He didn't believe in debts...at least collecting them...and if you were to speak to him about what you or your people feel you owe him, I feel he would respond something like this. 'Take care of yourself and your people. Do right by them, and stand against injustice and those who would do evil. By doing that, you will repay any debt you feel you owe me and then some.'"

"That does sound like something the Liberator would say," Xask said, "but we have tarried long enough. Vossk and the others will catch up to us. Qar'Zhosk awaits."

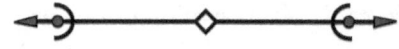

CHAPTER 5

The old trade road led deeper into the foothills until they reached a tunnel wide enough for three large, caravan wagons to pass side by side without touching. Metal gates that looked like wrought iron but with streaks of a strange red hue blocked entrance to the tunnel, and two massive dracons stood behind the gate, halberds in their hands and swords strapped to their backs. Deeper into the tunnel, Gavin could see sconces much like those in Tel Mivar lighting the space.

As Gavin drew close to the gate, he dismounted and approached the gate at Xask's side. The dracons behind the gate took one look at Gavin's medallion and unlocked the gates in haste. The gates unlocked, the dracons then swung them back against the tunnel walls and dropped to one knee, acting as impromptu gate stops.

Gavin sighed. "This is going to get old…fast," he said, not even bothering to whisper. "Please, stand. I won't have people kneeling to me."

"They are only-" Xask said.

"I know, following the oldest traditions. I respect that you feel you should honor my family, but not even my mentor—the man you term the Liberator—would have tolerated this for long. Neither of us are the type of people who seek personal aggrandizement. Like I said when we met Vossk, if you want to honor what my mentor helped you achieve, make the best of all you can. It's a far better memorial to him than everyone kneeling every time I approach."

"I understand your position," Xask said, "but to change such an ancient tradition is unheard-of and must be brought before the Council of Clans. We should address this matter with them."

Yay...more politics, Gavin thought, though he was careful to keep his reaction from showing in his expression.

GAVIN THOUGHT they would have a challenging time getting the animals to enter the tunnel, but the horses and pack-mules didn't seem to give the matter a second thought. The tunnel was just the right size for their shod hooves to make an odd echo as they trotted along.

"How far is it to Qar'Zhosk?" Gavin asked as he walked beside Xask.

"We have some distance to go yet. The cavern that became my people's home sits under the spine of the Godswall Mountains. There has been talk down through the centuries that we are another line of defense, making sure they do not tunnel through. The filth that has overrun Skullkeep has likewise learned not to delve too deeply."

"From what I've seen, I imagine your people can be fierce warriors."

Something in Xask's demeanor changed, and to Gavin's estimation, the air took on a slight chill.

Xask directed a sidelong look to Gavin as they walked, saying, "Those who have not seen us do war do not understand. Your apprentice, Mariana of Cothos, had it right when she said Lornithar made us to be shock troops...and we were well-made."

The moment passed, and Xask returned to her pleasant, welcoming self.

"We have not had to do war since the time your people call the

Founding, but every child goes through training that provides a basic level of skill and competency across our entire society."

"What can you tell me about your society?" Gavin asked.

"When we settled here, in Qar'Zhosk, we were fifteen clans. We lost one clan, Qar'Nyskyx, during a fierce raid into our lands by the filth from Skullkeep. Another, Qoh'Leskahl, betrayed us all to those exiled beyond the Godswall Mountains. To this day, we remember them in every Council chamber. One Clan Seat stands empty and another shattered."

"So," Gavin asked, "you rule yourselves through a council?"

"Yes," Xask replied, adding an affirmative nod. "Each city has its own Council of Clans, and all cities send representatives to Qar'Zhosk four times per year to address and consider any matters pertaining to us all. Otherwise, each city's Council of Clans is trusted to handle routine matters, but each city may call for a Grand Moot, during which every Council and many representatives of the people gather to discuss matters of emergency or great importance. In my life, I have only seen one Grand Moot."

"Really? May I ask what it discussed?" Gavin asked.

"We withdrew from the world during our last Grand Moot."

Gavin stopped, blinking. "But...I thought your people withdrew from the world shortly after the last Archmagister died."

"Yes," Xask said. "Your understanding is correct. After a year passed without Bellos naming a new Archmagister, the leadership of my people decided that the naturals transgressed in some major way, causing the gods to abandon the world."

"Wasn't that something like 600 years ago?" Gavin asked.

Xask nodded once. "I am 1,246 of your years old, and it is common for one of my people to live well into their second millennium. In fact, most consider dying at 2,000 to be dying before one's time."

Gavin felt like he'd been punched in the gut at the enormity of what Xask said.

"So...on average...it's been between three and four generations for you since the Godswar?"

Xask nodded. "Yes. It is not ancient history for us, as it is for you naturals. Many of our current elders *spoke* with the survivors of that horror."

Gavin took a deep breath and let it out as a heavy sigh. "I think I need time to process that."

"As you will," Xask replied. "I shall be here when you are ready to resume conversation."

* * *

AFTER ALMOST AN HOUR OF TRAVEL, the tunnel opened into an immense cavern, filled by a city. The cavern itself seemed to be an ellipse, somewhere between a compressed circle and egg-shaped, and it was enormous. The only way Gavin had an indication of the far side of the cavern was by looking at the city's lights far off in the distance.

On the left side of the cavern—from Gavin's perspective, a massive waterfall cascaded down to a pool in a raging cataract of white water and soft green light. From the pool, the water became a river running through the city before it disappeared into the cavern wall.

"Wow…why does your water glow?" Gavin gazed at the distant falls.

"Ah, yes. Erin's Falls continue to be a mystery to our people still yet today. We could never learn why it glows the way it does, but it does not appear to harm us…as the pool and river are our primary source of water."

"Erin's Falls?"

"Yes. We named the waterfall for the arcanist who helped us divert the underground river to become our water source. She was very accomplished in her craft."

"This is amazing," Gavin said, his voice just above a whisper.

"Gavin," Lillian said, her voice full of awe and wonder, "look up."

Gavin glanced at Lillian and, taking in her expression, lifted his eyes to the cavern ceiling…and gaped. A massive illusion effect covered the cavern's entire ceiling. It was faded and flickering, and there were patches where the illusion broke down and showed stalactites hanging far above. From what Gavin could see, it looked as though the illusion was supposed to mimic the sky outside the cavern, but that made little sense, unless....

"You guys need sunlight for Vitamin D, don't you?" Gavin asked, turning to Xask.

Xask turned to face Gavin, and though her features were the most alien Gavin had seen since waking up in the world, he could tell she was confused.

"What is *Vitamin D?*" she asked, glancing from Gavin to his apprentices and back. "I've never heard of that."

"It's...well..." Gavin took a deep breath to keep from showing his frustration. The gray mist had enclosed his mind once more, and he no longer understood what Vitamin D was.

Lillian was quick to step into the moment, saying, "Gavin says things, sometimes, that we don't understand. We can't really explain it."

The mists in his mind faded, and Gavin smiled. "A person's body needs specific compounds to survive and thrive. It gets most of these from food, but some, the body can make. Vitamin D is one the body can make, and exposure to sunlight is crucial to its production. I don't know anything about dragons, but if your people are indeed part human, I would imagine the sunlight requirement came from that."

Xask nodded. "I'm glad to have found you. You understand the problem. Many of our young were ill until we cycled them outside the cavern on camping trips. Even if you correct the city's sky, we will continue the camping trips. The young ones seem to enjoy them very much."

Gavin closed his eyes and concentrated on the resonances he felt from the illusion through his *skathos*. He knew at once what the problem was; the effect was breaking down from imperfect anchoring.

"Who made your sky?" Gavin asked.

"The arcanists who taught my people to wield the Art, along

with a few of the more promising students," Xask said. "If you want specific names, we must examine the archives."

"But it wasn't my mentor? The one you call The Liberator?"

"Oh, no. As far as we know, he was never aware of the problem. The records show that, by the time we started feeling ill, he had already moved south with the Army of Valthon to relieve the siege of Vushaar."

"I thought so," Gavin said. "It doesn't feel like his work."

"May I ask what you mean?"

"Well, first off, you need to understand that I'm not even close to the level of mastery my mentor displayed, but one of the things I've seen about long-term, perpetual effects like this is that the effect needs to be anchored to something permanent. The protections built into Mivar Estate back in Tel Mivar are anchored to Lillian's bloodline; if the Mivar line ever dies out, those protections will cease to exist as well. I imagine it's the same with the other estates of my friends' families. Now, keep in mind this is just after a brief examination, so I could be totally wrong here. It feels like the effect used to produce your sky wasn't anchored well, and that's why it's breaking down after all these years."

Xask stared at Gavin in silence for several moments before saying, "I almost begrudge the time it will take to introduce you to the Council of Clans. You need to meet with our arcanists as soon as possible."

CHAPTER 6

Gavin was used to people reacting to him—specifically his House—with awe and unease, but those experiences did not prepare him in the slightest for the reactions of the people as Xask led him and his friends through the streets to meet with the leadership of the Thirteen Clans. First, the moment they saw the Glyph of Kirloth, they knelt to one knee and bowed their heads. Then, after Gavin and company passed, they stood and watched until Gavin walked out of sight. Some even followed the group. By the time they reached the cupola-styled pavilion that Xask indicated was their destination, a sizeable following had developed in their wake.

Fifteen stone chairs formed a semi-circle around one side of the pavilion, and the first thing Gavin noticed was that one chair was crumbled and blackened. Another chair sat empty. Thirteen dracons filled the remaining seats.

Xask whispered for Gavin to wait until she called for him. She stepped forward into the cupola and bowed deeply to the assembled clan leaders.

"Honored Leaders," Xask said, "I have returned with one who can repair our sky."

"That is good," one of clan leaders said. "The illness is spreading. More young ones are becoming sick, even those who have been outside."

Another clan leader said, "We trust you did not inform whoever you brought of his or her fate once the work is complete. We could not trust their work if they know they will die upon completion."

Gavin heard some gasps behind him. One of them sounded like Kiri. He wasn't about to allow a group of people he didn't even know to contemplate killing him and his people. Even if he were not Kirloth now, that just wouldn't be permissible.

"Honored-"

Before Xask could complete her statement, Gavin stepped into the cupola, saying, "There's a problem with your death sentence."

Seven of the clan leaders erupted to their feet without paying full attention to Gavin. One of them said, "How dare you interrupt our deliberations! You have no place here!"

"If you think I will stand and await an introduction to a group of people planning my death after asking for my help, you're more senile than you look. You better think long and hard about deciding you'll try to kill me and mine. I don't respond well to threats, and I don't do half measures."

"You stand deep within our territory, human," another standing clan leader said, his voice sneering even if his facial muscles couldn't carry through on the expression. "Do you think you'll ever leave here alive?"

Gavin stepped into the cupola and lifted his left hand, cupping it as if holding an apple. Within a heartbeat, an orb of iridescent power hovered in the air above his palm, its color shifting like a kaleidoscope almost faster than the eye could follow.

"I think I'm prepared to burn myself out eradicating your race from the world, if you persist in this heedless fallacy, and I promise you...you'll die first."

At this point, a shred of wisdom entered one of the leader's minds, albeit one who was still seated, and she lowered her eyes to examine Gavin's medallion. Her eyes widened, and she fell from her seat to the floor, kneeling and pressing her head against the marble flagstones. Her actions were so pronounced and startling that the other clan leaders examined Gavin, searching for what inspired such a reaction. Those still seated processed what their eyes showed them faster than their enraged counterparts, and they too prostrated themselves before Gavin.

"How dare you dishonor yourselves before some corrupted outsider!" Xask's own clan leader said, his voice harsh and loud. The spectacle had already carried to the crowd that had followed Gavin and his friends through the streets, and it didn't require exceptional hearing to notice the angry whispers stalking back and forth through the crowd like a hungry predator. Those 'common' people knew who those leaders disrespected, and everyone was too focused on the spectacle in the cupola to notice members of the crowd sending runners off into the city.

"You dishonor all of us!" Xask said, moving to stand snout-to-chest with her clan leader and glaring up at him. "Has all sense left you? You threaten the Scion of the Liberator! I am appalled to know you carry my blood. No recompense imaginable can erase the dishonor you've dealt our clan...and our people."

"None of the Liberator's line exists in the world, old crone," the leader of Clan Qar'Kirloth growled, staring down at Xask. "Your age has addled your wits and allowed this charlatan to deceive you. This impertinence is only the latest of your offenses, and I shall take much enjoyment seeing you staked at last."

Gavin eyed the clan leader, and he detested what he saw. He turned his head to the right and said over his shoulder, "Lillian, bring the others and stand on either side of me. Declan, the elves, and Kiri stay back in the shadows."

Mariana and Wynn soon stood on Gavin's left side, and Lillian and Braden stood on Gavin's right.

"I suppose some would say it's not my place to butt into what is an internal matter," Gavin said, "but I appreciate Xask since we met earlier this morning. I'm not sure what these 'offenses' you mentioned are, but until I have a clear understanding, nobody's staking anyone.

"In all truth, you are correct; I am not in the direct line of the man your people call the Liberator. However, I am the distant descendant of his brother Gerrus, the brother who took his family to the Refugee World, and the Liberator himself trained me in the Art after he named me his heir."

Gavin stepped forward and, moving Xask aside, reached up and delivered a backhand slap to the clan leader. The shock of the strike drove the clan leader's snout to the side, more than the strength of the blow, and he turned to face Gavin, his nostrils flaring.

"You are an affront to all decency and civilized behavior," Gavin said, "and I challenge you."

"You insolent worm! How dare you strike me! I'll kill you right-"

"You cannot," a new voice spoke. Gavin turned to look and saw the six clan leaders who had prostrated themselves now standing. It was the female who first prostrated herself that spoke. "He has challenged you. You must accept his challenge or refuse it. No other actions are permitted."

"That's not *entirely* true," another clan leader said. This speaker was a male, short for a dracon and stooped with age. "We must determine the truth of this man's identity before the challenge can be accepted or denied. It is a matter of our oldest traditions. If this man is indeed of the Liberator's line...well...that would force us on a different path, and the challenge would be void."

"How so?" Gavin asked, oblivious to the seething dracon standing not even a foot away from him.

"It is a matter of the oldest traditions that the Liberator and all those of his line are sacred to our people and to be rendered all the honors our people can conceive. If you are who you appear to be, these clan leaders have egregiously violated that tradition, and there can only be one response."

"And how do we prove I am who I appear to be?"

"I am ancient even among our kind," the stooped clan leader said. "I've studied the ancient texts of our home's founding. If you will permit me, I shall prick your flesh with a claw and ask you to touch one of our pavilion's pillars."

Gavin's right eyebrow quirked upward. "And what will that do?"

"If you are who you appear to be, the proof will be immediate. If you are not—if you are some charlatan who has managed to fake a House's medallion after countless centuries—nothing will happen."

Gavin shrugged and extended his hand to the dracon. "Sure. Why not? Want to prick my finger or thumb, or do you prefer my palm?"

The ancient clan leader lifted his left hand and used the claw on his index finger to draw blood on Gavin's index finger. He gestured to the pillars of the pavilion. Gavin turned and walked over to the pillar nearest him and pressed his bloody finger to the marble.

For a heartbeat, nothing happened.

Just as Xask's clan leader clenched his fist to proclaim his triumph, a deep **THRUM** resonated outward from the pavilion, and any wizards in the city felt a powerful Evocation erupt into existence. A bright radiance lit the immediate area around the pavilion as runes lit up along the edges of the streets moving outward through the city. At each intersection, the Glyph of Kirloth appeared twenty feet in the air. This effect radiated outward until the entire cavern was bright as day, lit by countless Glyphs of Kirloth and those runes along the streets.

Gavin looked at the glyph of his House hovering over the closest intersection, and he stepped out of the pavilion and looked above it. About ten feet above the center of the curved dome, a Glyph of Kirloth—easily thirty feet across—blazed bright. He stepped back inside the pavilion and looked at the ancient clan leader.

"Was that what was supposed to happen?" Gavin asked.

The ancient clan leader smiled and nodded once. "It was a protection built into the foundation of our city by the arcanists of the time. They wanted to ensure there could be no question whether the Liberator or one of his House stood before us."

"And what happens to them now?"

The ancient clan leader turned to regard those clan leaders who had surged to their feet in a rage. "For six of them, they will be stripped of their rank and wealth and will serve their clans as best their fellows will allow. I fear they will be little more than pariahs. For the leader of Qar'Kirloth, however, the traditions are clear. His offense is such that no other path than staking is possible."

"To the Abyss with you! I will never submit!" the leader of Qar'Kirloth drew a dagger that Gavin or Declan would've considered a short sword and lunged at the ancient clan leader.

Gavin calmly invoked a Word, *"Thymnos."*

The leader of Qar'Kirloth froze, but his momentum carried him forward in a fall. The ancient clan leader stepped to one side and allowed the disgraced (and paralyzed) clan leader to strike the floor.

The remaining six clan leaders who had surged to their feet looked at their former associate and sighed almost as one. They removed a mantle from around their shoulders and draped it across the chairs they had vacated. They bowed to the remaining clan leaders, turned to bow to Gavin, and vacated the pavilion.

Four dracons entered the pavilion, removed the mantle from the paralyzed leader of Qar'Kirloth, and draped that mantle across the clan's chair before carrying the paralyzed dracon out of the pavilion.

The remaining clan leaders looked at one another for several moments before the ancient one sighed.

"We must now fill seven seats. Never in all our history has this ever occurred."

Gavin shrugged and pointed at Xask with his left thumb, saying, "Well, I don't know if it's any of my business, but Xask seemed to represent your people well on the journey here from our camp."

The remaining clan leaders looked to one another in silence for several moments before turning almost as one to regard Xask. At long last, the ancient clan leader turned back to Gavin.

"We will spend most of the day tomorrow meeting with the clans and organizing replacement clan leaders. I would ask Xask to conduct you and your fellows to the hostel we once maintained for traveling merchants and diplomats. Despite its lack of use over these last six hundred years, we have maintained it in good condition, and you may rest there while you assist us with our sky."

Gavin nodded. "Very well. Where will I work on repairing your sky?"

"Xask will conduct you to the workplace of those who are striving to solve the problem in the morning. I've always found it best to begin new projects at dawn."

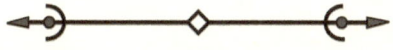

CHAPTER 7

The next morning found Gavin and his apprentices standing just inside the doorway of a room large enough to be a classroom. Several chalkboards made of a dark slate hung on wheeled stands around the room. A large rectangular table with rounded corners occupied the center of the space, scrolls and stacks of parchment covering the tabletop. Three dracons stood in front of one chalkboard. From what Gavin could hear, they argued over various methods to repair the sky effect.

"Good morning," Gavin said, after standing unnoticed by the dracons for some time.

The dracons turned almost as one to regard the source of the interruption.

"Who are you?" the dracon on the left said.

"And how did you get in here?" the dracon on the right added.

"I'm surprised you're still alive," the center dracon joined the discourse. "We've been killing trespassers for a long time now."

"My name is Gavin Cross, and I've been asked to assist with your sky. These are my friends and apprentices: Lillian, Mariana, Wynn, and Braden."

The dracons eyed Gavin in silence for several moments before their eyes widened. They smiled and moved with haste to approach Gavin and his friends.

"So glad to meet you! Xask said she'd found someone to help, but she didn't give us any details as to who. I'm Nahskar," the center dracon said. "This is Ghrax," indicating the left dracon, "and Ysk," indicating the right dracon.

"Have you ever worked with a perpetual effect?" Ghrax asked.

"That depends on your definition, I suppose. I've invoked several composite effects and spent time examining the protections built into the manor wall at the Mivar Estate in Tel Mivar."

"Composite effects?" Ysk said. "You've invoked composite effects? How is that possible?"

Gavin almost sighed. He didn't mind helping the dracons, but he also didn't want to spend two weeks in needless discussion. Hoping that his full identity would forestall further questions instead of instigating more, he withdrew his wizard's medallion from within his tunic, dropping it to rest against his sternum. His apprentices did likewise.

"I was trained in the Art by the man your people term 'The Liberator,' and I'm told he was my uncle...albeit many, many times removed. Don't ask me to teach you any spells, because my mentor only had me work with Words of Power."

The dracons stared at Gavin's medallion in silence for several moments before they examined the medallions of his friends.

At last, Nahskar spoke. "I remember the day the Clans voted to withdraw from the world and the old alliance. I remember the death of Bellock Vanlon, the last Archmagister, and I remember many years before that. In all my wildest imaginings, I never considered the day would come when Kirloth and his Apprentices would once more walk upon the world together. I know not what brings you to this part of the world, but I assure you we are grateful beyond measure you would take time out of your journey to assist us. Tell us what you need, and you shall have it."

Gavin nodded. "You're welcome, and please, do not feel you have to stand on any ceremony. My name is Gavin, and I'm happy to share what I know."

.   .   .

GAVIN LED everyone over to an unused chalkboard. Ysk provided a collection of chalk with haste, and Gavin wrote 'Current' at the top of the chalkboard and underlined it. He then turned to the four humans and three dracons watching him.

"I think the best way forward is for us to understand the current situation as best we can. It's apparent that the effect that has served the dracons for millennia is breaking down, and I wouldn't be surprised if it fails within the year, given the rate of its degradation. Let's examine that effect and diagram it on this chalkboard behind me, as best we can. We'll start with our *skathos* and move on to Divination if we must."

The three dracons looked to one another and stepped off to one side, whispering. After the quick conference, Ysk and Ghrax left with some haste as Nahskar returned to the group.

Gavin turned and made a mark on the chalkboard that looked like a dash or minus sign. He then turned to Lillian, saying, "Lillian, focus on your *skathos*. Tell me what the sky effect feels like to you."

Lillian closed her eyes. After several moments, she said, "It feels like Illusion," Gavin wrote the rune for Illusion by the dash, "and maybe Divination," Gavin made a plus sign followed by the rune for Divination, "all wrapped around Conjuration." Gavin made another plus sign and the rune for Conjuration.

Gavin worked his way through each of his apprentices, getting them to report what their *skathos* told them about the failing effect and writing that on successive lines. Then, he closed his own eyes and concentrated on his *skathos*. He didn't know if his apprentices were not as sensitive as he was or if they had difficulty describing what they felt, but while their descriptions covered the gist of the effect, Gavin felt nuances their descriptions lacked.

"Okay," Gavin said and opened his eyes. Seeing there were many more dracons in the room than there had been when he closed his eyes startled him. "Oh…hello."

Nahskar stepped forward and said, "Please, forgive us, milord. It has been many years since we had access to anyone trained in

Words of Power, and we would very much appreciate you permitting our arcanists to attend this work. It would be very educational."

Gavin shrugged, saying, "I don't mind. It surprised me." He fell silent for a few moments. "Who all here besides my friends and I would qualify as a wizard?"

Most of the dracons raised a hand.

"Okay. Of those, have any received any training in the Art? Do you feel comfortable trying to diagram your sky effect using your *skathos*?"

Most of the dracons lowered their hands, but six hands remained in the air.

"Very well. You'll work with us. Nahskar, I need enough charcoal and parchment for myself, my friends, and these dracons. Hmmm...I don't see any chairs. Well, I don't want to wait while we find some. *Nythraex.*"

Every wizard present felt the resonance of Gavin's invocation slam into them like a rushing wall of ice-cold water. A few dropped to one knee, gasping for air, as chairs made of solid wood with no tool marks or fasteners appeared around the table.

"Everyone who indicated they felt comfortable diagraming the sky effect, find a seat. Let's get this party started. The rest of you, gather around and watch."

Ghrax and Nahskar hurried to clear the table as Ysk provided charcoal pencils and fresh parchment. They then occupied the last three open seats around the table.

AN HOUR LATER, the last dracon finished her diagram, and Gavin collected them. All the diagrams bore many similarities, and a few (including his) were more detailed than the others. Gavin showed all the diagrams to everyone and praised them for their work. He then returned to the 'Current' chalkboard, wiped away his earlier writings, and drew a diagram of the existing effect that was a composite of all the diagrams on parchment.

Once he finished, Gavin turned to the group, saying, "Okay. This is where we are...right now. As you can see, the single greatest flaw to this effect is a lack of an anchor, and I believe that lack is the main reason it's failing today. Unfortunately, my training and studies have not indicated it's possible to change such an effect to include an anchor after it's set, especially this long after it's set, so we will break this apart and construct a new effect, one that is anchored. That effect should serve the dracons well for quite some time to come."

"How are we going to break apart the existing effect without causing mass panic among the people?" Nahskar asked, as several dracons nodded. "Yes, we have streetlamps for nighttime, but even patchy and failing as it is, the people are used to seeing the sun above them."

"It will have to be a composite effect," Gavin said. "The first part will dispel the existing effect, while the second will create and anchor the effect that replaces it. We could do it separately, but as you said, people might panic when the cavern goes dark. So, I say we don't let the cavern go dark."

The dracons around the room looked to one another. Gavin wasn't too adept at reading their facial expressions, but their body language suggested anxiety.

"Is something wrong?" Gavin asked.

"As far as I know, none of us have ever worked with composite effects before," Ghrax said.

Gavin smiled. "Well...this will be a learning experience for everyone, then."

* * *

OVER THE FOLLOWING DAYS, Gavin worked with the dracons and his apprentices to design the effect that would replace the dracons' failing sky. While he welcomed input from everyone, Gavin treated it as a learning exercise, with most of the final design for the effect being his. Eight days passed while Gavin and the others completed the preparatory work, but at long last, the design was ready.

. . .

EVERYONE GATHERED around Gavin and his apprentices as they made ready to invoke the composite effect that would replace the dracons' sky with a more permanent, more reliable, and more effective solution. The final design revolved around Divination and Transmutation. Using Divination, they would create a specialized scrying sphere that would fill the cavern's ceiling, and the Transmutation would both bind the effect to the dracon bloodlines and change the scrying sphere to be more of an actual window to the outside sky, instead of just an image of it.

The final invocation would use four Words: a Word of Tutation to dispel the existing effect, a Word of Divination to create the scrying sphere, a Word of Transmutation to change the scrying sphere into a kind of window or one-way portal, and a Word of Transmutation to anchor the effect to the dracon bloodlines.

Gavin gestured for his apprentices to assume their positions around him, their right hands touching one of Gavin's shoulders while their left hands rested on the shoulder of the person to their left. They had practiced speaking in unison in their rooms at night, as Gavin didn't want anyone to embarrass themselves in front of the dracons.

"Sound off when you're ready," Gavin said.

"Ready," Lillian said.

"Ready," Braden said.

"Ready," Wynn said.

"Ready," Mariana said.

"On my nod," Gavin said as he closed his eyes and focused on the effect he wanted to create. The picture firm in his mind, Gavin nodded once.

"*Klyphos-Klaepos-Zyrhaek-Rhyskaal,*" five voices intoned together.

The massive resonance of the composite effect slammed into every wizard present, driving most to their knees. It affected Gavin the most, the invocation savaging him to the point that he bled from both nostrils as he collapsed to his hands and knees. After a few moments, Gavin forced himself back to his feet and accepted an offered rag to wipe away the blood running down his lips; once his nose stopped bleeding, he whispered another Word, "*Idluhn*," to incinerate the bloody rag.

Looking up to survey their handiwork, Gavin saw no open or fading patches in the effect above the city, and the effect stretched from one edge of the cavern to the others.

"That is the best our sky has looked in ages," the ancient clan leader said as he broke through the ranks of those around Gavin and his apprentices. "On behalf of all our people, I thank you."

"Well, it's not without drawbacks," Gavin said. "You'll now share in the seasons of the outside world. When it rains outside, it'll rain here. You'll have snow as well and, perhaps, even wind."

"We'll have weather?" one dracon nearby asked, her voice filled with awe.

"Yes. You'll have weather. I'm glad you build your houses with roofs. That'll be even more important now."

"Come," the ancient clan leader said. "We have prepared a feast in your honor."

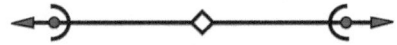

CHAPTER 8

The next morning, Gavin and company set out from the dracons' city, and they found themselves surrounded by a rather large escort. They chatted with those dracons closest to them among the throng and made good time through the tunnel. It wasn't even mid-morning yet when they left the tunnel for the wide-open skies. They bade farewell to the dracons and wended their way out of the foothills, intent on returning to the old trade road that traveled from Mivar Province in Tel to Thartan Province in Vushaar.

"THAT WAS a good thing you did for the dracons," Elayna said as they rode.

Gavin nodded. "I suppose there are some who would argue that the dracons are a relic of a time long past, and therefore, we should not have helped them. The thing is, though, they didn't choose to be made. They didn't choose to exist. They're people, just like the rest of us, and if a little effort and a nosebleed are all it takes to ensure they can remain in their ancestral home, I see no reason not to spend that effort and survive that nosebleed."

"Grandmother would be pleased."

It wasn't long before Declan once more handed off the reins of his horse to Braden and pulled his lute from his back. Within moments thereof, they traveled to the accompaniment of some of the finest melodies in the known world, strummed by one of the world's finest bards.

* * *

DAYS PASSED, and the party crossed into Vushaar without interference or any sign that the Lornithrasa were once again on their trail. The days were pleasant for traveling, and Declan's proficiency with the lute made the journey more enjoyable.

THEY WERE four days into Vushaar and camped for the night when a man stumbled into the pine thicket that served as a waystation and their campsite. Sweat soaked every visible surface of his body, and he gasped for air as he collapsed to his knees just outside the camp's ward.

Gavin, Declan, and Sarres walked to the edge of the ward to see if the man still lived. At their approach, he struggled to lift his head, saying, "May I please have some water?"

Declan and Sarres looked to Gavin, who nodded, and Declan went back to the camp.

"What is your name, neighbor?" Gavin asked. "How come you to be this far out?"

"Forgive me, but I don't know which side you support," the man said as he pushed himself to his knees. "I'd rather not go into any detail. I'm much obliged for the water."

It was then that Declan and Kiri returned with a small jug of water. Declan stopped at Gavin's side, and Kiri stepped to the edge of the ward to pass the jug to the man.

"Thank you, young-" The man froze as he lifted his eyes to the woman handing him the water jug. His eyes bulged, and he was on his feet in an instant, his hand going for the dagger at his side. "Run, Princess! I'll hold them off!"

Sarres drew his own blade and moved to leap to Kiri's defense.

"Hold fast, Sarres," Gavin said and focused his gaze on the dagger. "*Zyrhaek.*"

A slight tightening of his eyes was the only sign Gavin felt any pain whatsoever as the man's dagger fell away as iron filings and leather wrapping.

"You mind explaining why you'd pull a blade on my friend... especially after we've been kind enough to share our water?" Gavin said, moving up to stand beside Kiri.

"Friend?" the man said. "You're no friend; you're her captors!"

The man lunged forward and made a grab for Kiri. Gavin sighed and took a step back. The moment the man reached the perimeter of the ward, glowing runes appeared in the ground at the perimeter's edge. There was a crackling sound as a shimmering wall of lightning rose from the runes, and a spark erupted out to strike the man in his chest. The man crumpled to the ground without even a cry. A small thunderclap rumbled across the camp, and Gavin, Kiri, Declan, and Sarres could smell a faint trace of ozone.

"Is he...dead?" Kiri asked, her hand flying to her mouth.

Gavin shook his head, saying, "Of course not. Well, not unless he has a weak heart. Declan, do you mind checking him?"

The bard stepped outside the ward and knelt at the man's side. He pressed fingers to the man's neck and nodded. "He lives, just like you said."

"Very well. Bring him inside the ward. Your wardstone should protect him as long as some part of your skin touches his."

Without another word, Gavin turned and walked back to the campfire.

"Was that a lightning strike?" Mariana asked as Gavin returned.

Gavin shook his head. "Someone collapsed outside the ward

and asked for water. When he saw Kiri, he went all weird, calling her 'Princess' and acting like we were her captors. He lunged at Kiri, and the ward shocked him into unconsciousness."

Gavin resumed his seat on a felled log as Sarres and Kiri arrived, Declan a few moments behind them. Declan laid the man down next to the logs and sat across the fire from Gavin. Sarres went to Elayna's side, and Kiri stood at the edge of the rough circle made by the felled logs. Her eyes scanned all those present, but they lingered on Gavin.

The silence that descended on the camp as Gavin and Kiri looked at one another was heavy and almost awkward. When no one spoke, Gavin broke the silence.

"So, 'Princess,' is it?" he asked.

"Gavin-" Lillian said.

"No, Lillian. It's time," Kiri said. She moved to sit on the unoccupied log, at a forty-five-degree angle to Gavin's right, and released a heavy sigh. "Gavin, my full name is Kiri Muran."

Gavin blinked. "So, this Terris that Valera asked me to help?"

"My father. He knew the civil war was coming, and he sent me to Tel...to be safe, of all things. I never knew who I was supposed to meet on the Tel Mivar docks; we never made it that far."

"From his reaction, I'm guessing your people think you dead with the rest of your ship's people," Gavin said. "This might complicate things."

Then, scanning the faces of his fellow travelers, Gavin realized something. Only Mariana, Wynn, and Braden shared his surprise. He locked eyes with Declan, saying, "You knew?"

Declan remained silent for a few moments before nodding once. "Yes."

Gavin shifted his attention to Lillian. "And you?"

"I found out during those days you were gone...after Marcus," Lillian said.

"I recognized her from a visit to Vushaar I made with my sister," Elayna said, drawing Gavin's attention.

Gavin's eyes flicked to Sarres, who shrugged and said, "I had no idea who she was, if it matters. There just isn't too much that surprises me anymore."

Gavin nodded and looked at the unconscious man on the fringe of the camp. "So, who's he?"

Kiri shrugged. "I don't know. I've never seen him before in my life. Gavin, I-"

"It's okay, Kiri. Don't worry about it." Gavin pushed himself to his feet and walked toward the horses' picket.

Kiri rose to follow him, but Declan speared her with a glance and shook his head.

GAVIN FOUND himself standing beside Jasmine. He retrieved the brush he'd used to groom her when they made camp and started brushing her down again. She didn't seem to mind the second brushing.

A part of him wanted to feel betrayed that his friends had known such a crucial piece of information about Kiri and had not shared it with him. He especially wanted to be angry with Declan, who served him as one of his Wraiths. The Wraiths were *supposed* to provide him with information after all.

The longer he worked with Jasmine and considered the matter, though, he realized they had acted just as he would. Elayna probably assumed he already knew, and besides, the elves were so new to their group that Gavin didn't blame either of them for not saying much. They were still developing the mutual trust already enjoyed between everyone else. No...if he had known about Kiri's background, Gavin would've considered it her story to tell. He would've let the decision of who knew rest on Kiri's shoulders.

Tired of brushing down Jasmine, Gavin returned the brush to the saddlebag and stepped over to the food stores, retrieving an apple. Jasmine's interest in the apple was rather apparent.

"Hold on. I'm going to cut it for you first," Gavin said, though Jasmine gave him a look that suggested she wasn't too worried about whether he cut it up first or not. The small knife Gavin carried on his belt made short work of quartering the apple, and Gavin placed one quarter in his palm and held his hand out to Jasmine as flat as he could make it. The apple disappeared in a chomp and a slight brushing of her lips against Gavin's hand.

"I thought you might like that," Gavin said, offering another apple quarter in his left hand as he reached his right hand back to rub Jasmine's neck.

The fourth apple quarter had just disappeared when Gavin heard footsteps behind him. He looked over his shoulder and saw Mariana a slight distance away.

"He's waking up, Gavin."

"All right," Gavin said, before turning back to Jasmine. "I've got to go. Have a good night, okay?"

Jasmine chuffed and pushed her nose against Gavin's chest.

Gavin turned and saw Mariana staring at him. He quirked his eyebrow in a silent question.

"It is almost scary sometimes how you seem to communicate with that horse."

Gavin chuckled as he passed Mariana on the way back to the campfire. "Jasmine's a good friend. I guess you could say we bonded while traveling after Marcus's death."

GAVIN RETURNED to the campfire and found the man sitting on the ground, leaning against one of the felled logs and looking wild around the eyes.

"So, neighbor…care to explain why you tried to attack my friend?"

"Attack?" the man said, frowning his confusion. "No. I tried to free her."

"Well, I can promise you she's as free as she'll ever be until I find a way to remove that brand from her shoulder. I don't care whether you believe me or not, but you've not made the best impression. I must confess that I'm conflicted. Part of me wants to kick your ass out of our camp and ask my Elven associate to bombard you with arrows until he can't see you anymore. Another part of me wants to have another associate spend some effort and sweat digging a shallow grave outside the ward, and the last part of me just wants to say, 'hell with it all,' and go to sleep. I know which option I favor, but I'm a little curious about your vote."

"I...I can't die yet. I need to reach Governor Zentris in Thartan."

Kiri looked up at that. "Why do you need to reach Uncle Zen? Who are you?"

The man licked his lips as a nervous tic and pulled his eyes away from Gavin. "Your Highness," he said, "my name is Seb, and I serve your grandfather as a stable-hand. The Roensils are using the upheaval of the civil war to make a grab for your family's land. The settlement the old king forced on them has never sat well, and frankly, they seem to be expecting your father to lose. Master Clay-mark sent me to Thartan to alert Governor Zentris and beg aid. How many days until I reach the city?"

"I'm pretty sure you're not where you think you are," Gavin said, before shifting his attention to Declan. "We crossed into Vushaar...what...four days ago now?"

Seb looked like he wanted to faint. "You mean I've been heading *north*?"

Declan nodded. "We're at least a week from Thartan, maybe two...and that's if we ride hard."

Seb slumped against the log, his expression forlorn and dejected. "I've failed. I'll never be able to bring back help in time."

"Gavin," Kiri said, "may I speak with you?"

Gavin pulled his attention away from Seb to face Kiri. He saw the angst on her face and suspected he knew what she wanted to say. He nodded and followed her to the far side of the campfire.

"Gavin, I feel bad about how you found out about who I used to be," Kiri said, wringing her hands and looking at the ground, "and I feel like I have no reason to ask this of you. But..."

"You want to divert to your grandparents' farm and help them defend against these Roensils." Kiri's eyes shot up to look at Gavin, as he continued. "Kiri, everyone has a right to their own secrets, and I don't fault you for protecting that one. If I'm completely honest, it would've been nice to find out about it some other way, but it is what it is. I left Tel Mivar to help your family. There's no reason we can't help both sides of your family while we're at it."

Kiri's smile would've lit an overcast night bright as a day at high noon.

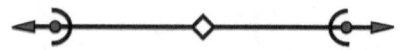

CHAPTER 9

"Oh, my," Kiri said, her utterance almost a gasp. "I don't remember the manor looking like *that.*"

They were stopped at the crest of a small hill over-looking the manor of Kiri's grandparents. The manor below looked eerily reminiscent of the fortified Sivas manor. Several work parties labored at reinforcing the manor wall and increasing its height, while two elevated guard-posts flanked the main gate. Sentry towers also now stood at each corner of the manor wall and at the mid-point of each side. Structures that looked to be barracks and an armory sat back near the stables, and many armed individuals patrolled the land inside the manor wall.

"It looks like a fortified camp," Lillian said.

"Master Claymark accepts as a fact that the Roensils are coming for him," Seb said from his somewhat-precarious perch atop one of the pack-mules. "He's doing everything he can to defend against them when they come."

Gavin scanned the various work being done, and a half-smile curled one side of his mouth as he said, "Well, I daresay we'll be able to add to his defenses...if he'll have us. I think we'd best make ourselves known from the outset. Let's take a moment to don our robes, and we'll wear our medallions outside our clothes."

A SHORT TIME LATER, they approached the manor's gate. Now close enough to make out details, Gavin saw that of the two people in each guard-post one held a longbow and the other a crossbow.

As they came within fifteen feet of the gate, one guard said, "That's close enough. State your names and business."

"My name is Gavin Cross, and I am Head of House Kirloth. I am here to offer the help of my associates and myself to the master of this manor."

"Wait there," the guard said. He signaled a guard patrolling nearby and sent him to the manor house to request the master's presence at the gate.

A few minutes later, two men in tailored work clothes approached the gate. One looked to be on the upper end of middle age, his skin weathered and wrinkled with his dark hair mixed with gray. The other was young, and the family resemblance was enough that Gavin thought he was the older man's son.

"I am Natan Claymark, master of this manor, and this is my son, Paul. What's this about you offering your help? How did you even know of our situation?"

"Your man Seb got a bit turned around and headed north instead of south," Gavin said as he stepped down from Jasmine. Kiri dismounted too, careful to keep her hood pulled low over her head. "He collapsed at the edge of our camp a couple nights ago, and once he recovered, he explained your situation. I diverted from our destination to offer you our help at the request of my friend... who also happens to be your granddaughter."

"You'll have to do better than that, young fool," Natan said. "My granddaughter died at sea over two years ago."

"No, Grandfather, I didn't," Kiri said, approaching the gate and pulling back her hood. "Hi, Uncle Paul."

Before anyone else could react, Natan had the gate unlatched and stood at arms' length in front of Kiri. He grasped her shoulders in his large, calloused hands, and he looked her all over in disbelief, his green eyes glinting with unshed tears. He pulled Kiri into an embrace, holding her tight.

"Oh, little Kiri…I thought we'd lost you, girl." Natan released Kiri and, turning to his son, said, "Look who's come home."

Paul smiled and knelt to one knee, saying, "Your Highness, welcome home. It has been too long."

"Uncle Paul…you know Father and I don't require family to kneel when it's just us."

"Ah, but it's not just us…is it, Your Highness?" Paul said. "I count fifteen people within earshot and another fifty within eyesight."

"Quite right," Natan said, kneeling as well.

Within moments, a wave of kneeling went out from the area surrounding the gate as those present followed their master's lead.

"Oh, stand up," Kiri said, her voice carrying just a hint of exasperation. "I'm trying to keep a low profile as we travel through Vushaar."

Natan and Paul pushed themselves to their feet, and soon, all those present did so as well.

"Kiri makes a good point," Gavin said, approaching Natan and Paul. "Forgive me, but we need to make sure none of your people will carry any tales of Kiri's return."

Natan grimaced. "There was a time I'd vouch for anyone wearing my colors, but with the Roensil threat, I've had to expand my retinue faster than I'd like. How would you make sure?"

"Muster your people in the courtyard, here, and have them divide themselves into five lines. My apprentices and I will see to the rest."

* * *

EXPERIENCED MAGES HAD access to a spell called 'Divination of Truth.' It was a Fourth Circle spell that surrounded the target in a gray aura when cast. For the duration of the spell, that aura would turn blazing white for truth or bright, malevolent red for a lie. Gavin had no scrolls of the spell, but because he had learned of the spell during his studies and the spell's progenitor during his perusal of Mivar's Histories, Gavin knew he could duplicate the effect by invoking a Word of Divination.

While Natan mustered everyone (including the workers who were reinforcing the walls) in the courtyard, Gavin showed his apprentices the Word they would invoke to duplicate Divination of Truth. He then showed them the Word of Tutation they would use to dispel the effect upon successful verification of the individual's loyalty to the Muran line first and Natan Claymark and his family second.

It took most of the afternoon to work through all those present, but it was worth it. They discovered five guards with questionable loyalty to the Muran line who were spies for the Roensils and ten people who were far more loyal to Natan Claymark and his family than the Muran line. In other circumstances, that could have proved problematic, but because Natan's oldest child and daughter had married Terris Muran, those ten individuals were far more loyal to Kiri than her father.

"Thank you for showing me who I could trust," Natan said, facing Gavin and his friends. "I suppose I shouldn't be surprised the Roensils infiltrated my guard force; I'm just glad none of them worked on any of the wall improvements."

"Now that we have them," Gavin said, "would you like to see if they know anything of the Roensils' plans?"

"I've never been fond of torture, good sir. I feel it provides unreliable results."

Gavin smiled. "Oh, we don't need to torture them. We'll start with a simple Divination of Truth to see if they have any knowledge of Roensils' plans. Hopefully, we'll find at least one who does not, and we can use that one as a lesson. The others should be much more helpful at that point. Pity mind-readers don't exist; we could pluck the information we wanted right out of their heads."

"When you say use one as a lesson, what do you mean by that?" Natan asked.

Gavin turned his attention from the five guards sitting on the ground, tied at the hands and feet, to face Natan. "Are you sure you want to know?"

"I see. I'm not comfortable harming any of them. We don't need the information that badly."

"I was trained in the Art and in what it means to be Kirloth by the man who dueled Milthas and founded the Kingdom of Tel. The family employing these men seeks to kill you, your family, and your people. If Kiri is here when they come for you and they find her, they'll kill her, too.

"There was a time I would've agreed with you…that there are some things that no one should ever do, no matter the provocation or the end goal. I am not that man anymore, Natan, and the only way you'll stop me from using these men to ensure Kiri's safety is demanding I leave your lands."

"I'm not a religious man," Natan said. "I believe in hard work and making your own fate through perseverance and doing to others as you would have others do unto you. I cannot expect others to show kindness to me if I don't show kindness to others. Yes, these men are working for the family that seeks my death and the death of my family, but that doesn't change my values. I won't let you torture these men."

Gavin gazed into Natan's eyes in silence for several moments. If any of those men escaped, they would take the knowledge that Kiri lived with them. Gavin wasn't ready for the world at large to learn Kiri lived, especially through a family determined to eliminate her grandfather's line just to make a grab for land. Still, if he killed them, what would that make him? He'd killed Sivas more out of strategic need than any pique, revenge, or anything like that, and the truth of it was he didn't regret killing Sivas in the least. As he stood there looking Natan in his eyes, Gavin knew he wouldn't regret killing those five guards, either…not even a little bit. There was nothing for it; Gavin needed advice.

"A few moments please, Natan," Gavin said and turned to his

fellows. Gesturing for them to follow him, Gavin walked far enough away for their conversation to be out of earshot.

"WHAT IS IT, GAVIN?" Lillian asked when they'd gathered.

Gavin focused on Kiri, who faced him with a knowing expression. "Kiri knows."

Lillian turned to Kiri, saying, "Well?"

"He's debating killing those men," Kiri said. "A clean death wouldn't be torture, and the knowledge I'm alive would be safe. But I doubt it would secure my grandfather as a friend; he might tell us to leave, even knowing he needs our help."

"Trust me, Kiri," Gavin said. "Your grandfather will always love you. Nothing will ever take that away. But *I*—on the other hand— don't care in the slightest what he thinks of me. Those guards present a possible source of information regarding Roensils' plans and a threat to you through their knowledge. I am certain the proper course of action is to wrack those men's body and souls until they're begging to tell us everything they know. Barring that, they should not leave this estate alive…not with what they know."

"Gavin," Kiri said, "people will learn I'm alive regardless of what we do. If nothing else, word will spread once I'm home and at Father's side again."

"Yes, that's true," Declan said, "but we have to cross over half your country to deliver you safely back home. Knowledge that you're alive and trying to make it home would create many complications and might very well lead to failure. It makes little sense to save the kingdom from Ivarson's rebellion if you're killed on the way to the capital."

"Gavin and Declan are right," Elayna said. "Until you're within the palace walls in Vushaar, our greatest protection is the world at large thinking the Crown Princess is dead. All it would take is one crossbow quarrel, one arrow, or a caster capable of death magic, and the Muran line is ended." She turned to look Gavin right in his eyes. "It's no secret anyone bearing the mantle of Kirloth is capable of a level of ruthlessness the common person would never consider, and the sad, unfortunate fact is that this world needs that ruthlessness from time to time. It's the sacrifice you make so we don't have to. Be the Kirloth your mentor trained you to be, Gavin, and follow your conscience."

Gavin looked to each of his associates who hadn't spoken, offering them each a chance to weigh in. None of them did.

"Very well," Gavin said, turning and walking back to Natan, Paul, and the five guards.

"Natan," Gavin said, stopping to stand about eight feet from Natan and his son, "I respect your convictions and your morals, but I do not share them. These men represent a threat to Kiri so grave they could jeopardize our chances of seeing Kiri safely home if they lived, and I cannot think of any kind of assurance they could give that would stay my hand." Gavin shifted his attention to the five men and invoked a Word, "*Thraxys.*"

A slight tightening around his eyes indicated Gavin's discomfort as the five men died. Natan looked at the five corpses, his expression horrified.

"How could…you killed those men!"

"Yes, I did," Gavin said, "and I won't apologize for it. Kiri is safer with them dead."

Natan turned to look at Gavin, and Gavin saw judgment and condemnation in his eyes as he said, "You're a merciless man, Gavin Cross; may the gods save you from ever needing mercy yourself."

Natan turned and walked to the manor house, his head low.

Gavin watched him go and, in the corner of his eye, saw Paul turn from looking toward his father to look at him. He shifted his attention to Kiri's uncle.

"For what it's worth, I understand your choice," Paul said. "I don't think I could have done it, but I understand it."

Paul then turned and walked after his father.

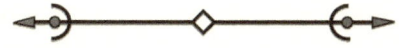

CHAPTER 10

A short time later, Gavin and his friends sat around a large table with Natan, Paul, and the leaders of Natan's guard force.

"Do we have any information on when the Roensils plan to move against you?" Gavin asked.

Natan still looked unsettled, but he rose to the occasion and shook his head. "We know they've been hiring mercenaries, and their selection criteria isn't too specific."

"See lightning and hear thunder?" Declan asked, drawing a chuckle from Sarres.

"Pretty much," Natan said. "For all I know, they're building a raiding force. We're one of the largest grain producers for the country, and it wouldn't take much to ruin us."

"I don't see that," Sarres said. "From everything we've discussed, this Roensil is only attacking you *for* the land itself. It gains him nothing if his attack spoils the land. Describe the Roensil who's in charge, please."

"He's a great, hulking brute of a man," Paul said. "In his younger days, he killed several in brawls with one punch. Unfortunately, he's not stupid, either. He has an almost feral cunning about him, and he doesn't suffer fools. His oldest son was little more than a simpleton, and when the boy ruined a business deal for the family a third time, the old man wrung his neck."

Sarres nodded in silence. After a few moments, he lifted his head to face Natan, saying, "He'll come for you here, then. It'll be a straight-up fight. He may have a few surprises in the way of tactics, but what your son just said leads me to think this will be as much of a lesson about what's in store for any who oppose him as a grab for your family's land."

"There have been rumors he's selling grain to Ivarson's troops," Natan said. "I don't want to believe it, myself. The Roensils were one of the most loyal families for many decades, centuries even. The original homestead came from a land grant by one of His Majesty's ancestors many, many years ago for honorable service above and beyond the call of duty."

Just then, a knock heralded the entrance of Natan's majordomo. "Milord, there's an itinerant trader at the gate, asking to speak with you. He says he has information you need."

"I find this very suspicious, Father," Paul said.

"It is odd; I'll grant you that."

Gavin shrugged. "I'll speak with him at the gate, then. If there's nothing to it or if he's a panhandler looking to sell tall tales for coin, I'll toss him a few silvers and send him on his way."

Natan regarded Gavin with undisguised puzzlement. "Charity from Kirloth?"

"I take no joy from killing, Natan," Gavin said as he pushed himself to his feet. "but neither do I avoid its utility."

GAVIN FOLLOWED the majordomo to the manor wall's gate. A man stood there, dressed in shabby, road-worn clothes, and he looked to be on the upper end of middle age. Salt-and-pepper hair lay matted and greasy against his scalp, and Gavin smelled him some fifteen feet from the gate. In his left hand, he held the reins of a pack-mule loaded with bulging sacks and all manner of random items.

"Master Claymark is indisposed," Gavin said as he approached the man, "but I promise whatever information you give me will reach him."

"Weel now," the man said in a raspy, weathered voice, "ain't ye just th' soul o' kindness." The man scratched at his right hip for a moment before shifting his attention to his left arm. As the man pushed back the sleeve of his filthy tunic to scratch his left forearm, Gavin saw a Wraith tattoo on the man's left wrist.

"Been a long time since I seen a wizard o' yer House, boy. Are ye the real thang or just some jumped-up puppy all full of piss 'n vinegar?"

"Oh, I'm real enough," Gavin said. "Now, do you have that information or not?"

"I been trading my circle, seein' all the settlements north of Thartan. I kin make enough to pay for the whole trip tradin' spices at the Roensil estate, and I never seen that place as empty as it was, just th' other day. The missus, Lady Roensil she likes to be called, told me her man and his people were out on a ride and just left enough to keep the manor safe. The man at the gate said Old Man Roensil left a few days ago with something like seven hundred men."

Gavin nodded, saying, "Thank you. I'm not sure we have anything to trade with you, but I appreciate the information." He retrieved his coin purse and started to withdraw a handful of silvers but then changed his mind and extended a gold piece to the trader with his right hand. "Here, take this for your trouble. You might want to be some distance down the road, sooner rather than later."

The trader wrapped his right hand around Gavin's and pulled Gavin into a tight embrace. The smell came closer to knocking Gavin down than any of his recent invocations.

"Why, thankee! Yer powerful generous and kind, ye are," the trader said. He leaned into Gavin's ear, still shaking Gavin's hand like a man who'd never seen a gold piece before and whispered, "Roensil has seven mages with him, Milord. He hired them a month ago and has had them preparing for an assault on this estate."

The trader released Gavin and stepped back, palming the gold piece and tucking it away in a pocket. "Thankee, good sir; thankee. Blessings of the gods be upon you and yours."

He turned and started to lead his mule away from the gate.

Gavin turned and saw the majordomo stepping back from Gavin, his expression a grimace.

"Run up to the house and bring me a couple cakes of soap, please," Gavin said, before turning back toward the trader. "Master trader, hold a few moments more, please."

"Oh, kind sir, yer already too generous," the trader said. "No need to trouble yerself for anything else." He stopped, though.

The majordomo soon returned with two cakes of soap and handed them to Gavin. Gavin walked over to the trader and placed the soap in the man's hand, braving the stench to lean close and whisper, "Your smell would empty a graveyard, no necromancy required. Take a bath. You should give serious thought to burning those clothes, too, and if I have to send the entire Thartan chapter to see to the job, I'll make sure they scrub you down with a wire brush."

The trader winced.

Gavin patted him twice on the back and left him.

"Did that trader have anything worthwhile to say?" Natan asked as Gavin re-entered the discussion.

"Roensil left his estate a few days ago with upwards of seven hundred men. He also hired seven mages, and he's had them preparing for a month."

"Seven hundred men?" Natan asked. "That can't be true. Why, we don't even have a quarter that number under arms! He'll roll over us like we're not even here."

"Declan," Gavin said, "how long would it take seven hundred men to travel here from Roensil's place?"

"No more than a week. Did the trader say how old his information was?"

"No. He didn't have many specifics. He just knew they were coming."

"We're putting a lot of faith in some panhandler," Paul said. "What are the chances Roensil sent him to feed us misinformation?"

Gavin's mind drifted back to the Wraith tattoo on the man's left wrist and shook his head. "That's not possible. I'd sooner believe the sun would rise in the west."

"You're awfully certain of that trader's veracity," Natan said. "What do you know that we don't?"

"Many things," Gavin said, "just like you know many things I do not."

Lillian leaned close to Gavin and whispered, "What about the dracons? You made quite an impression on them. Think they would help with the defenses here?"

"That's a good idea. It doesn't hurt to ask," Gavin said and directed his attention back to Natan. "I may have a line on some troops who would be friendly to your cause. I will speak with them and ask for their help."

"If it takes more than a couple hours to reach them, I wouldn't bother," Natan said. "From the sounds of it, they will overrun us before you'd make it back."

Gavin chuckled. "I wouldn't worry about being overrun, Natan. After all, the fight hasn't even started yet. While I'm seeing to those additional troops, Lillian speaks for me in all things."

"Are you sure about that?" Lillian asked, her voice a whisper.

"I wouldn't have said it if I wasn't sure," Gavin said, not bothering to whisper. "Take care of Jasmine for me."

"You're not taking a horse?" Paul asked. "How can you hope to make it back in time?"

Gavin pushed his chair back from the table and stood, saying, "If I know where I'm going, I don't *need* a horse. *Paedryx.*"

Gavin's invocation slammed into those wizards present as an arch of sapphire energy rose out of the floor. When it reached its full height, the center of the arch flashed, becoming a doorway to another place. Gavin stepped through, and the arch vanished as if it had never been.

* * *

GAVIN STOOD in the cupola pavilion at the center of the dracon city, facing the assembled clan leaders. He smiled and nodded once at Xask, who now bore the mantle of her clan's leadership.

"We did not expect to see you again so soon," the ancient clan leader said.

Gavin shrugged. "I did not expect to encounter a situation that required me asking for your help."

"What is the situation you speak of?" Xask asked.

"Do you remember my friend Kiri?" When the clan leaders nodded, Gavin continued. "Her grandfather, Natan Claymark, is a large wheat and grain supplier in northern Thartan Province, just across the border in Vushaar. A longtime rival is using the civil war to move against the Claymark family with the intent of eliminating the family and seizing their lands. The rival has mobilized a force of seven hundred mercenaries and seven mages to attack the Claymark estate, and while my apprentices and I can see to the mages, Claymark has no way to secure sufficient reliable men-at-arms to fend off this assault, especially since he'd need to ensure anyone he hired would protect Kiri's secret."

"And so, you came to us," Xask said. "We left the world six hundred years ago when it became clear that the naturals had lost their way. Bellos's choice not to name a new Archmagister after the death of Bellock Vanlon was a sign to all who cared to notice that the naturals had lost the favor of the gods."

"I'm not asking you to return to the world. I'm asking you to help me help someone...just as I helped you."

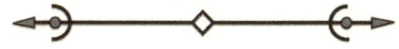

CHAPTER 11

"I think he has a few more than seven hundred mercenaries," Braden said, looking out over the mass of troops forming up a few hundred yards away from the manor wall.

"Looks closer to twelve hundred," Declan said. "He must've been repeating what he was told; I can't imagine the trader would get the count wrong."

"Roensil could've met another group before coming here," Mariana said. "The trader Gavin spoke with may have only seen seven hundred."

"Look-there's-a-group-riding-this-way," Wynn said, pointing.

Lillian sighed, saying, "I should go stand with Natan during the conversation. Make sure he knows he's not alone."

"I don't think you need to worry about that," Declan said. "He has about twelve hundred guests to keep him company."

Lillian, Paul, and Natan stood at the gate when the three riders bearing a flag of truce arrived. The man in the lead looked to be about Natan's age and the woman at his side about Paul's. The man wore chain-mail over padding and carried a sword at his right side.

The woman wore chain-mail, with a spiked mace at her left side. The third individual wore a red robe, and the silver runes on the cuffs of the sleeves indicated he held the rank of *Magus* within the Society of the Arcane.

"Well, Natan, are you going to be smart about this and save us all a lot of trouble?"

"There's nothing smart about giving away my family's heritage, Janson," Natan said, "especially when we both know you'll kill us, anyway."

Janson Roensil shifted his gaze to Lillian and smirked. "What's the matter, Natan? Couldn't you afford a real arcanist? Do you think four students can compete with my seven fully trained arcanists?"

The mage at Janson's shoulder looked at Lillian and jerked as recognition set in. He shifted his gaze over Natan's shoulder to where Wynn, Braden, and Mariana stood. Lillian saw him pale and say just loud enough to hear, "If they're here, where is *he*?"

"What are you blathering about?" Roensil said, looking over his shoulder to the mage.

"We may not have as much of an upper hand here as you think," the mage said, his eyes flitting from point to point. "Their mentor is missing."

"Their mentor? If you're trying to back out of the contract..."

"You hired me for my sage wisdom and council, and I'm telling you they're not students. They're *apprentices*, and I don't believe their mentor is all that far away."

"He's about four- or five-days' ride to the north," Lillian said, smiling up at the arcanist. "He went to see some associates about reinforcements."

"Four- or five-days' ride?" the arcanist said, frowning. "Why, there's nothing up there but...oh, you can't be serious! No one has survived the dracon lands in six hundred years."

Lillian shrugged, her smile shifting to a smirk. "Well then, you have nothing to worry about...do you?"

Roensil turned back to Natan, saying, "This is your last chance. Surrender now, and I'll let your servants live."

Natan shook his head. "Janson, if I honestly believed you'd

spare them *and* I felt our chances were hopeless, then I *might* consider your offer. We're not going anywhere."

"Suit yourself," Janson said and turned his horse, nudging the mount to a trot as he led his daughter and hireling back to their lines.

"Gavin had better show up," Natan said, once they were out of earshot.

"I'm not worried," Lillian said. "He'll return. You'll see."

* * *

GAVIN'S CONCERNS when he left the Claymark estate proved to be unfounded...*very* unfounded. Gavin expected he'd have to use all manner of persuasion and oratory to bring the dracons around to his way of thinking. Instead, he was having to turn people away. When the clan leaders put out the call that Kirloth had returned asking for their help, *everyone* responded, even the children and elderly.

Gavin wasn't about to take children into battle, no matter what their parents thought of the idea, and the elderly would make perfect babysitters while the parents were away. That still left him with several thousand volunteers.

Gavin rubbed his chin with his right hand as he looked out over the mass of people. He had no idea in the world what he would do with all these volunteers.

"What troubles you?" Xask asked, drawing Gavin's attention.

"I don't need this many people," Gavin said, "and I don't like leaving your city undefended."

Xask smiled. "You're applying your experience to us. Those younglings and elderly you turned away? They are more than suffi-cient defense for the city, and besides, we're not calling in the scouts. They may be disappointed they did not get to attend, but we have more than sufficient numbers for the task at hand. How do you want us organized?"

Gavin was afraid someone would ask him that. When 'his' army had moved against the mercenaries at Lake Yortun, Gavin had been more than content to allow the officers to handle all the organiza-tion and day-to-day management. The only times he'd had to inter-vene was when they brought a matter to him for adjudication, which didn't happen all that often…maybe three or four times.

"Honestly, I must confess to being overwhelmed. I fully expected that I'd have to beg and plead for your help; I wasn't prepared for this kind of response at all. Am I correct that the experience and leadership exists to handle the organization of the troops?"

Xask nodded. "You are."

"Then, I'm not about to horn in and disrupt what works for your people. Pass the word to get everything settled, and send two arcanists from each unit—however those units turn out—to me. I'm not sure how much time we have, but I know it's far less than we think."

A short time later, Gavin faced twenty-six dracon arcanists, and they ran the gamut of age and experience. They stood in the large workroom where Gavin had worked on repairing their sky.

"Okay. Forgive me for this being rough; we're working against the clock, and we need to get a move on. How many of you are wizards?" Twenty-six hands raised. "Excellent. Gather around. I have a few things to show you."

Gavin led the group over to one chalkboard and sketched out the runes representing two Words, one of Divination and the other of Transmutation.

"Now then, this is a Word of Divination. We'll use it to create scrying spheres to fine tune our point of arrival. The other is a Word of Transmutation we'll use to create the actual portals. Commit them to memory if you haven't already." Gavin waited until everyone was finished and pointed to one at random. "Time to check for understanding. I want you to step out of the group and create a scrying sphere over the table that looks down on the entrance to the tunnel leading to the city."

The dracon looked a little nervous but stepped over to the table. She took a breath and invoked the Word, "*Klaepos.*"

The scrying sphere that formed wasn't much larger than a window in a house, but it was a scrying sphere that looked down on the entrance to the tunnel. Everyone present could see the dracon standing behind the gate, looking rather bored, and there was more than one gasp of surprise.

"Very good," Gavin said. "Does anyone have questions?" No one did. "Very well. Let's rejoin the others and make ready to leave."

GAVIN LED the arcanists to the city's sporting field. The sporting field was the only space in the city large enough for the volunteers to muster with any ease. Gavin shook his head as he looked out over the mass of people, still not quite believing he was returning to Natan's place with almost sixty-five hundred dracons…all armed, armored, and ready to fight. Even after explaining the attacking force was only fielding seven hundred, the dracons would not be swayed; they wanted to show their support and gratitude to Kirloth.

Gavin watched the arcanists separate and return to their assigned units, and he was surprised that those units were not organized along clan lines. It seemed each clan had a specific affinity or affinities, and by drawing from all clans, each unit was stronger than what it would've been if it was made up from only one clan.

"There's so much I have yet to learn about this world," Gavin said, almost sighing. "Ah, well. Time to stop woolgathering and pick our arrival point. *Klaepos*."

Gavin's scrying sphere was much larger than the one created by the dracon, and it overlooked the entire Claymark estate. Gavin gasped at what he saw; the Roensils had many more than seven hundred mercenaries, and they were moving to assault the gate.

"Arcanists to me!" Gavin shouted, and those twenty-six soon stood before him. "I will place a magical marker where you are to create your portals. One at a time, step forward."

The first stepped forward, and Gavin took the dracon's hand in his left as he used his right to interact with the scrying sphere. The physical contact as Gavin placed the marker tuned the arcanist to the mark for easier recognition. Within two minutes, twenty-six arrival markers were placed; thirteen along the inside the manor wall and thirteen behind the assaulting force.

"Return to your units, and make ready. I want us all to arrive at the same time. Create your portals on my command."

The dracons nodded and returned to their units. They took up positions in the van of their respective formations and nodded to Gavin, signaling their readiness. Once everyone was ready, Gavin nodded once and said, "Now!"

Twenty-six dracons invoked the Word of Transmutation Gavin taught them, creating portals in front of their formations. Gavin hurried to one specific formation, moving to stand beside the dracon he'd instructed to create the scrying sphere.

"Let's go!"

* * *

NATAN SIGHED when he saw the Roensil force move toward the manor wall. They weren't ready, and they would not *be* ready. It looked like Gavin would not be in time, either.

"You should get your friends and get Kiri over the back wall," Natan said as he surveyed the approaching force. "They'll be too busy with us to notice your departure."

Lillian shook her head. "Gavin said he'd return, and he said he'd help you. We're not doing anything except shutting down those mages."

"Have some sense about you," Natan growled. "That's my granddaughter and the Crown Princess in the house, there! There's no call-"

Whatever Natan was going to say was cut off, as the compound sound of crackling energy all around his position drowned out his voice. Lillian cried out and wrapped her arms across her midriff as she struggled to stay standing, and her fellow apprentices did the same. Natan feared a magical attack, but as he turned to look at Lillian, what was going on behind him drew his attention.

Thirteen portals rose out of the earth, and no two of them

looked alike. Natan gaped as dracons streamed through the portals onto his land, and he laughed as his tension and fear evaporated upon seeing Gavin step through the portal right behind him, leading one of the dracon contingents.

The moment Gavin stepped through the portal, he invoked a Word, "*Thyphos*." A radiance above him drew Natan's attention, and looking up, he felt his jaw slacken at the sight: the battle standard of House Kirloth—at least fifteen feet wide—hovered above their heads some thirty feet in the air.

The dracons vaulted Natan's manor wall, almost like it wasn't even there and dressed their lines to repel the coming assault... which wasn't coming all that quickly now. Gavin climbed the ladder to one of the elevated guard-posts by the gate and used another Conjuration effect to ensure his words were heard across the valley.

"My name is Gavin Cross, and as you may have guessed, I am Head of House Kirloth. Any mercenary who lays down his or her weapons and kneels—arcanists included—will be granted mercy; I have no desire to bathe this field in blood today. My offer of mercy does not extend to the Roensils and any who steadfastly stand with them. You have fifteen minutes to decide. After that, anyone still armed or standing dies."

* * *

"Well, we're done," the arcanist said, looking from the dracons in front of them to the dracons behind them.

"How dare you!" Janson Roensil growled. "I paid you good money!"

"You paid me to provide magical support to what you described as an easy rout. This stopped being an easy rout the moment those portals opened, and if you think the seven of us can turn the tide against that horde of dracons—not to mention Kirloth himself—you're a damned fool. I don't mind giving my life for my family to eat, but I'd at least like to have a hope of surviving."

Before Janson could respond, the arcanist swung off the far side of the horse from Janson and knelt to one knee, lacing his fingers behind his head. He wasn't the only one, either. Mercenaries are, by far, the most pragmatic of professional soldiers. They don't fight for country; they fight for coin, and the best coin comes from victories…not wholesale defeats. Within ten minutes, the only people still standing were the Roensils atop their mounts (who were exempt from Gavin's mercy anyway) and a handful of Roensil retainers loyal to Janson and his daughter.

* * *

SEEING ONLY FIFTEEN PEOPLE—AT most—still standing, Gavin said, "dracons, hold your positions. I'll handle this."

Gavin cleared his mind of all thoughts except his intent, and he focused his entire consciousness on that intent. Then, he invoked the first Word he ever learned, *"Thraxys."*

The Roensils—Janson and his daughter—and the few fighters still standing fell to the ground, dead before their bodies struck the dirt. The Roensils' horses shied away from their riders falling away, and as the wind shifted to bring the scent of so many dracons—who happened to smell just like dragons to herd animals—to the horses, the rider-less mounts whinnied in terror and bolted at a full gallop.

A SHORT TIME LATER, most of the dracons were returned home, with only a couple formations remaining to keep an eye on the surrendered mercenaries. Natan stood at the now-open gate, staring at the bodies that were the only casualties of the so-called assault.

"What's to become of them all?" Natan asked when Gavin walked up to his side.

Gavin shrugged. "Honestly, I don't care…as long as they never accept coin to attack you or yours again. I will have a word with them to that effect, and then, I'll offer them a job."

"What should I do with the bodies?"

"I'll deal with them, too," Gavin said. "I think the remaining Roensils may need an object lesson."

ROBERT M. KERNS

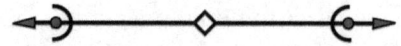

CHAPTER 12

"So, tell me why Declan and I aren't going with you?" Kiri asked, frowning at Gavin her fists on her hips.

"For one thing, if they found out you're still alive and I knew about them having that knowledge, I'd have to kill them. I've killed enough people today. Second, I thought you'd enjoy more time with your grandparents and uncle, and since I will have close to a thousand dracons with me, Declan stays with you."

Kiri let out a sigh and unclenched her fists as she lowered her hands from her hips. "That makes sense, I suppose, but I don't like your first response being killing anyone who learns I'm still alive."

Gavin shrugged. "We all have our burdens to bear. Once you're home with your father, I won't worry about it. At that point, you'll be inside the most secure part of the most secure city in the known world."

"What makes you say that?"

"According to Mivar's Histories, Vushaar withstood a siege led by Ak'Rython and Milthas's lieutenant for several years, before the Army of Valthon got around to breaking the siege. Unless Ivarson somehow has agents inside the city, we could make a leisurely stroll of your return home and still arrive before Ivarson breached the walls."

"You don't think Tel Mivar is more secure?"

Gavin shrugged. "I have no way of knowing. The city's defenses have never been put to the test. I'd like to think it's just as secure, but until there's a siege, we'll never know for sure. Now, enjoy this time with your family. I'll be back in about an hour or so."

GAVIN STOOD at the gathered corpses, his apprentices fanned out behind him. Gavin felt this next part was rather distasteful, but he saw no other way. After all, he'd never been to the Roensil estate.

Gavin knelt and pricked the finger of Janson Roensil, drawing a couple drops of blood. It took a few moments, given that the man's heart was no longer beating. Then, he stood and concentrated on the blood. He formed his intent in his mind and cleared away all other distractions. Then, he spoke the Word, "*Paedryx.*"

Savage pain tore at Gavin's guts, causing him to feel on the verge of vomiting, as an archway of sapphire energy rose out of the earth. The pain was worse this time, because Gavin didn't have a clear vision of his destination in mind...just the intent to open a portal to the man's home whose blood he held. Still, though, it seemed to work.

Gavin glanced at one of Natan's people, asking, "Is that the Roensil estate?"

The man was a simple stonemason, and his wide eyes and slack jaw suggested he wasn't all that comfortable around magic. Still, though, he gave Gavin a jerky nod.

"Thank you, good sir," Gavin said. He then directed his focus to the corpses and spoke another Word, "*Khrypaex.*" The gathered corpses rose on conjured cushions of air and hovered a bit closer to Gavin.

"All right," Gavin said. "Let's go."

He turned and led the floating corpses, his apprentices, and three formations of dracons through the portal.

* * *

"WHAT IS THE MEANING OF THIS?" Lady Roensil said, her tone gruff and haughty. Lady Roensil stood at the gate to her family's manor, and she looked every inch the Lady of the House. Her dress was made of expensive silk, its tailoring exquisite, and the hairpins that held her coiffed hair would pay a person's salary for a year, not to mention the rings, necklace, and earrings.

"I thought we should have a word," Gavin said. "I bring you the corpses of your husband, daughter, and various individuals wearing your colors."

The color left Lady Roensil's face as she looked upon her family's remains. "I'll have that Claymark's head for this!"

"That's what I wanted to discuss," Gavin said. "Allow me to introduce myself. My name is Gavin Cross, and I'm Head of House Kirloth. These individuals at my back are my apprentices, and the assorted souls behind them are the dracons who stayed behind to escort me on this errand. Claymark had nothing to do with their deaths...unless you count the fact that they were trying to kill him and his family to take their land. *I* killed your husband, daughter, and these retainers. If you want to swear vengeance on someone, it should be me. I honestly don't care, but I want to be very clear about this next part. If you continue the feud with Claymark that led to these deaths, I urge you to dig your own grave along with one for anyone else who lacks sense enough to see reason, because I give you my word. The moment you attack Natan Claymark or his people ever again, I'll see to your deaths myself...and depopulate your entire estate in the process. If you don't believe me, send people to Tel and investigate the fates of Baron Kalinor and House Sivas. Trust me; the information won't be hard to find."

Gavin directed a casual wave of his left hand as he said, "*Rhosed.*"

The cushions of air under the corpses faded, lowering them to the ground before dissipating.

"We now take our leave of you, Lady Roensil, and I ask you to heed well what I've said."

"You dare threaten me not ten feet from my gate? I should have you killed where you stand!"

"Lady Roensil, I did not threaten you. I stated facts and made you a promise. The fact you've attracted my attention should be threat enough."

Gavin started to open another portal, but he felt like experimenting. If he was right, he figured it would unnerve everyone watching quite a bit. He formed his intent in his mind and focused his entire consciousness on making that intent a reality. Then, he spoke the word, "*Paedryx*."

Instead of a portal, Gavin teleported himself, his apprentices, and every single dracon back to the land outside Natan Claymark's estate. In the blink of an eye, they were simply...gone.

* * *

BACK AT THE CLAYMARK ESTATE, Gavin thanked the dracons before their arcanists opened portals to return home. Then, he turned to consider the mercenaries who had surrendered. The more he considered offering them jobs, the more he doubted the logistics of the proposition. All his people were back in Tel, with those troops he'd stationed at the former Sivas estate being the closest. Still, he was always looking for loyal people, and if they wanted guaranteed work and were willing to travel to Tel, he knew his captains would evaluate them.

"All right, people, listen up," Gavin said, addressing the mercenaries. "I'm always on the lookout for competent, loyal people, and I'm willing to hire any of you who travel to Tel and pass the evaluations of my captains there. I need to know who will make the trip, so I can provide an introduction. The introduction will guarantee a travel stipend if you don't make the cut...for whatever reason. All who are interested, stand up and form a group to my right."

About three-quarters of the group moved to the new group.

Gavin nodded. "Very well. The rest of you, listen well. Claymark and his people are off limits. The next time you attack these people or their holdings, you'll have no mercy from me or mine.

Now, be on your way. You should be well away from here by nightfall."

Those mercenaries not interested in Gavin's employment gathered their belongings and left.

Gavin considered the mercenaries who wanted to try for his employment, and he didn't enjoy the thought of writing over five hundred introductions. Well, there was nothing for it; it was time to experiment again. He formed a picture in his mind of the introduction he desired, complete with writing and a Glyph of Kirloth that glowed as a signature. He added the specification that the introductions would dissolve when they were handed to one of his captains, and once his intent was clear and solid in his mind, Gavin spoke the Word, "*Nythraex.*"

A stack of parchment appeared in his left hand, all manifestations of his intent and identical to one another. Gavin divided the stack into fifths, distributing four stacks to his apprentices.

"Form five lines, and when you've received a parchment, be on your way. The closest posting of my forces is the Vischaene Vineyard in the Kingdom of Tel."

It took longer to get those five-hundred-odd mercenaries on their way to Tel than Gavin would've liked, and the sun was low on the horizon when he entered Natan's house. In the end, he didn't get to leave that day, as Natan insisted on Gavin and his friends partaking of Claymark hospitality. Neither Natan nor his wife was interested in seeing Gavin and his friends spend the night at a road-side camp after they'd done so much to help the family.

The next morning, Gavin and his friends resumed their travels after Kiri's grandmother and her kitchen staff provided an excellent breakfast and restocked their traveling supplies. Natan also insisted on exchanging Gavin's pack-mules for two pack-horses, since the horses would allow them to make better time than the sedate pace the mules tended to prefer.

As they stood at the gate, Natan approached Gavin, his expression stern as he said, "I've spent time thinking about what I've witnessed of your methods. I want no part of how you live your life to touch me or mine. I appreciate your help in ending the Roensil threat, but I'd prefer you not come by here ever again."

Gavin shrugged. "I have no problem with that, but you should be certain you'll never want to call on my help again. If this is how we leave things, neither I nor anyone who answers to me will help you again...not even to pick up a letter the postman dropped along the highway. Do you understand?"

Natan nodded once. "I do. Thank you for seeing Kiri home, and you'd best be on your way."

"Good day to you and yours, Natan Claymark," Gavin said, before turning to Jasmine and pulling himself into the saddle.

As they rode away, Gavin turned to Declan, asking, "You heard?"

"I did," Declan replied.

"Ensure everyone knows that Natan Claymark and his family receive no further assistance from us."

Declan nodded once.

Soon, the Claymark estate disappeared over the horizon.

"Did you enjoy your time with the family?" Gavin asked Kiri.

Kiri smiled like a little girl who'd received her first doll. "Oh, yes! It's been so long since I've been home. Seeing them...well, I feel like I'll make it home after all. The capital just seems so far away, especially with everything that's happening. It's easy to feel like I'll never see home again."

Gavin nodded. "On one side, I can understand that. Still, though, I'm surprised you feel that way."

"Oh? Why?"

Gavin turned to look Kiri in her eyes, saying, "Because I promised to take you home, and I always keep my promises."

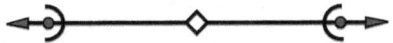

CHAPTER 13

They rode south for the most part, traveling through the grasslands and wheat fields of northern Vushaar. The weather was pleasant, with salty breezes blowing east off the Inner Sea, and the ladies, Wynn, Braden, and Declan sung to the accompaniment of Declan's virtuoso manipulation of the lute. Gavin and Sarres felt discretion to be the better part of valor in that venue, but Wynn's steady tenor surprised everyone. Gavin would've thought the nervous energy Wynn exuded would've prevented him from keeping even halfway-decent time, soon possessing considerable evidence to the contrary.

ABOUT FOUR DAYS south of the Claymark estate, they were riding through rolling fields, and topping a small rise, they saw a child running toward them, a small lad with light brown hair. Some distance back, four men ran in pursuit. The boy reached them in short order, and Kiri gasped when she saw him.

"Help me!" the boy screamed as he ran. "Please, help me!"

Gavin slowed Jasmine and dropped to his feet. The boy ran up to him and threw his arms around Gavin's waist. "Don't let them take me back; please, don't let them take me!"

Gavin gestured to Sarres and Declan. "See to the men chasing him."

With the small boy clinging to him, Gavin turned as best he could and surveyed the area. A small copse of trees stood not too far to the west, and he could see some fallen trees among them. Gavin hefted the boy up onto his horse in front of the saddle and climbed astride the animal himself.

"Come on," Gavin said. "Let's go over there, so we can at least be in some shade while we sort this out."

THERE WAS an aged fire pit at the center of the copse of trees, and from the position of the fallen logs coupled with the nearby spring, it was clear they had found another waystation. Gavin dismounted and tied his horse to a tree, before turning and lowering the boy to the ground. The others soon dismounted and secured their horses, but no one was prepared for the boy's reaction when he saw Kiri.

"Kiri!" His face lit up, and he charged her with his arms wide, soon clutching her leg in the kind of bear hug only a small child can produce. "What are you doing here? Uncle Zen said you went away."

"Well, Garrett, my trip was cut short, and I'm on my way back," Kiri said as she extricated herself from the boy and knelt to embrace him.

Kiri soon broke the embrace and led the boy over to a log, where she sat and pulled him onto her lap. She looked to each person in turn, but she focused on Gavin.

"His name is Garrett," Kiri said, "and he's the nephew of my father's oldest friend, Zentris. Zentris is like an uncle to me, too, and he's been the governor of Thartan Province for as long as I can remember." She looked down at Garrett before continuing to speak. "Garrett, what are you doing all the way out here by yourself?"

"They took us, Kiri, me and Naida. They weren't nice, either. I think they were going to do something to Naida before one woman with them pulled her knife on them."

Garrett's words kicked off a fury in Gavin's soul unlike anything he could remember in recent months. He walked over and knelt in front of Kiri, eyes locked on Garrett.

"People took you from your uncle, Garrett? You and your sister?"

"Yes, sir."

Gavin nodded. "Do you know why they did it? Who they worked for?"

"I don't think so. They never talked around us a whole lot, but I heard them say something about a general one time they thought we were asleep."

"They must have abducted the children to force Zentris to support Ivarson," Mariana said from where she stood not too far away.

Declan and Sarres arrived at that point.

Declan said, "They were fierce fighters. Each one fought to the death."

Gavin nodded his acceptance before shifting his gaze to Sarres. "Can you back-trace the boy's path, find out where he came from?"

Sarres gave Gavin a look that spoke volumes. "The way the vegetation is disturbed, *you* could back-trace the boy's path."

"Go, then," Gavin said, "and when you reach the end of the trail, scout the area and find a suitable place for a camp. Be as stealthy as you can. I'd prefer that camp to be on the western side, so we have unhindered access to Thartan."

Sarres nodded and left.

Gavin turned to Declan, saying, "Go to Thartan, and contact your fellows. They couldn't have abducted the governor's niece and nephew without help inside the city. I want your people to identify everyone associated with the plot. Once that's done and confirmed, bring enough people back to our new camp to conduct Kiri and the boy to Thartan. Your ward-stone will guide you once I set up the camp's ward. Take those horses for re-mounts if you think they can handle it."

Now that it was evident they'd be spending time within those trees, Gavin suggested everyone see to the horses.

THE HORSES CARED FOR, Gavin set up the wards, taking a small stone from the ground to become Garrett's ward-stone. Sarres returned a short time after dusk, and Gavin could tell the day had been tiring for him.

Sarres flopped on a log across from where Gavin sat. He withdrew his waterskin from its place on his belt and took a long pull.

"I tracked the boy's path to a run-down manor about two leagues south of here," Sarres said. "Whatever it might have been, that place is now a fortified camp. Oh, sure, they do a pretty good job of acting like a manor under guard because of all the instability, but there isn't anyone working the fields. And, we're farther south than we thought we were. I found a hilltop on the southern side of the manor that was tall enough for me to see Thartan in the distance; where we are now is about a day and a half of easy riding from the city."

"Did you find any suitable locations for a camp closer to Thartan?" Gavin asked.

"Not really," Sarres said, shaking his head. "We're about an hour past the fringe of the manor's sentry patrols right now, and they have a lot of men skulking through the countryside between the manor and Thartan. They're obviously worried about anyone trying to sneak into the manor from the south and west, and they have spread their people so thin on the north and east sides, it's a perimeter in name only."

Gavin turned to where Kiri sat playing with Garrett. "Kiri, do you know of a manor or plantation about a day's ride north of Thartan? Someplace that would be run-down from lack of care?"

Kiri's brow furrowed in thought for several moments before she nodded. "The only place I can think of is the old estate of Thanis Velsharin. He was a petty trader playing at being a merchant prince, and he died of somewhat mysterious circumstances about five years ago…well, seven years ago now. I didn't realize anyone had bought his place. Why?"

"Whoever now owns that manor is involved in the children's abduction," Gavin said, "and I think that's where Naida is being held."

Kiri looked down at the boy beside her. "Garrett, did you escape from a big house not too far south of us?"

"Yeah, there were a lot of bad men there. I wanted to get Naida out, but I didn't know where they were keeping her."

Gavin turned to Sarres, saying, "Get parchment and ink. Chart out what you remember of the compound, and we'll look at it in the morning. I think we all could use sleep."

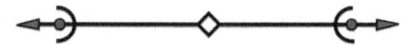

CHAPTER 14

I t was after nightfall when Gavin felt himself being gently shaken awake. He blinked his eyes to clear away the sleep, and there was just enough light to see a dark form leaning over him.

"It's Declan," the bard whispered. "My associates await us outside the camp."

Gavin rose and followed Declan as best he could through the stand of trees. The trees' canopy was so thick, what would have been an otherwise moon-lit night was a pitch-black hole in the world. Eight people stood beside horses on the outskirts of the camp; there was just enough light for Gavin to see three of them were women. Their matte-black leather armor made them look like nothing so much as three-dimensional shadows.

All eight bowed deeply at Gavin's approach, but only the one closest to Gavin spoke.

"Milord," he said, his voice barely above a whisper, "it is an honor to meet you. My name is Athis, and I serve you as an officer in Thartan's town guard."

He stood just slightly taller than Gavin, but he was lanky and thinner. Gavin tried to make out further details, but there simply wasn't sufficient light.

"The honor is mine, Athis; I am Gavin Cross. I had planned to send the princess and governor's nephew back to Thartan, but from what my scout reports, the terrain is fairly well saturated with scouts from the manor. Do you think the nine of you could stealth into the manor house, locate the governor's niece, and extract her to this camp?"

Athis turned to his group, and Gavin heard them discussing and debating the matter. After a short time, Athis turned back to face Gavin.

"Under what rules of engagement would this extraction occur, sir?"

Gavin took a deep breath before turning to pace a short distance, thinking. Gavin recognized and admitted that he stood at the top of a very slippery slope. He thought it too easy to fall into bad habits only possible because of his power.

Gavin stopped his walk to reflect on his thoughts. Up until that moment, he hadn't admitted to himself that he did indeed have a considerable amount of power, both personally and in the world at large. It was a very sobering thought, and it was that realization— more than anything else that had crossed his mind—that decided his course of action. He turned and walked back to the nine people awaiting him.

"Athis," Gavin said, "how many people would you need to capture everyone on that manor?"

Not even the limited light could hide Athis's surprise from Gavin. "Excuse me, milord, but did you say capture?"

"Yes, I did. I had thought to make an object lesson of those people by removing them from the face of the earth, but I think it would be a far better statement for their entire group—minus those four Sarres and Declan killed earlier—to be found hogtied in what-ever barracks facility they have. Do you have access to sufficient people to make that happen?"

Athis broke out into a feral grin. "I can send a message to the rest of our people in Thartan. They can head out and secure the scouts between the city and the manor as well as help us with what's left to do on the manor once they arrive there. I consider the extraction of the niece to be my top priority, but I think we can achieve your secondary objective, sir. With your leave, I'll send that message and be on our way back to the manor. I'll send the niece here with the ladies and Declan."

Gavin considered the situation with the camp's wards. He didn't want the ladies arriving and having to spend whatever was left of the night outside the wards, but Gavin couldn't take the steps necessary to provide ward-stones. The Word of Power he'd have to use four times would surely wake every wizard in the camp, but an idea suddenly popped into his mind.

Huh, Gavin thought as he retrieved a small stone from the ground at his feet. *I wonder if it would work.*

Gavin pulled his knife and scratched the rune the ward-stones had and then nicked his thumb, swabbing the rune with his blood. He handed the stone to Athis as he said, "Try to walk to that nearest tree behind me. If you feel pressure against your chest, stop, and back up."

Athis walked to the tree and back. "Was I supposed to feel something?"

Gavin smiled, felt like cheering. "Guess not. I'll make a few more stones to see the girl safely here. Athis, I want everyone involved in this. Leave enough people in Thartan to round up any conspirators there as well."

THE NEXT MORNING, Gavin awoke early. When he rolled over in his bedroll, he saw four women—three in worn leather traveling clothes and one youngster just starting adolescence. He assumed the youngster to be Naida, and he smiled at seeing her deep in sleep.

"How was it?" Gavin said as he sat beside the women, his voice quiet.

The closest to Gavin made small gesture of nonchalance. "It could have been worse. We had a terrible time getting her out of her cell; it took an oath from us that Garrett was north of the manor with Kiri before she would even allow us near her."

Another woman moved closer to Gavin and began to whisper. "Milord, I have received word from Thartan. We were successful. All targets have been gathered in an abandoned warehouse on the fringe of the city with sufficient evidence to prompt the proper questions; matter of fact, it was the same warehouse they used to stage the job and be a safe-house until they could smuggle the children out of the city."

"Good," Gavin said. "Who can we trust in the city?"

"In this climate, I wouldn't trust anyone but the Cavaliers who make up the Governor's personal guard."

Gavin nodded. "Get word to the Cavaliers to investigate the warehouse and manor. While you're at it, arrange for a meeting with Zentris...something very low key. He won't want to see anyone right now, but make it something suitably important but very boring, the sort of thing no one would notice. I want to return those children as soon as possible."

THE AFTERNOON TWO DAYS LATER, a trade deputation from the Kingdom of Tel entered the north gate of Thartan. There was such an uproar over various important public officials being found bound in a warehouse that no one bothered to look too closely at the group of 'diplomats.'

Gavin couldn't help but compare Thartan to the city he had already come to think of as home. A faint miasma hung over the city from the street lamps that had burned pitch the night before, and the structures were brick-and-mortar construction. Whereas the structures of Tel Mivar were a testament to the power and majesty of the Art, Thartan existed only through mortal toil. Gavin couldn't decide which he preferred.

THE GOVERNOR's office was lined with mahogany paneling, and the upholstery of his furniture was a soft exquisite velvet. The Governor's desk sat on the left side of the room, and large windows opposite the door stood open, allowing a breeze and light in from the mansion's courtyard.

Zentris looked up at the group's entrance, and upon seeing Gavin, his expression immediately became shrewd. Zentris was a man of middle years, what hair he had left going gray. He was a touch on the short side, and he didn't seem to have as much of the paunch Gavin had been accustomed to seeing on middle-aged, powerful men. His eyes couldn't help but reveal the man's intelligence.

"You're no trade ambassador from Tel," Zentris said as he rose to his feet. "Who are you, and why shouldn't I call the guards?"

"Calling the guards would be a very bad thing, Governor," Gavin said. "Doing so would call attention to a certain someone we've taken great pains to make nondescript."

"Really," Zentris said, the tone of his voice making his word a statement. "Who are you hiding?"

"Me, Uncle Zen," Kiri said as she stepped around Gavin. Naida walked beside her and held her right hand, and Kiri carried a dozing little Garrett in her arms.

Zentris blinked his surprise at seeing Kiri alive, but his focus soon shifted to the children with her. All semblance of Thartan's Governor vanished, replaced by the man who had cared for his brother's children ever since his brother, sister-in-law, and own son had died at sea. He didn't so much kneel as fall to his knees and held out his arms. Naida released Kiri's hand and ran to her uncle. Kiri nudged Garrett, and upon seeing his uncle, the boy squirmed free of Kiri (not that she was trying to keep him) and ran to join his sister.

For several moments, nothing existed beyond the reach of Zentris's arms, not even the nine people standing in his office. Gavin watched the man do his dead-level best not to cry, and he realized he was glad only four people had died in the efforts to free and return the children. It was good that such a worthy moment wasn't tainted by a bloodbath, and he found that those thoughts warmed his heart.

This is what my power shall stand for in this world, Gavin thought as he watched Zentris and the children, *the small victories that mean so much more. It is a far better legacy for Marcus than anything else I could have imagined.*

Zentris pulled Gavin from his thoughts by rising to his feet and sending the children to one side of the room. His examination of Gavin was speculative, and he included Gavin's fellows in that speculation as well. It was clear he had no idea how Kiri fit into it all.

"Money seems insufficient for the kindness you've rendered my wife and I, stranger."

Gavin smiled. "Watching your reception of the children and seeing their reaction to you paid any debt that might have existed, assuming that I'm so crass as to want a reward in the first place."

Zentris shook his head in disbelief. "Who are you people?"

By now, Lillian and the other wizards stood to Gavin's right, and almost in unison, they withdrew their medallions from inside their tunics. Zentris's eyes went to each medallion in turn, moving down the line.

"Roshan...Wygoth...Cothos...Mivar, and...and Kirloth?" Gavin knew the moment Zentris recognized his House's glyph, for the governor reacted just how Gavin had come to expect from those familiar with the House glyphs: sheer, unadulterated awe laced with both fear and respect.

Gavin stepped forward and extended his right hand to Zentris. "My name is Gavin Cross, sir."

Zentris's eyes went to Kiri. "We all thought she died, drowned with the rest when the *Sprite* went down at sea."

"I washed ashore on some driftwood," Kiri said, "where I was found by a group of slavers. I was traded back and forth for two years before Gavin found me."

"I'm so sorry. I can't imagine what you've survived." Zentris walked over and sat on the edge of his desk, running his hands back over his head. "My real concern now is all the people who saw her and the children. This grand edifice is more like a seat of government than an actual residence, and you must've passed any number of gossiping functionaries who could recognize Kiri at a distance, let alone five feet."

"They didn't see the Crown Princess carrying your niece and nephew, Zentris," Gavin said.

"Oh, what did they see?"

Gavin turned and gestured for Lillian to speak. He could've answered that question himself, but Lillian still wasn't comfortable with the knowledge that she was destined to walk the halls and corridors of power. He thought it would do her some good to get a little practice dealing with a foreign dignitary, even if the interaction took place under somewhat unorthodox circumstances.

"They saw an unremarkable and most unappreciated secretary weighed down with the papers and documents any trade deputation simply must have, sir," Lillian said. "I didn't think it would work myself, but Gavin really outdid himself with the illusion he wove around Kiri and the children."

"And everyone believed what they saw? No one saw past the illusion?"

Mariana stepped forward to speak at that point. "Sir, I serve Tel as a Battle-mage, and part of my training has been how to protect those individuals who need it...what to watch for among a crowd, how people try to hide reactions, that sort of thing. No one we passed gave any reaction that Kiri even existed, let alone taking enough time to examine the illusion for any flaws it might have had. Her identity is safe."

"I see. Well, under the circumstances, a banquet honoring the intrepid heroes hardly seems the proper course of action, but I don't like it. You should be recognized for what you've done."

Gavin waved away the concern. "If you would reward us, blame the children's return on the brave and loyal Cavaliers. Isn't it obvious? Those poor souls they apprehended in the warehouse across town gave all manner of testimony on their nefarious scheme."

Zentris shook his head once more before resuming his gaze at Gavin. "You are an odd one, Gavin Cross; there's no denying that. My assistant was quite flustered at the mysterious appointment that simply appeared on my schedule this morning, and those thirty-odd people didn't tie themselves up."

"Don't ask too many questions, Zentris," Gavin said, responding to the man's shrewd gaze with an enigmatic smile. "Accept matters for what they are: an astounding windfall for Muran loyalists."

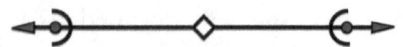

CHAPTER 15

Eight days after leaving Thartan, they camped on the western shore of a small lake. A castle stood on a hill overlooking the eastern shores of the lake, and even at their present distance, it was clear the castle was little more than ancient ruins. While Gavin set about establishing the wards for the camp, Declan and Sarres sought their meal that evening.

Later that night, they were sitting around the fire, singing to the accompaniment of Declan's lute when a massive Evocation resonance erupted somewhere nearby.

"Gavin," Lillian said, "what was that?"

"A powerful wizard just invoked an Evocation effect," Gavin said, turning toward the ruins off in the distance as he continued, "and it came from there."

Declan walked over to stand beside Gavin. "I don't know about you, but I'm not exactly fond of leaving an unknown wizard of apparent power so close to us while we sleep. How about we investigate it?"

Gavin stared off toward the ruins in the distance, thinking through the situation. He didn't like either option, really. Still, they were already vulnerable. Establishing the camp's wards created a subtle but noticeable Tutation effect where there hadn't been one before, which meant they were a bonfire on a dark night to anyone capable of feeling the ebb and flow of the Art.

"I'm leaning in favor of Declan's thoughts unless anyone else wants to talk me out of it."

Rather than speak, the elves walked over and began donning their armor. Mariana went over to her things and removed her light armor and Battle-mage vestments and began donning those as well. Declan saw the others' actions and changed into his matte-black leather armor.

THE CURTAIN WALL WAS A CRUMBLING, shattered ruin that stood in ragged sections around the promontory upon which the keep had been built. No sign of the portcullis or gate remained in the gate-house, and even the gatehouse itself was superfluous, as the curtain wall had collapsed for thirty feet on either side of it. Script Gavin didn't even recognize was chiseled into the arch of the gatehouse's entrance.

Kiri was riding beside Gavin, and she stopped and examined the script. She was silent for several moments, her expression thought-ful, until her eyes widened.

"We have to leave here...right now," Kiri said, backing her horse away from the ruined castle.

Everyone stopped and turned to face her.

Gavin was the first to speak, asking, "What's wrong?"

"We're no longer in Vushaar. For that matter, where we camped probably isn't either."

Gavin glanced at the others before resuming his focus on Kiri. "Kiri, how could we no longer be in Vushaar? We're almost in the center of your country."

"I don't know when it started, but in records dating as far back as three thousand years, the Vushaari crown has recognized a three-league area centered on a ruined keep as sovereign, foreign soil. Roads pass through the territory, and travelers, traders, and such aren't molested. But bandits never survive nor does anyone who enters the keep. This is that keep. I recognize the script on the gate-house from an artist's rendition I saw in a book back home."

Before anyone else could speak, a Conjuration effect washed over them. Gavin could tell that, while the effect was focused on them, it originated somewhere else.

"Hello, there," a disembodied voice said. *"You've been standing at my gatehouse for quite some time, and I thought I'd extend an invitation. I'm rather busy at the moment, so I've not bothered with a scrying yet, but I'd really like to know whether you're bandits, raiders, or simply travelers. Besides, you have some wizards stronger than I've met in quite some time. I'd enjoy a conversation...if I end up not killing you after all. Oh...and please, don't run. You wouldn't reach Vushaari territory before I'd catch you, and chasing bandits down for extermination is so bothersome."*

Everyone turned to Gavin as the young wizard regarded the keep a short distance beyond the gatehouse. He sat atop Jasmine, his expression and mannerisms resigned.

"Well, that tears it," Gavin said at last, a sigh following his words. "Sarres, take point, if you please, and Mariana, please join him. Sarres, watch for physical traps; Mariana, magical traps. Declan, please assume rear guard. Kiri, I want you in the center of the formation, and I would like Braden, Wynn, and Elayna with you. Lillian, now that I'm thinking about it, be on rear guard with Declan."

Gavin nudged Jasmine to a walk and led the group to the steps of the keep. Hitching rails stood on either side of the keep steps, and Gavin looped the reins around the left rail after dismounting.

Once everyone had dismounted and secured their horses, Sarres and Mariana led the way into the keep. The doors themselves were in obvious disrepair. The door that was still on its hinges had large gaping holes, but at least the one lying against the wall was still in good condition...as long as one overlooked the absence of hinges.

Remnants of furniture, carpets, and decorations lay strewn hither and yon, and the group's entrance into the keep startled a roosting flock of birds into flight. Sarres and Mariana led the group toward a staircase only to find that the first dozen feet of said staircase were all that remained.

"Okay," Gavin said. "I'm not liking this at all. Hold here for a moment, everyone."

Gavin stepped back and cleared all thoughts from his mind as Marcus had taught him all those months ago. The effect he wanted to achieve could not be done with one Word alone, which necessitated a composite effect. He carefully chose the two Words he would use, and having focused on his intent, he spoke those Words, "*Nysphaes-Gozdrahk.*"

The invocation hit Gavin square in his guts, but a fierce grimace was the only outward sign of his pain.

"*Well now...isn't that a surprise,*" the disembodied voice said once more. "*I've not felt that family's mastery of the Art since last I stood with my old friend, Amdar. Directly across from the keep's entrance, you will find a hidden access to a staircase leading down. I shall be cautiously optimistic, young wizard, and disable the stairs' traps. I very much want to meet you now.*"

Gavin couldn't keep from lifting his shoulders in a shrug as he shook his head, saying, "I know just as much as you guys about what's going on, or who's on the other end of that voice. I'm still not sure we should trust it."

"What was it that you did?" Mariana asked. "That didn't feel like a normal invocation."

Gavin shook his head. "It was a composite effect of Tutation and Conjuration. The Tutation effect provides better than average protection against magic, and the Conjuration effect basically created an invisible shroud of armor around us. We have about an hour before this effect dissipates."

"Then, we should not waste time," Declan said, as he turned and headed toward the opening in the wall. Gavin and the others followed.

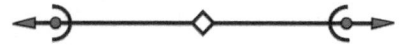

CHAPTER 16

The stone staircase circled downward for an interminably long time. The stones were precisely shaped to follow the curvature of the staircase, but unlike the masonry of Tel Mivar, these stones showed indications of mortar. The staircase as a whole was well lit, but the light had no apparent source; the wizards of the group recognized a Conjuration effect permeating the staircase.

The doorway at the bottom opened into a well-appointed cavern, divided into sections based on the purpose of the space. The cavern was comfortably cool, though not as damp as one might have expected. Plush carpets lined the floor, and they stood at the edge of a sitting room.

An individual arose from one of the armchairs that faced the hearth in the sitting area and walked closer to the group. It looked like nothing other than a long-desiccated corpse. There was no flesh or muscle around the skull, and two pinpoints of orange light blazed in the skull's eye sockets. What flesh remained was dry and cracked, but there was next to no flesh at all.

"Ah, hello there!" the individual said during the approach. The speech was accented by an eerie clacking of teeth. "I must say,

Young Kirloth, I was not expecting one of your House at all. Why, I wasn't even aware any youngsters of your House remained in Drakmoor."

The voice was decidedly masculine, even though there remained no visible way of discerning to what gender this individual had once been born.

"Gavin," Mariana said, her voice laced with fear and awe, "what is he?"

"Ah, Lady Cothos," the individual said, "I would expect you of all people to recognize me. I'm somewhat disappointed that you don't." He turned to face Gavin. "So, young man, I'm curious to hear how you shall answer your comrade's question."

Gavin's expression was thoughtful and analyzing. He folded one arm across his midriff, while placing the fingers of his other hand against his lips. "You said you've stood in the presence of my family's power before, and you know the House Glyphs. Kiri said the Vushaari crown regards the territory three leagues in every direction centered on this keep as sovereign, foreign soil, and I've never before seen the script carved into the stone of the gatehouse. You must be Othron; there's no one else you really could be, not with your...well...your distinctive appearance."

The individual clapped his hands together. "Excellent, Young Kirloth! It's very good to meet you. I am indeed Othron. You know, if you ever make it to Tel Mivar, you should visit a man the locals call Marcus. He's a kinsman of yours, and I'm sure he would appreciate meeting you."

Gavin's expression fell just a bit. "Sir, Marcus trained me in the Art, and I'm sorry to inform you that he died a few months ago."

Othron's shoulders slumped. "K...my old friend is dead? How did it happen?"

"I don't have all the details, but from what I do know, he was confronted by two deqs of the Lornithrasa. They were apparently looking for me, though I can't imagine why, and killed Marcus when he refused to lead them to me."

"I'm sorry," Lillian said, her voice quiet, "but I'm having trouble placing the name."

Elayna said, "Othron was a contemporary of Kirloth and Bellos. A knowledgeable wizard strong in the Art, he is widely debated as the equal to Kirloth in mastery, if not better."

"Bah!" Othron said. "I was never Amdar's better in terms of the Art, not even his equal. He lived, breathed, ate, and slept the Art; I merely used it. But, we've carried on so." Othron gestured toward a sitting area with several armchairs and a sofa or two. The upholstery's fashion was long out-of-date, but the furniture looked as though it hadn't aged a day. "Please, make yourselves comfortable, and we'll proceed with the introductions."

Once seated, Gavin introduced his friends, saving Kiri for last.

"Well, well, well," Othron said, lounging in a green velvet armchair, "you're quite some distance from home, Your Highness, and I must say you picked a rather dicey time to return. Surely, Terris wanted you safely away from all this nonsense."

Kiri nodded. "He sent me to Tel, but my ship was lost at sea. I've spent the last two years as a slave."

"That's very unfortunate. My apologies, Your Highness," Othron said. "I have beds available, and I don't use them myself. I'm not exactly one for sleeping all that much anymore. You're quite welcome to spend the night here, rather than at that rocky road-side camp."

Gavin started to decline politely, but the dreamy expressions on the ladies' faces at the mention of an honest-to-goodness bed changed his mind. "Why, thank you, Othron. We'll be glad to accept your hospitality...just as soon as we see to our horses in the courtyard."

Othron dismissed the matter with a wave. "Don't worry about that. My spectral servants can see to them."

Othron rose to his feet and led them to the sleeping areas. As they walked, Othron asked Gavin to stay up just a bit longer, to which Gavin agreed.

Once everyone else was safely tucked away in their own rooms, Othron led Gavin to the library. That room in the cavern was easily sixty feet by sixty, filled with rows upon rows of bookshelves, and they were full for the most part.

"This is impressive," Gavin said as Othron led him over to a reading area, "but I get the feeling it's not why you asked to continue our conversation."

Othron shook his head. "Oh, no. I didn't want to alarm any of the others, but I've been hearing whispers, for decades now, that the Necromancer is finally preparing to move. I know for a fact that Marcus was the last of his line in this world, but here you are, a true-born son of House Kirloth. Now, one of my old friend's brothers is accounted for...Marin. He stands within the ranks of the divine, but Marin was the youngest and Amdar the eldest. Oh, Amdar was Kirloth's given name, by the way. I don't know if he ever told you.

"The middle brother, Gerrus, had a wife and children when the Godswar erupted, and he had no desire to run off to war. When Valthon and Nesta gathered the refugees wanting to flee this world and the war, Gerrus took his family and joined them. Amdar never forgave Gerrus for what he saw as abandonment and betrayal. I would bet my soul jar you descended from Gerrus's line; it's the only thing that makes sense."

"In that case, how did I end up in this world?"

Othron shrugged. "I think the gods have a plan for you, and I think that plan involves the siege of Vushaar. The old alliance is preparing to go to war against the King of Tel. I can't blame them, honestly; the man's an unmitigated ass. However, that war will weaken the forces of everyone involved. The Necromancer already has Tel; the king yips when he says 'bark.' The Necromancer is now trying to gain control of Vushaar. If that happens, war will be inevitable, and the old alliance will be too weak to defend ourselves when the armies of Lornithar march through Hope's Pass."

"Why would they do that after all this time?" Gavin asked. "I could see them invading within the first century or so, but it's been six thousand years."

"For all his shortcomings, Lornithar is no fool. He's not about to start a fresh war until he's certain he can win. To even have a chance, he must locate and destroy the foundation artifacts of his prison, and to the best of my knowledge, there is only one account of the meeting that decided where those artifacts would rest."

Gavin sighed and leaned against a book case. "Let me guess...it's in the Royal Archives of Vushaar."

"Just so."

"Ivarson, then, is working for the Necromancer...who is in turn working for Lornithar?"

Othron shrugged as he walked over to a nearby bookshelf. "I doubt we're lucky enough for matters to be so straight-forward, but I do know for certain General Ivarson is the Necromancer's pawn. The Necromancer sent five wizards to bolster the man's siege force. I don't know if they've arrived as of yet, but they will within the month." Othron turned his attention to the bookshelf, scanning the spines. "Ah, here we go."

Othron pulled three tomes from the shelf and turned to Gavin, extending the books to him. "These were placed in my care by your mentor more years ago than I like to remember. As you are his heir, they now belong to you. I fear you will have need of them before this matter is settled."

Gavin accepted the books and examined the covers. Two were bound in unmarked, brown leather, but gold leather bound the third.

"What are these?" Gavin asked.

"The gold leather volume is Bellos's work to catalog all known Words of Power just prior to the eruption of the Godswar. The other two are experimentation journals that record Kirloth's work on composite effects and wizardry on the battlefield."

"Thank you," Gavin said as he shifted the books to a better grip.

"You're quite welcome," Othron said, turning to lead Gavin back out of the library. "Unlike me, you still need to sleep, and I imagine I've cost you enough of yours. Let me show you to your bed."

THE NEXT MORNING, Othron saw them off from the steps of the keep. The horses appeared as though they had been well cared-for and seemed thoroughly rested. Their first stop was what would've been their camp for the night. Gavin collapsed the wards and collected the ward-stones while everyone gathered what items they'd left inside the wards. Once the ward-stones were safely distributed between his saddlebags, Gavin sat on a felled log and pulled out the map of Vushaar and the compass, looking it over while the others finished collecting their belongings.

"What do you think?" Declan asked, sitting down beside Gavin.

Gavin sighed. "Well, we're just about due east of the capital. We could start angling south-southwest, but if I'm reading this map right, the trails we want don't open up until the southern edge of the Sarnath Hills. I think we should make our course about three points west of due south; that should put us right at the southern end of those trails. How long do you think it'll take us to reach the hills?"

"Well, we've been making about thirteen to fifteen leagues per day, and given where we are, I'd say we're looking at one and a half to two weeks."

"Just what we need...more time to be discovered. Well, there's no help for it, I suppose."

The others signaled ready to depart, and Gavin rolled up the map before returning it to the map case and then both the case and the compass to his left saddlebag. He hauled himself into the saddle, and once everyone was mounted, Gavin nudged Jasmine up to a trot.

* * *

THEY WERE six days out from Othron's keep, and they were making camp beside a brook that wandered through the wooded, rolling hills of that region. Gavin set up the ward-stones and activated the wards straight-away before busying himself with helping to make the camp live-able. After dinner, Gavin and the wizards broke off for another study session. Declan and the elves were playing quiet tunes and humming to them.

Off by herself, Kiri sat wrapping her hair around a finger. For several days now, even before meeting Othron, Gavin was occupying an increasingly greater amount of her attention. She noticed that she smiled more often when she thought of him, and as she looked back on a conversation with her aunt a few years back, she feared where her emotions were dragging her. She needed to think, needed to walk her thoughts out. The others were focused on their respective tasks; none of them noticed her leaving camp.

HOURS PASSED. The study session ran long, but they were being so productive Gavin hadn't wanted to stop. Besides, the elves and Declan had managed to entertain each other during the extra time.

"Has anyone seen Kiri?" Gavin asked, looking around the camp.

"She was here not too long ago," Mariana said, now looking around herself.

Lillian walked over to Gavin and laid a comforting hand on his shoulder. "I wouldn't worry about her, Gavin. She's had some stuff on her mind, and she'll be fine as long as she stays inside the wards."

"Shall I go find her?" Sarres asked as he walked up to Gavin and Lillian.

Every fiber of his being shouted for Gavin to say yes, but he wasn't exactly rational where Kiri was concerned anymore.

Gavin walked over to the ward-stones that formed the fire circle. He walked around the stones until he found the one he wanted, then knelt and touched it. He spoke Kiri's name and waited a few heartbeats.

"She's still inside the wards," Gavin said as he returned to his feet. "Let's not interfere. Besides, she knows how far the wards extend, and I'm willing to trust her judgment."

* * *

IT WAS A CALM, pleasant morning that was swiftly approaching noon. Birds chirped in the distance, and the slight breeze carried the scent of the pine trees all around them.

"So, who's going to wake him?" Mariana asked, her eyes on Gavin's sleeping form.

"Don't look at me," Wynn said, emphatically shaking his head. "Braden, you can do it."

Braden lifted his hands and backed away. "Not a chance. Lillian, you've known him the longest, and he likes you."

A short distance away, the elves and Declan watched the wizards' discussion with a certain amount of amusement. The situation overall was not funny in the least, but nonetheless, observing the wizards' impromptu game of hot potato provided some slight entertainment.

Declan pushed himself to his feet and walked over to the quartet, saying in a soft voice just loud enough to be heard, "If you four don't quiet down, the question of who wakes him will be rather moot."

"Huh?" Wynn asked, lifting his eyes to meet Declan's gaze.

The sleeping form began to stir, and Declan's mouth curled into a sardonic grin. "Too late."

THAT NIGHT, Gavin did not sleep well at all, and he did not feel the least bit rested when he finally opened his eyes. He clawed his way to his feet.

"Oh, goodness," Gavin said, as he stretched and blinked his eyes against the morning sun. "That was not the best night's sleep I've had on this trip. Why did you people let me sleep so long?"

When he turned around, Gavin found everyone but Kiri standing not too far away. Each person looked like he or she had something to say, and it was just as apparent that none of them wanted to speak.

Lillian finally stepped forward. She was wringing her hands. "Kiri's gone, Gavin; slavers took her."

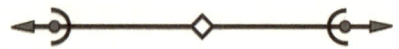

CHAPTER 17

"Show me." Gavin said. "Take me through what you know step by step."

Sarres and Declan looked to each other and nodded in unison. They then turned and started walking away from the camp-fire. Gavin followed. They walked in a southwesterly direction, and before too long, Gavin felt himself leaving the wards. They walked farther southwest until they arrived at a semi-clearing surrounded by clumps of undergrowth. There were signs of a struggle.

"From what the tracks show, a six-person raiding party was moving southeast and came upon Kiri here," Declan said. "There was a fight of some sort, and Kiri was eventually subdued. However, there is some good news. These raiders were apparently from one of the bands that my associates have infiltrated, because we found these artifacts under a hedge-plant over here."

Declan led Gavin over to a plant and bent it away to expose the dirt at its roots. Symbols were scratched into the dry topsoil, and there was a handkerchief tied around the trunk of the shrub.

Gavin turned to the group and took in their countenances. They still feared him; he could see it, but he was past the rage, past the raw emotions that would've led to immediate violence.

"Please, don't take this the wrong way, but I would appreciate it if you could give Declan and me some privacy for a few moments."

The others withdrew a distance, and Gavin knelt in front of the symbols.

"What do these say, Declan?"

"They're basically an identification of the Wraith and a statement that she will protect Kiri. She recognized the Glyph of Kirloth in Kiri's ward-stone and suspected you would be coming for her. I've examined the handkerchief as best I could, and it seems to have a few drops of blood on it."

Gavin nodded, untying the handkerchief from the trunk of the shrub. He rose to his feet and motioned for the others to re-join.

"What is it, Gavin?" Lillian asked as they once more stood at Gavin's side.

Gavin's eyes never left the handkerchief as he spoke. "It's a way to find Kiri and track the filth that took her."

Gavin led them over to the center of the clearing. He stopped and held the handkerchief in his left hand. It was hard to do, so hard to do, but Gavin managed to clear his mind of everything but his intent.

I will see the owner of this blood.

The intent firm in his mind, Gavin spoke a Word of Divination, "*Klaepos.*"

His anger, rage, and fear were so great, the massive pain he should've felt was a mere echo, and the resonance of his power slammed into his apprentices' guts like a giant's fist.

Wynn and Braden collapsed to their knees, the wind driven from their lungs. Mariana was staggered, but being older with more experience around the Art, she was more resilient. Lillian only stayed on her feet through sheer force of will.

By now, a sphere of air in front of Gavin easily ten feet in diameter was beginning to shimmer and ripple. As far as most workings of the Art go, the effect was a gradual one, and Gavin didn't need to wait for it to complete.

· · ·

KIRI FOUGHT with all her might to hold back the tears every fiber of her being wanted to shed. The rope that bound her hands was rough and tight; she expected the skin around her wrists to be torn and bleeding before long, and her left cheek ached worse than she could ever remember. There had to be a nasty bruise; she didn't see how her face could feel like it did without one. That wasn't so bad, though. Bruises heal. The worst part was the slave collar that chafed her shoulders and neck.

Kiri sneaked a glance at the woman who rode beside her. She looked vaguely Vushaari, but despite the dark hair, her complexion was light enough Kiri wasn't sure. The way she had stood up to the men about to gang-rape Kiri was the one thing that gave Kiri enough strength to keep from breaking down.

There were six of them in the raiding party, and they were riding hard. Kiri didn't understand how they hadn't killed their horses. They-

Don't react, Kiri. She heard Gavin's voice in her mind, clear and distinct, and hope welled up within her soul. *No one can hear me but you. The woman who rides beside you is one of my agents, and she will protect you. They will probably do a great number of things to break your will, but please, don't despair. I'm coming for you; I swear on my life that I am.*

The faint touch Kiri felt in her mind faded away.

GAVIN PULLED his hand from the scrying sphere and dispelled it. He turned to find everyone facing him, waiting.

"Don't just hear what I'm about to say; listen well, and understand me before you answer. I could teleport us all to Kiri's location right this instant, and we could free her. But that would not soothe the anger and rage that threatens to devour me. I will follow this band of slavers back to wherever they base their operations, and I will eradicate the entire force from the face of this world. People will speak of their fate in terrified whispers for a thousand years.

"This is not vengeance; this is not punishment. This is an object lesson to the world that I will not tolerate attacks on people who bear the glyph of my House. I do not take your participation for granted. If any of you disagree with my intent on whatever grounds, I can respect that and will send you to whatever destination you desire, and your departure will not change my disposition toward you in the slightest. You are my friends, and I would do no less if it were one of you we saw in the scrying sphere. I'm going back to camp; you have until I'm packed to decide."

THE GROUP WATCHED Gavin walk away in silence for several moments. It was Mariana who spoke first.

"We're guests in a foreign country," the battle-mage of House Cothos said. "We don't have the authority to intervene, and I'm active military personnel in a unit attached to the Army of Tel. This could have very bad repercussions, and Tel and Vushaar aren't exactly the close friends they used to be. I realize we just intervened in a feud between two families, but one could argue we were operating at the behest of the Crown Princess."

"Mariana," Sarres said, waiting until the battle-mage was looking at him before continuing, "I don't think he cares."

Elayna nodded. "I have no doubt whatsoever that he would do the same if it were one of us captured by slavers, but we all know there couldn't have been a worse person they could have abducted. I don't see as how we have any option. I fear what will happen if we're not there."

Braden shifted his eyes from the distant figure of Gavin to face the elf. "What do you mean? You believe Gavin will commit some kind of atrocity if we're not there?"

Elayna met Braden's gaze. "Young man, I doubt there's anything we can do to prevent that, but it will not be as bad as Kirloth's treatment of the men who murdered his family. No, I fear something worse. For all his knowledge and mastery, Gavin is still very much an untried wizard; he's still learning how far he can push himself with the Art. I saw my brother, Kantar, go through the same stage in our youth. We need to be there to watch his back, in case he pushes himself too far."

"What really bothers me," Lillian said, "is this woman he

claimed as an agent. How could Gavin have possibly cultivated a network of agents so quickly?"

"I-dunno," Wynn said. "Could-he-have-inherited-them-somehow?"

"Agents...inherited agents..." Mariana said, her voice distant. With no warning, her body went rigid, and her eyes rolled back into her head.

"*It was the eighth day of the fourth month in the old calendar,*" Mariana said, but the voice was not her own, masculine and with an odd accent. "*To counter the growing threat of the Lornithrasa, Kirloth formed the organization known as the Wraiths. He captured one Lornithrasa and wracked that man's body and soul to shatter the bonds Lornithar had created, then placed the man under a geas to share all he knew about the Lornithrasa with this new force. Those who became the first Wraiths of Kirloth were chosen based on two criteria: some natural talent at stealth and a certain moral indifference toward such deeds as murder.*

"*Throughout the Godswar, the Wraiths of Kirloth saw to those tasks that no one wanted to admit made the Godswar easier to win. In the wake of the Founding, Kirloth re-purposed the Wraiths to act as the personal intelligence agents of the Archmagister of Tel, though they never strayed from their training as masters of stealth and subtle violence.*"

Mariana staggered as she came to her senses. She closed her eyes and sighed, saying, "Dammit! That hasn't happened since I was a child."

"We should be moving if we want to catch Gavin," Declan said and started walking toward camp.

The others moved to follow, but Lillian stayed close to Mariana.

"Are you okay?" Lillian asked. "What was that?"

"I'm fine, just a little mad at myself," Mariana said, her stride unsteady as she walked. "We don't like to discuss this, but you probably deserve an explanation. Each of our families have certain legacies from our ancestors who fought in the Godswar. Some, like House Mivar's affinity to the Art, were bestowed by Bellos at his ascendance, but in my family's case, it's a legacy of Cothos himself."

They were almost to the edge of the wards now, and Mariana's gait had normalized, her voice stronger and closer to normal.

"Cothos was so horrified by the Godswar that he felt we should always have a record of what transpired and why we fought in the first place, and he felt Mivar's Histories were too bland, too detached. He spent over two years constructing the composite effect to achieve what he wanted, and when he completed it, half of that effect created a matrix of knowledge within his mind that was a perfect and complete record of the Godswar...down to the smallest detail.

"Now, Cothos was mortal, and he knew it. What's more, he wasn't comfortable at all with idea of following Othron's path, so the other half of his composite effect bound that matrix to his family line. Some of you may have heard the term 'the Lore-keepers of House Cothos.' Every member of my family has that perfect record of the Godswar, but I don't think Cothos truly considered what he was doing, how binding this composite effect to living beings would affect the generations. You see, besides the history of the Godswar, each member of my family has an affinity with one specific subset of knowledge. Because of that affinity, we are an archive for that subject. For example, my mother's affinity is metal-lurgy; if her physique would allow it, she could be a better black-smith than the best dwarf in Stonehearth."

"That-can't-be-fun-at-all," Wynn said as he walked. "What's-your-affinity?"

Before Mariana could speak, Lillian gasped, her eyes wide, and she ran to get ahead of Declan. When she passed Declan, Lillian started walking backward toward the camp, her eyes intent on the bard.

"When Gavin asked us to step away...he was having you trans-late those symbols under that bush. What were they, some kind of secret code?"

"Lillian," Braden said, "what are you talking about?"

"Declan's a Wraith," Lillian said. "I just figured it out."

Declan stopped walking. His posture never changed, but he sighed. That sigh was laden with resignation.

"I was really hoping you wouldn't start connecting dots," Declan said. He turned to faced everyone as he spoke. "My oath to the order requires me to kill any who learn of our existence. But...you are his friends, and he was going to tell you of us when we first set out on this journey. I convinced him otherwise. Swear to me that you will never tell another soul, living or dead, of what you now know, and I will follow his trust in you. Before you swear, be certain that—should you ever betray his trust—we will know, and you will die. It may not be immediate. It may not happen for years, but if you choose to betray his trust, you will die at hands of a Wraith one day."

Each person swore never to betray Gavin's trust, and there was no mistaking Declan's pride. "'Tel will never fall, not so long as the Great Houses stand together.' Do you recognize the quote?"

Mariana nodded in silence.

The others looked back and forth between themselves. It was Braden who broke the silence by asking, "Well? Who said it?"

"Bellos," Declan said, "the last time He appeared in the mortal world...just shortly after the death of Bellock Vanlon."

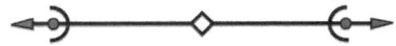

CHAPTER 18

The slavers met up with several more raiding parties as they traveled generally south. The evening of the third day, the much-larger raiding band arrived at what had once been a farming estate, which the slavers had fortified into a collection and distribution center. There were archer towers and sentry patrols. The former animal corrals now held the slaves, one for the men and the other for women.

The slaver in charge of the raiding party walked back and pulled Kiri from her mount. The woman who had ridden beside her the past three days started to object, but the slaver glared up at her.

"Stow it," the slaver said. "You've been so close to her the past three days, it's enough to make a person wonder if maybe you're not a little sweet on her."

The woman smirked. "She's not my type. I'm just trying to keep you idiots from taking any actions you'll come to sorely regret later."

The slaver frowned as he pulled Kiri to her feet by the rope attached to her collar, asking, "Now, what's that supposed to mean?"

"She wasn't wandering around in the night up there. Even now, riders are coming for her, and while you've sealed your fate regardless, there are fates worse than death. The one coming for her would see to that if he finds her…overly mistreated. Trust me on this."

The man glared at the woman as she sat astride her horse, and his fist clenched around the rope attached to Kiri's collar. At last, he released the rope.

"Fine; have it your way," the slaver growled. "Take her up to the manor. I'm sure the one running this mess will want to say hello."

THE WOMAN DROPPED from her mount with a cat-like grace that drew Kiri's attention. The last person she'd seen move like that was Declan. The woman approached Kiri, withdrawing a small key from her belt; she inserted that key into the lock securing the collar, and a quick flick of her wrist released the latch. A small cloud of dust rose as the collar landed on the ground.

"Thank you," Kiri said, her voice quiet. "How do you know he's coming for me?"

"Because I helped him find you," the woman said as she took hold of Kiri's upper left arm and started guiding her toward the house. "Besides, we both know he'd come for you regardless of whether I helped him or not."

EXQUISITE FURNISHINGS FILLED the halls of the manor. Lamps with gold filigree, crystal chandeliers, fine tapestries and carpets, and porcelain tea service on silver platters were but a few of the lavish items the slavers appropriated from the former owners. The woman led Kiri to a set of double doors that slid back into the walls, which were currently closed. Muffled voices carried through the doors, which were soon no longer muffled as the woman pushed the doors wide.

"What's the status of the next shipment for Ivarson?" a woman asked as she leaned over the massive dining table that had become the centerpiece of an impromptu logistics center. The woman stood out among all other Vushaari. Her form—though attractive—wasn't up to the level of Kiri. Her skin—though smooth and cared for—

bore the common Vushaari olive complexion. No. What made her stand out among most other women in Vushaar was her wavy, blond hair.

Kiri jerked as she recognized the woman's voice.

"We should have enough with the batch the raiding parties brought in just now, once we brand them," a man said. "I'm told a detachment from the army is already on the way to retrieve them. We should have them ready for conscription when they arrive."

The woman leaning over the table said, "Very well. I don't want there to be any snags. Ivarson is just starting to get the siege established, and I want him to have plenty of bodies to throw at the Cavaliers. I paid good money for the soldiers he's keeping as the core of his force, and I'd rather not have the Cavaliers whittle them down too much. After all, I'll need a new royal guard when I take the throne."

"Milady, the special slave the outriders spoke of is here," the man said.

"Oh? What's so special-" The woman stood up from leaning against the table and lifted her eyes to the pair standing just inside the door, and Kiri found herself looking at her half-sister, Kaila Claymark.

In the months following the death of his wife, Rionne, Terris asked his wife's younger sister, Callie, to help him with his young daughter. It was perhaps inevitable, given their close proximity and Callie's pleasant personality plus her obvious love for her niece, that a lapse in judgment or two would occur. Not even two years after Rionne's death, Kiri's half-sister was born.

Kiri stared at her sister, unable to understand what she was seeing. Kaila didn't visibly react; she just stared into Kiri's eyes, and Kiri couldn't help but notice how dead her sister's eyes looked.

At last, Kaila sighed. When she spoke, her voice was tired, resigned almost. "You're supposed to be dead. I just knew it was too much to hope that incompetent arcanist would get it right."

"What?" Kiri asked, unable to believe what she was hearing.

"You really believed a storm fierce enough to sink a Vushaari corsair came out of nowhere during the season we hardly ever have storms on the Inner Sea? By the gods…you're even more naïve than I thought."

Everything crashed down on Kiri at once, and it was too much. It was just too much. "You? You arranged for the *Sprite* to sink?"

"Well, of course, I did. I-"

"*Why*, Kaila? Why would you do this? What did I ever do to you?"

"You existed," Kaila said, her voice developing an edge as her hands clenched into fists. "Do you think I never noticed how everyone fawned over you? Oh, Crown Princess Kiri, she's so wonderful! She will be a great Queen someday! All while my mother—your own aunt—was little more than a hired hand, being your nanny!" Kaila stopped and visibly worked to regain her control. "Well, I never realized how unfair it was until I was approached one day to act as an agent within Father's court, but then, it occurred to me. My father was King. I could be the Crown Princess, too. And I thought everything was working so well. After all, you died at sea with the *Sprite*. Ivarson was maneuvering people he could trust into unit commands in Father's army. It was all coming together…except for the small fact that Father never named me Crown Princess. I guess I got tired of waiting and decided to take what is my due."

"Kaila…what happened to you?"

Kaila gazed at Kiri a few moments longer with her dead eyes before she jerked her chin toward the door. "Take her to the cells in the basement. I think I want her close at hand to enjoy my triumph in the capital."

* * *

GAVIN RETURNED to camp having scouted the slavers' base with Declan and Sarres and found unexpected guests at the fringe of the wards. Four individuals in armor stood on the northwest edge of the camp. Three were men, one visibly much older, and the red-haired woman's eyes led Gavin to believe hers was a soul that had seen far too much.

"I'd like to know what you think you're doing here," the older man said. "This is sovereign Vushaari soil."

Gavin sighed and shook his head. He was not in the mood for pointless posturing. "We're saving a friend from these animals. Back off. By this time tomorrow, they won't be a problem anymore."

"Just who do you think you are?" the woman asked. "You're one man, and there are at least two hundred slavers down there."

Gavin stood his ground, eyeing the new arrivals and their equipment. Their armor was blacked out, and a lot of their gear was mismatched. It was only the tattoos on their upper left arms that marked them as Cavaliers.

"You four look like you're on a stealth job," Gavin said. "What's your interest in that camp?"

"Pike off, wizard," the woman growled. "You still haven't identified yourself."

Gavin chuckled, shaking his head. "Such manners...not exactly welcoming on my first trip to your country." The woman glared at Gavin and moved as if to push through the wards. "I am Gavin Cross, Head of House Kirloth, and I don't recommend trying my wards. I hear death isn't all that pleasant. Now, would you be so kind as to return the favor?"

The older man directed an appraising look at Gavin but held his silence for several more moments. Finally, though, he spoke. "I'm Roth Thatcherson, and it is my honor to serve in the personal detail of King Terris Muran."

"Thatcherson?" Gavin asked, not able to keep from smiling. "My mentor introduced me to a friend of his named Thatcherson in Tel Mivar, the Royal Priest of Tel."

Roth nodded, saying, "He's my older brother. Who is your mentor?"

"Have you ever met a man who went by the name Marcus?"

Roth nodded once more. "Those slavers, or people they work for, managed to spirit away King Terris's younger daughter. They say they will kill Kaila Claymark if he doesn't surrender to the general besieging the capital."

"And it's your job to infiltrate the camp and retrieve her before anyone's the wiser?" Gavin asked.

"Yes," Roth said.

"Your job will be far easier if you join us," Gavin said. "We just returned from scouting the farm, and I plan to attack just a little before dawn."

"This is the most far-fetched horse pucky-"

Gavin glared at the woman, his patience used up. "Listen, lady, I don't know what I did to sour your disposition so, but honestly, I don't really care. You stand before scions of the Great Houses of Tel, and it would behoove you to show a little more respect."

"I have yet to meet one of you freaks worth the shit on my boots," the woman said, her voice rising, "and I'll not-"

Something in Gavin's eyes drove a spike of fear through Roth Thatcherson's soul. He placed a hand on his comrade's shoulder, saying, "Tanna, that's enough. Stand down."

"Roth! This is our-"

"Tanna," Roth said, leaning close but still speaking loud enough for everyone to hear, "I'm trying to save your life. You're no good to the King dead, especially if you bring it on yourself and embarrass him in the process. House Kirloth and the Muran line go back to the Godswar. His family has more history with the King than you ever will."

LATER THAT NIGHT, they sat around a dark fire pit chatting. As close as they were to the slavers, no one was willing to risk being discovered because of a campfire. Mariana, Lillian, Wynn, and Braden sat with the two younger men from the Cavaliers. Declan, Gavin, and Roth sat together, and the elves conversed with the woman.

The sun was just inching below the horizon when a lone figure approached the perimeter of the wards. Gavin looked up and smiled as he recognized her. He stood, walking to the edge of the wards and handed her a ward-stone he had prepared while conversing with Roth.

The woman stepped through the wards and approached the camp. Everyone looked up at her arrival.

"Ladies and gentlemen," Gavin said, "this is one of my agents infiltrating the slavers. She will be providing us valuable information."

Over the next couple hours, the woman briefed everyone present on the guard shift rotations, sentry paths, and where Kiri was precisely located. Gavin and his friends noticed she made a point of not identifying the friend Gavin had come to rescue.

"That is all I can tell you," she said finally, "except for one last part. Your new associates won't like this."

"Oh? How so?" Gavin asked.

"Kaila Claymark wasn't abducted from the palace. She left of her own accord, using the ploy of abduction to set up an alibi for her. She is allied with Ivarson and is running the slaver camp below as we speak."

"What?" Roth said, his eyes wide. "I don't know who you think you are, but you should think very carefully about maligning the daughter of Vushaar's king."

Gavin shifted his attention to Roth, saying, "Calm yourself, Cavalier. If you have a problem with her, you have a problem with me." Gavin turned his attention back to his agent. "Can you arrange for Kaila to be in the same cell as our associate?"

"Easily, milord."

"See to it, then, and gather yourself and anyone else you want spared in there as well. I will begin the attack just before dawn, and except for whomever is inside that cell, only slaves and horses will leave here tomorrow."

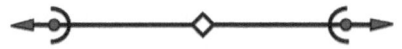

CHAPTER 19

Gavin stood on a small knoll just beyond the perimeter of the plantation. The first rays of the sun were just starting to peek over the horizon to the east, and his friends and the Cavaliers stood arrayed behind him. In his hands, Gavin held the rough diagram of the plantation the woman had drawn the night before.

"The barn has been converted into a barracks," Gavin said, more to himself than anyone present. "That has to go first."

Gavin's next actions surprised all those watching. He knelt to one knee and bowed his head. "I am not an overly-religious man, but Bellos, I ask thee for the strength and will necessary to see these events through. My plan is a far-greater working of the Art than any I have ever attempted, but the life of someone very dear to me is in danger. If I must trade my life to see her safely home, then I gladly make that offer. Please, help me see her home."

Gavin took a deep breath and pushed himself back to his feet. He ran through his mind every mental image he could envision of what might have happened to Kiri had his Wraiths not infiltrated these slavers. The anger and rage stoked the fires of his soul once more and provided a barrier against the pain he knew would be coming. Then, he cleared his mind of everything but the anger, rage, and a crystal-clear image of his intent. Gavin next spoke three Words of Power, blending them together to form one long polysyllabic Word, "*Luhrhym-Rhyskaal-Idluhn.*"

The resonance of the composite effect struck Lillian, Braden, Wynn, and Mariana so hard and so fast that they collapsed to their knees and retched, almost blacking out. As she fought to keep from retching again, Lillian wondered what in all creation could have required that much power. She didn't have to wait long to find out.

A small, swirling storm was developing around the barn-barracks. Dirt, rocks, slavers, fence-posts, weeds, water-troughs, and more were caught up in a maelstrom. The walls of the barn started to cave inward, and the crack of the roof's spine was audible even at Gavin's distant position when it broke and began drawing in as well. The swirling cloud pulled tighter, tighter, and had anyone present possessed the proper knowledge, the space around the barn would've evinced an eerie similarity to the event horizon of a black hole.

While the barn and most things surrounding it continued to swirl into a tighter and tighter sphere, the slave pens and slaves within them—not thirty feet away—remained untouched, though the slaves were doubtless terrified by the maelstrom from which they could not run.

The maelstrom at last reached a kind of critical mass, and with a crack like that of lightning, the maelstrom exploded in a shower of dirt, rocks, wood, people…well…pieces of people, and various other bits. A rather large spar that had once been part of the roof's rafters flew toward Gavin like a guided missile, but Gavin stood his ground and watched its flight with nonchalance. Just as the others were registering the danger and starting to dive aside, the spar struck an unseen barrier and fell to the ground in a pile of what looked like saw dust.

An eyeball fell out of the sky and landed about three feet to Gavin's left with a soft *squish*. Gavin turned his head and regarded the item in silence for a few moments.

"Well, I think it's safe to say that the garrison is no longer a problem. Now, it's time to deal with the house and what perimeter patrols remain."

Gavin pulled the handkerchief that held a few drops of Kiri's blood from the sleeve of his robe. He held the handkerchief in his left hand with his fingers and thumb touching the dried blood, and he concentrated on the intent of seeing Kiri. He then spoke the Word of Power to re-create a scrying sphere, "*Klaepos.*"

The sphere shimmered into existence on Gavin's right, and it showed an image of Kiri and a number of others huddled in a small cell, their expressions terrified. A blond woman lay off to one side unconscious, bound, and gagged.

At seeing Kiri, Gavin felt his anger start to wane, but it was too soon; there was still too much left to do. Gavin looked to the plantation house, and by now, a number of people were milling about on the veranda, probably rather concerned about the recent lack of a barracks. Gavin focused on them, pushed through his mind images of the despicable acts those people had done, and he managed to hold on to his rage.

Gavin took a deep breath and slowly released it. He ran through the sequence of everything he wanted to happen, picturing each event individually before weaving them together as one. Once he was confident in his focus, Gavin took another deep breath. The two Words he wanted to use were already on the tip of his tongue, and he spoke them, "*Sykhurhos-Idluhn.*"

The severe resonance of Gavin's previous composite effect served as a bit of a buffer, and this new invocation did not savage his fellow wizards. Still, this invocation's raw power rattled their bodies and souls and struck the breath from their lungs.

In the scrying sphere, the stone blocks of the cell took on a soft-white radiance just moments before red lines of power drew across every seam of the house, such as between shingles or pieces of paneling. The lines grew in radiance until they made it almost impossible to face the house before they seemed to wink out, and for a very brief instant, the slaver camp was pure calm. The next instant, the plantation house exploded. The instant after that, all that remained was a starburst blast pattern centered on a stone cube with an iron cell door in one side.

Gavin nodded once and said, "Okay, people, fan out. There should be at least one survivor somewhere down there, and I want that survivor. Once we have one confirmed, kill any more you find."

"How dare you!" Tanna said. "This is sovereign Vushaari soil, and any survivors we find will face the King's justice!"

Gavin turned, and everyone recoiled from what they saw. Gavin's flesh was now the pallor of death. His eye sockets were sunken and dark, as if he'd gone months without sleep, and his eyes themselves looked dead, devoid of that tell-tale spark of life.

"Do as I say," Gavin said, "or you can tout the King's justice in the halls of the dead. The choice is yours."

Tanna bristled and drew in a fresh breath, but Roth placed his hand on her shoulder and leaned close to her right ear.

"Tanna, you mean nothing to him right now, and the King's jurisdiction here even less," Roth whispered so low only she could hear him. "Do as he says."

Tanna ground her teeth together and glared at Gavin. "Fine. Have it your way now, but sometime, you'll get yours. I swear it."

Gavin turned and walked off the knoll toward the distant stone cube.

"Declan, I'll need you to pick the lock on that cell," Gavin said over his shoulder. "The rest of you, find me a survivor."

* * *

KIRI LOOKED up at the sound of the lock clicking. The door swung open, and she couldn't keep from smiling at seeing Declan standing in the doorway. But something was wrong, and it took her a few moments to process what the wrongness was. Sunlight shouldn't be streaming into the cell from the doorway; there used to be a stone wall with sconces about six feet from the cell door. Curiosity overcame her fear, and Kiri walked outside her cell for the first time in a day and a half. She walked into a wasteland.

The plantation house possessed a well-manicured lawn when

she entered the building that would become her short-lived prison, having flower beds and shrubbery arrangements as well. It was all gone now, both the house and the landscaping, given way to a blast pattern unlike anything Kiri had ever seen before. The barn was gone, too. There was not even any debris large enough to say for certain that it was from the house, the picket fence, or the barn.

"By the gods…" Kiri managed to say, little more than an empowered whisper. "They…the wizards did this for me?"

Declan watched her with care, paying special attention to her reaction and state of mind. He needed to see her honest response to his next words. "No. *He* did this…alone and unaided."

"Gavin did…" Kiri's left hand shot out, grabbing Declan's right wrist. "Where is he? Is he okay?"

Declan couldn't decide whether to credit his years as a bard and that love of acting and entertaining or his years as a Wraith, but he knew Kiri saw no hint of his relief and happiness that he had not seen disgust or revulsion in her reaction.

"He's near what used to be the barn," Declan said, gesturing with his left thumb. "As for whether he's okay, that remains to be seen."

Kiri moved to one side and saw a number of people had already gathered in what had been the center of the plantation, including the woman who had protected her on the ride back here. She glanced over her shoulder and saw a woman in matte black leather armor at her side, leading Kaila, and she wondered how she had missed those others moving past her. That, however, didn't keep her from hurrying to join them.

GAVIN LOOKED DOWN on the sole survivor of his attack on the compound. The man looked to be just slightly older than Gavin himself, with a shaved head and dark eyes, but a hunk of his left forearm had been ripped away, exposing the bones.

"Milord," a whisper at Gavin's side drew his attention to the woman who had slipped out unseen the night before, "I know you saw the signs of what poor treatment I was unable to prevent, and I thought you should know that he was the one who did it."

"Is that so?" Gavin asked. When the woman nodded once, Gavin gave the man a dark smile that held no mirth at all. "How poetic, then."

"Whatever torture you have in mind, you'd better hurry," the slaver said. "I'm not long for this world."

"Oh, no," Gavin said, his voice far more harsh than his fellows had ever heard it. "You see, the whole point of an object lesson is for others to learn from it, and how could anyone learn from this, if no one is left to tell the tale?"

Gavin invoked five Words of Power, "*Thyskhahs-Khraezax-Sykhurhos-Thyskhahs-Uhnrys*", and the man began screaming. Everyone watched as the flesh of the man's left arm withered and blackened to a lifeless husk of its former self across an agonizing period of several seconds.

Once the immediate pain of the transformation receded, the slaver looked back up at Gavin as he gasped for breath.

"Yes, that's right; you feel completely healthy, aside from what remains of your left arm," Gavin said. "That's the only form of healing arcanists can do, you see. It's one of the uses of Necromancy, taking what is alive and shifting that life force to something else. Honestly, that sort of thing is frowned upon in polite society nowadays; it isn't all that kind. It was a bit tricky, too, considering that I was healing the rest of you with what life remained in your arm, but I think I managed it rather well."

"You're daft as a loon, if you think I'm going to thank you for that or do anything you want," the slaver said through gasps for air.

Gavin chuckled, the malevolent mirthless smile returning to his mouth. "You don't have a choice, really. You see…the necromantic healing was only the first third of that composite effect. The second was the equivalent of a geas and contingency, and the final third was what happens if the terms of the geas are ever unfulfilled."

"What have you done to me?"

"You must never stay in one settlement—whether trading post, village, town, or city—for more than five consecutive days, and every time you enter a settlement as I previously defined, you must recount the story of what happened here today…but more important, you must tell them why."

"I know why…you're bloodthirsty monster!"

"Do you remember the woman you happened across at night six days ago? She was walking alone and put up a half-decent fight? The woman this lady at my side wouldn't let you pursue more intimate entertainments with?"

"Yeah…"

"That woman is my friend and, beyond that, very dear to me, and all of this is a warning or, as I said earlier, an object lesson. This and worse is what awaits anyone who attacks my friends or those I have placed under my protection. My birth name is Gavin Cross, but you may call me…Kirloth."

Gavin was pleased to see the expected reaction in this man as well, or perhaps, especially in this man.

"Oh, yes…you should know what will befall you should you fail to tell your tale. I would imagine what you feel now and felt in your left arm is rather unpleasant. Right now, you will age normally, never suffer disease or any form of physical injury, and you will live a normal lifespan. However, if you ever enter a settlement and tell no one of what happened today, who did it, or why, the rest of your body will wither and die to match your arm, and you will live with that pain until the end of time. Now, go. You have a lot of traveling to do."

The man scrabbled to his feet and headed northwest. Gavin watched him as he went. He knew he should probably feel some remorse over the doom he had just levied upon that man, but Gavin couldn't find any remorse within himself, not a shred. As he watched the distant man hobble over the small hill out of sight, Gavin wondered if that lack of remorse made him a bad person.

"Gavin," Sarres shouted as he leaped down from the sole tree to survive the destruction, "we have troops incoming! The outriders are twenty minutes away, at best!"

"There's no time," Gavin said, as he scanned the desolate landscape around them. His eyes finally came to rest on Kaila. "Who's she?"

"She's…she's my sister, Gavin. She orchestrated all of this and has allied with Ivarson," Kiri said. "It will break my father's heart when he learns of this." Kiri's eyes widened just a bit, then hardened, and she looked into Gavin's eyes. "Gavin, I would spare my father the pain of ordering her execution for treason, and it would kill my aunt, too." Kiri squared her shoulders. "Kaila Claymark is a traitor to Vushaar, and the penalty for treason is death. As Crown Princess of Vushaar, I ask you, Kirloth, to carry out that sentence forthwith."

Gavin didn't even blink as he spoke the Word, "*Thraxys*." Kaila collapsed to the ground, like a puppet whose strings were cut.

"What are you doing still standing around?" Sarres said, skidding to a stop at the side of the group. "Those outriders are going to be here any minute."

"There's nothing for it," Gavin said. "The only way we'll survive is not to be here when those troops arrive. Kiri, give me your hand, and I want you to focus every facet of your mind on home…someplace large enough to receive all of these slaves besides us. Can you do that?"

"Gavin…you look like you have one foot in the grave already. I'm not-"

"If you have another option—a better option—then put words to it! We're losing time!"

Kiri sighed and took Gavin's right hand in both of hers. As she lifted his hand, Gavin's sleeve slipped back, revealing a forearm almost completely black from the Void-scar. Kiri closed her eyes.

This is going to be nine kinds of bad, Gavin thought before he cleared his mind of all thought, focusing on his intent. Once his intent became a solid image in his mind, excluding all else, he spoke the Words, "*Ikrhys-Paedryx*."

* * *

THE PALACE COURTYARD served as both an ingress to the palace complex and a parade ground for the Cavaliers on those rare occasions they paraded. At just before noon on a bright sunny day, the courtyard was devoid of life...except for four Cavaliers acting as 'ceremonial' guards and the various shrubs, flowers, and small trees the groundskeepers labored to keep alive.

Despite all their training to be the elite troops of the Vushaari army, the Cavaliers stood stock still and gaped at the sight of almost five hundred people and several horses appearing in the courtyard out of thin air. There was no poof of smoke, no fanfare...nothing. They were just suddenly *there*.

"DID WE MAKE IT?" Gavin asked, his voice a raspy whisper.

"Yes, Gavin, we did," Kiri said as alarms began ringing all throughout the palace compound.

"Good." Gavin's eyes rolled back in his head, and he collapsed. He would've struck the flagstones with a bit of force, had Declan not acted with haste to catch him.

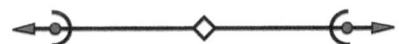

CHAPTER 20

Q'Orval deBentak had seen a great many things in his life. Some good and several not so good, but the sight before him as he pushed through the ring of Cavaliers in the courtyard stopped him more thoroughly than an arrow or crossbow quarrel. The Cavaliers ringing the group that arrived out of nowhere had their swords out. Five of the newly arrived group had their swords out as well, and an additional four held orbs of incandescent, kaleidoscopic power roiling and seething above the palms of their hands. Those four stood at the cardinal points around the mass of people—who were very clearly slaves for the most part—with their backs to the group at large. One look at the silver medallions resting atop the sternums of those four told Q'Orval who the far more dangerous people were…without one shred of doubt.

"What's the meaning of this?" Q'Orval demanded, shouldering his way through the ring of Cavaliers.

"It's an assault on the palace, Lord Chamberlain!" one of the Cavaliers said, her voice urgent.

"Do none of you recognize Roth Thatcherson, second in command of the King's personal guard?" Q'Orval asked. "I would think you owe him a bit more respect than this, not to mention the arrival of such august guests as the Heirs of the Great Houses of Tel. Unless I miss my guess, you lot skate on precariously thin ice just now."

"You're not wrong," a woman wearing the Glyph of Mivar said, her eyes never leaving her section of the ring. "One wrong move, and they all die."

"If you're not assaulting the palace, what could possibly be so important you'd react with this level of threatened violence?"

"As our mentor likes to say, we don't make threats," Lady Mivar said. "We make promises."

The movement of a figure out from behind Roth and his team drew Q'Orval's attention, and he froze, feeling very much like his heart had seized.

"They're protecting me, Q'Orval," Kiri said.

"Kiri? Is that really you?" Q'Orval gasped. "We all thought you dead!" The reality of the situation dawned on Q'Orval, and his expression turned fierce. "Sheathe your swords, all of you...now! You've committed treason by drawing steel on the Crown Princess."

None of the Cavaliers moved.

Kiri looked around the group and sighed, saying, "Lillian, if you please? I'd rather none of them died, though."

"*Pharhyk*," Lillian said, and the orb of power above her right palm flashed as every weapon carried by the Cavaliers forming the ring around them dissolved to iron filings and leather wrapping.

"That wasn't the Word Gavin normally uses," Mariana said from her position.

"I don't think I'm strong enough for *that* Word yet," Lillian replied. "As strong as Gavin is, he can bull his way through most problems. Besides, I think I've heard somewhere that the effect is shaped by the invoker's intent."

Wynn and Braden snorted their laughter.

Q'Orval felt he was missing a good part of that exchange, but it was a matter for another time. He smiled as he returned his attention to Kiri, saying, "Come with me, Princess; I think there's someone who will want to meet you. Roth, can you and your associates see to these disarmed individuals? I'm sure the King will want a moment of their time in the very near future."

"What of these refugees, Q'Orval?" Kiri asked as Roth directed his team to begin rounding up the disarmed Cavaliers. "We couldn't leave them where they were. A contingent of troops from Ivarson's army was on the way to collect them as conscripts."

"We'll take care of them, Your Highness; I promise. In all truth, I'm not quite sure how, right this moment, but we will. Oh, if you don't mind, I'd like to arrange quarters for your friends where they can freshen up before meeting the King."

"Offended by our clothing already, Q'Orval?" Kiri said, a teasing sparkle in her eyes as a grin threatened to curl her lips.

"Not at all, Your Highness," Q'Orval replied with aplomb. "I just know what it will mean to your father to see you again, and I'm sure he'd rather that be as private an affair as possible."

"Declan, could you bring him here, please?" Kiri said over her shoulder before returning her attention to Q'Orval. The crowd shifted and parted behind Kiri, and Q'Orval felt his eyes widen when he saw none other than Declan the Dandy approach Kiri's side.

"But…you went on an expedition to the eastern archipelagos! I'm told the crowd at Birsha almost collapsed the pier."

Declan shrugged with one shoulder, despite the unconscious form he carried. "A convenient fiction, old friend. Older allegiances required my service for a time, and I needed to disappear."

"Q'Orval," Kiri said, drawing his attention back to her, "I want you to take very good care of this man Declan is carrying. He's the only reason I'm safe, and what's more, he's the only reason any of us were able to avoid that conscription party I mentioned."

"He shall have the best care, then," Q'Orval said. "If I may ask, who is he?"

"Gavin Cross," Kiri said, "Head of House Kirloth."

Despite all his years at court, Q'Orval blanched. His eyes flicked to the Heirs and took in the brown robes students wore and remembered the Lady Mivar's casual mention of a 'Gavin' and how much stronger he was than her.

"It seems I was right, after all," Q'Orval said.

"What do you mean?" Kiri asked.

"When I decided those four are the most dangerous people in the courtyard."

Roth approached Kiri's right shoulder at that point and nodded, saying, "If they're even a tenth as dangerous as Gavin, don't ever give them reason to prove it."

"Yes, well," Q'Orval said, swallowing hard, "let's get you settled and take Her Highness to the Royal Apartments."

* * *

THE PRIVATE STUDY of Terris Muran, King of Vushaar, came close to being the size of a suite. Unlike a suite, it was all one room, and with the exception of large windows looking out over the city, every wall sported a tall bookcase. Every shelf of every bookcase was full, and some were full almost to overflowing.

Terris Muran sat in his favorite armchair, reading a treatise on siege warfare that was penned by one of the finest generals Vushaar had ever produced. As interested as he was in the work, though, the sound of Q'Orval clearing his throat immediately drew his attention.

"What was the alarm about, Q'Orval?" Terris asked as he marked his place in the book and set it aside. "I can't remember the last time I've seen the Cavaliers in such an uproar. They hustled me out of the throne room like there was a fire next door."

"We had an unannounced arrival in the courtyard, Your Majesty," Q'Orval said. "I'm afraid it required my intervention to establish our new guests' welcome. Well, sire, they weren't all guests, in all truth."

"'Your Majesty,' Q'Orval...really? You haven't addressed me as Your Majesty when we're alone since I first ascended the throne," Terris said, pushing himself to his feet.

"Yes, well...we're not alone, Your Majesty," Q'Orval said, and Terris thought he detected a slight strain of amusement in his old friend's tone.

"Not alone? Why didn't you say-" Terris's voice stopped when he spun to offer proper courtesy to whomever was with Q'Orval. He was in the midst of giving himself a thorough dressing down for the breach of hospitality when his eyes locked on the person standing beside Q'Orval.

"Kiri?" Terris asked, his breath coming in ragged gasps. "But, you're...I mean...we all thought..."

Kiri almost sprinted the short distance to her father and threw her arms around him, pulling him into the tightest embrace she could ever remember giving anyone as she spoke in a soft voice, "I'm home, Father. I missed you so much!"

Terris couldn't stop the tears rolling down his face, tears he'd never allowed himself to shed when he thought he'd lost his daughter at sea. "But...how? Everyone said the *Sprite* sank."

"It did, Father," Kiri said, her voice muffled just a bit by Terris's tunic. "I washed ashore on a piece of driftwood. I don't know how I survived."

"Well, I'll spend some extra time offering thanks to Marin, for seeing you safely ashore." Terris clutched his daughter in his arms, and his tears began to wet her hair as he rested his cheek on her head. "It took you two years to make it home? Couldn't you have gotten us word somehow?"

"I'm sorry, Father. I wasn't...I...when I washed ashore, there were people on the beach, Father. They were slavers, and they didn't rescue me."

"What?" Terris gasped, shifting his hands to Kiri's shoulders and pushing her out to arms' length to get a better look at her. Tears streamed down her face, same as his. The traveling clothes she wore were well made, but the fabric stopped just a slight distance from the left side of her neck and curled down below her collarbone to circle her torso without covering her left arm or shoulder. She was completely decent; not even the most rigid prude could say otherwise, but her left shoulder and arm were bare, displaying the slave mark for all to see.

Kiri bowed her head, and Terris saw her jaw trembling. "I'm sorry, Father. I...I couldn't stop them!"

Terris pulled his daughter back into his arms and held her tight. "What? You think I don't want you, now that you're a slave? Do you honestly think anyone will *ever* call you a 'slave' where I can hear of it? You're my daughter, Kiri. As long as you're alive and healthy, everything else is dross."

Kiri giggled as Terris felt the tension leave her. "You might have some competition when it comes to chastising anyone who calls me a slave, Father."

"Oh, how's that?"

"Well, the man who technically owns me—according to the Slavers' Association—is rather determined that I be free, and... well...people step around him for *very* good reasons."

"Has he-"

"Oh, no, Father! He's never laid a hand on me. Why, when we first met, he even refused to sleep in the same bed as me...even though it was the only bed we had. He made a mattress out of blankets on the floor."

"I think I'll have to meet this man. Just who is he? And is he part of those unannounced guests Q'Orval mentioned?"

"He's why you have those unannounced guests, Father. We were at a slaver base several leagues southeast of here, with an army on the way from Ivarson to conscript the slaves they'd gathered so far. He used my memories of the courtyard to teleport us there before the outriders could arrive and overwhelm us."

"I've never heard of a mage with that kind of power," Terris said. "Why, I've never even heard of the Teleport spell being used that way."

"He's not a mage, Father. His name is Gavin Cross, and he's Head of House Kirloth. Teleporting us here on top of everything he did at the slaver camp took everything he had. He collapsed as soon as I told him I was home and safe."

Terris pushed Kiri back just enough to see her eyes, saying, "And if you hadn't been safe?"

"He probably would've killed himself ensuring that I was, and I'd be afraid to find out what all he'd take with him."

"As soon as he's ready, I certainly want to meet him, but that's for later. Come over here, and sit with me."

Terris pulled Kiri—who didn't require much pulling—over to the sofa in front of the east-facing window. He sat and, once Kiri sat at his side, put his arm around her as she rested her head on his shoulder.

"Now, I want to hear everything that's happened with you these last three years."

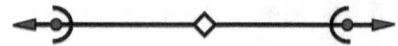

CHAPTER 21

Birds were chirping somewhere close. That was the first thing Gavin's mind processed as he returned to consciousness. The headache resonating throughout his skull like the peal of a blacksmith's hammer upon an anvil followed a close second.

"I really have to quit waking up in beds with headaches," Gavin said, more of a groaning whisper than any kind of well-formed speech.

"At least you're waking up at all," a deep baritone said from somewhere off to his right. "How do you feel otherwise?"

It took all Gavin's strength and will to lift his arms enough to put his hands on his head a few moments. "Far too weak, but nothing else seems apparent right now."

Gavin blinked open his eyes and found himself in a room with banks of windows in two adjoining walls. Those windows were open, and a blue bird chirped on a tree branch right outside the window directly in front of Gavin. The room itself was elegant with tasteful furnishings in an emerald color scheme. A cedar armoire stood against the wall off Gavin's right shoulder, and a dresser with a mirror, wash basin, and water pitcher stood beside the armoire.

The room's door was to his left. A chair sat at the right side of the bed, and the seat's cushion showed it had seen extensive recent use.

A man of average height and build with salt-and-pepper hair stood at the window to Gavin's right. He wore a gray shirt over tan trousers and boots, and the belt at his waist looked incomplete without a scabbard hanging from it. The man turned and, sipping from the goblet in his right hand, walked over to stand near the bed.

"You gave us all quite the scare, young man," he said, his voice a rumbling cascade, "but none so much as the princess I think. It took my personal word that I would stay with you until she returned to get her to keep her tutors' schedule. Would you like some water?"

"Not just yet, I think, but thank you," Gavin said. "I'm thirsty, don't get me wrong, but I think it would only make me sick given how I feel with this headache."

"The court wizard, Fallon, said to ask you about your power... how it felt to you and such. He said that was very important to ask as soon as you awoke."

Gavin nodded and laid his head back to consider the issue. For the first few moments, he felt none of the tell-tale tingling within him, but he settled his mind and concentrated on his body. To his surprise, the headache started to fade, giving way to the gradual return of that tingling sensation. And sure enough, at the core of the tingling, Gavin found the seed of power that made him a wizard.

"It's there," Gavin said at last, "but it's still very faint. I can feel it getting stronger, but it's very slow. It'll probably be days before I'm back to where I was."

The older man nodded and opened his mouth to speak. Before he could utter a word, though, the door flew open, and a blond-haired man in an orange and green velvet doublet and green hose stormed into the room.

"Your Majesty, I'm sorry to interrupt, but the Merchant's Guild is..." He stopped and took in the bewildered expression Gavin was directing at him. "Oh my, you're awake. Looks like the Cavaliers will win the pool after all."

The man standing beside the bed sighed. "The Merchant's

Guild can wait; after all, we are under siege. Be a good fellow, and go find my daughter. She's supposed to be with her tutors in the Archives, but it's always difficult to tell with her. Once you find her, please tell her Gavin's awake."

"Yes, Your Majesty, at once." The courtier turned and strode from the room, afresh with royal mandate.

Gavin turned his head to face the man beside his bed, but it was a slow process, almost a force of will just to start the motion. "I feel like I should be moving to the floor to bow, but turning my head to face you took the most of what effort I can muster."

The man regarded Gavin in silence for a few heartbeats before he stepped around to sit in the chair at Gavin's side. He placed his hand on Gavin's shoulder as he said, "Young man, you returned my daughter to me safe and whole, and from what I hear, you were a far better friend to Kiri than she had any right to expect to find in Tel, given her status at the time. You don't ever have to bow to me. Besides, your mentor never did."

Gavin couldn't keep from chuckling, though it was weak. "My mentor won a duel with a god. No offense, but what is a king compared to that?"

Terris laughed, a smile staying with him. "You have a point. I've often wondered how he must've seen the rest of us."

"I don't know about how he saw people in general, but I do know how he saw you and your family."

"I'm honestly not sure I should ask."

Gavin smiled and shook his head as best he could. "No, no. I'm sure it's not what you think. I can't remember the precise wording he used in the journal where he really discussed his continued association with the Muran line, but in his own way, he cared for your family, quite possibly as much as the Great Houses of Tel."

The door erupted open with such force it banged against the stop, and Kiri entered with most unseemly haste for a lady, let alone a crown princess.

"Father? Maervin said…" Her voice trailed off as she saw Gavin slowly turn his head and smile at her. She saw how weak the smile was, but she also saw *him*, the Gavin she first met and felt she truly knew. Her father no longer existed, and the fact that there was not a chair on Gavin's left side bothered her not at all. She knelt and took Gavin's hand in hers.

"How are you feeling?" Kiri said. "Do you need anything?"

"Kiri," Terris said.

After a long moment, Kiri turned to look at her father. "Yes, Father?"

"Come over here, and sit in the chair. The stone tile floor isn't good for your knees, and besides, the Merchant's Guild is waiting for me."

Terris rose and started to walk toward the door, as Kiri stood and moved over to the chair. The king was about half-way to the door when Gavin spoke.

"Terris, this may not be the best time, but there's something you should know."

Terris turned to face Gavin, his expression neutral. "Yes?"

"Do you remember Valera, the *Magus* of Divination who paid her respects at your father's funeral?"

Terris nodded. "Oh, yes. Rionne and I were truly touched that the Society sent someone."

"She may have offered the Society's condolences, but they didn't send her," Gavin said. "She was your grandfather's youngest sister."

Terris blinked, his jaw dropping just a bit. "What? That's impossible. All the records indicate my grandfather had only brothers."

"Your great-grandfather didn't agree with Valera's decision to pursue her career with the Society; he saw her training in Divination as a corrective measure to bring her visions under some semblance of control and felt very betrayed when Valera said she preferred her studies to court life. Marcus tried to reason with him, but he would have none of it. He had her stricken from every Muran family history on pain of death for anyone who disobeyed."

"I have no reason to disbelieve what you would say, but I have a very hard time believing this," Terris said.

"When I get back on my feet and find my satchel, I'll bring you what is most likely the sole copy of the true Muran genealogy for that period in your family's life. Marcus stole it before the scribes could destroy it, and when I realized I would be traveling here, I decided to try my best to correct that injustice."

"Your satchel is in this armoire, Gavin," Kiri said, going to the armoire and withdrawing the near-bottomless satchel that had traveled with him from Tel. She placed it on the bed beside Gavin.

"The Muran Genealogy," Gavin said before pushing his hand into the satchel as best he could. He pulled out a book whose cover was stylized with the calligraphy and inlay of a royal genealogy, and he laid it on the bed at his left side. "Take it. I will respect whatever decision you make."

"I know what you want me to decide," Terris said as he held the book in his hands, staring at it.

"Just because I have a preference doesn't mean I'm trying to coerce you in anyway. You are an adult and, what's more, a sovereign monarch. Your course is your own to choose, but we all nudge each other from time to time."

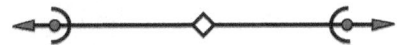

CHAPTER 22

Gavin spent the next four days in bed, except for the necessary trips to the privy. The first such trips were agonizing, his body so far beyond fatigue he could barely move his limbs. By the evening of fourth day, Gavin was starting to move with some renewed strength and independence, and he began exploring. His room was in the northeast tower of the palace; he knew that much from his conversations with Kiri and her father. What he was not prepared for, however, were the Cavaliers stationed at every hallway intersection.

"May I help you, sir?" the Cavalier at the intersection closest to Gavin's room asked as Gavin stopped and looked down each hall of the intersection in turn.

Gavin smiled. "No, I don't think so. I'm just exploring. Is it common to have Cavaliers stationed at every intersection throughout the palace?"

"No, sir," the Cavalier responded. "We're only stationed throughout the royal residence."

"Oh," Gavin said, his voice quiet. "Thank you."

.   .   .

IT WAS ABOUT mid-morning of the fifth day that Gavin felt up to an extended exploration. He bathed, donned his clothes, and poked his head out the window to gauge how many floors were below him. Then, Gavin left his room in search of someone he knew.

The corridor outside Gavin's room was tiled with an off-white ceramic tile, and he passed several mahogany doors, crafted much like his with an artistic design carved into the door's face. About every ten feet hung a portrait; given that the names under each portrait all ended with 'Muran,' Gavin felt safe in assuming these were Kiri's ancestors.

He soon found the central staircase, a spiral affair of solid stone masonry. Gavin admired the craftsmanship that had gone into the staircase, but he couldn't help thinking how easy it would've been to construct with the Art. Looking out his window, Gavin thought he was on the fourth floor, so he kept ambling down the stairs until he reached what he thought to be the main floor of the palace, the third set of closed doors below his own floor.

Gavin stepped through the closed doors and found Cavaliers in full battle dress standing on either side of the doorway. He nodded politely to them and proceeded on his way. Just as he was walking out of earshot, Gavin heard one of the soldiers whisper to the other, "That's the wizard who destroyed the slaver camp."

Gavin turned the corner and found himself on the shore of a veritable ocean of people. Within the waves of souls, Gavin identified court functionaries, common folk, guards, and some who represented the capital's middle class. A woman in a crimson velvet dress with a silver waist-cord soon noticed him and nudged the man at her side, whispering intently and nodding her head toward Gavin.

Just when Gavin thought the pair were about to break from the crowd and head his way, Gavin saw someone he knew at last. He smiled as Roth Thatcherson broke out from the crowd and started walking his way.

"Gavin," Roth said as he extended his hand to the young wizard, "it's good to see you up and around. How are you feeling?"

Gavin couldn't keep from shrugging. "Honestly, I've felt better, but it's better than what I expected."

Roth put his armored arm around Gavin's shoulders, a wary eye on the nobles moving to talk with the young wizard. "Well, I'm sure you'll continue to mend. So, were you feeling a little stir-crazy?"

"Just a bit. I explored my hallway yesterday, but this morning, I woke up feeling restless down to my bones."

"Well, I'm on my way to a meeting of the city's defense council. Why don't you come with me?"

They soon cleared the vestibule, and Roth removed his arm from Gavin's shoulders. They walked down a tiled hallway, a Cavalier stationed every few yards, until they reached an archway with double doors. A Cavalier stood on either side of the closed doors, each in full plate armor with a sword strapped to their backs and holding a halberd in the hand closest the doors.

"Who is this?" the guard Gavin assumed to be senior asked as Roth approached the doors.

Roth paused for a moment and smiled. "You mean to tell me you haven't heard of Gavin Cross? Maybe you've heard of the new Kirloth?"

Both guards paled just a bit, the far guard even going so far as to glance Gavin's way.

"If you would like," Roth said, "I can step inside and bring His Majesty out to discuss Gavin's attendance."

"No, sir," the senior guard said. "As commanding officer of Her Highness's personal guard, I'm confident we can trust your judgment."

The guards shifted their halberds to their opposite hands and heaved the large doors open. Gavin found himself entering a room with maps lining the walls and a massive chart comparing troop numbers on the far wall. A round table dominated the center of the room. Several individuals sat around that table, and as Roth and Gavin neared it, Gavin saw it was recessed and held a scale map of the city…complete with the troop formations making up the siege.

"Ah, Roth, so good of you…" Terris's voice trailed off as he looked up from the table and saw Gavin at Roth's side. "Gavin, I wasn't expecting you to be on your feet so soon. How are you feeling?"

"Tired, Your Majesty, but stir-crazy. Roth found me on the fringe of a crowd in a vestibule-type room a short distance from here."

Terris looked to Roth, and Roth said, "He was standing on the fringe of the petitioners, Your Majesty. One of the lesser nobles had already recognized him, so I decided to save him. And I thought his insights might be of some use. Forgive me, sire, if I overstepped my bounds."

"Insights?" A rough, slurred voice roared. "What insights could a waif younger than my grandson possibly have?"

An utter silence dominated the room as Terris turned to confront the older man who had just spoken. Gavin saw an older man in an ill-fitting uniform of the Vushaari army, with salt-and-pepper hair and a monocle over his left eye. Medals and ribbons adorned both breasts of the uniform jacket, but the sloshing wine glass in his left hand marred the dignified mien just a bit.

"General-" Terris said.

"Your Majesty, please forgive my interruption," Gavin said, "but the slur was directed at me."

Terris turned to face Gavin once more. "Very well, Gavin; I will yield the floor on one condition."

"Yes, Your Majesty?"

"Don't injure him."

Gavin frowned. "Why, of course not, Your Majesty. After all, the mess would stain the tile." Gavin shifted his body to face the old man fully, and he said, "Sir, I will grant you that I have no formal military experience. However…"

Gavin's voice trailed off as his *skathos* flared. The flare was no more than a small candle, but then again, Gavin wasn't exactly his normal self. He closed his eyes and concentrated on the feeling. In an instant, he knew. He ambled to the table and pointed to a section of the city's wall between the east and north gates.

"That section of the wall is no longer there; Ivarson's wizards have just revealed themselves."

"How much of the wall is gone, Gavin?" Terris asked as Roth stepped to Gavin's side and leaned heavily on the table.

Gavin shook his head; he felt like his strength was leaving him. "I don't know. I've recovered just enough to know it was a disintegration effect. Matter of fact, I'm pretty sure I know the Word of Transmutation they used."

"You say 'wizards?' Plural? As in more than one?" Roth asked.

Gavin nodded. "I've yet to meet the modern wizard who could invoke the Word that would do this alone; it's simply too powerful. Besides, during our journey south, I encountered…well, a friend of the family…who informed me that Ivarson would be receiving five wizards to reinforce his army at some point."

Gavin didn't seem to notice the worried glances that circled the table.

Just then, the doors flew open, and a young man wearing cloth under-armor that bore the crest of the Vushaari army ran into the room. He collapsed to his knees, gasping for air.

"Your…Your Majesty," the young man said, "the rebels have wizards, sir; they just destroyed a section of the wall!"

Roth turned and walked over to the young man. Roth lifted him to his feet and gently shook his shoulders. "You make a report before the king, boy. Stand up straight, and do a proper job of it."

Terris walked over and stood beside Roth. "It's okay, Roth; he has the look of a man who just ran all the way from the outer walls. Young man, tell us what happened, everything you can."

"The wall just collapsed to dust, sire! I ain't never seen anything like it. There's a hole in the city's wall at least a hunnerd yards wide; there's no way we can keep 'em out of the city. They're forming lines now for an assault. The Apprentices arrived just after the wall collapsed, and they-"

"Excuse me," Gavin said, "but who did you say arrived?"

"The Apprentices, yer lordship…Kirloth's Apprentices. Beggin' yer pardon, sir, but they've been calling themselves that…all four of 'em."

"You were saying, son?" Terris prompted.

"Yes, sire. Sorry, sire. The Apprentices, well, they arrived right after the wall turned to dust. They said they were going to try to re…rec…reconstitute it."

Just then, Gavin felt a faint tremor of magic from the same direction as the powerful Transmutation effect earlier. "They're doing it wrong," he said, his voice barely above a whisper.

"I don't understand, Gavin," Terris said.

"Lillian and the others…they're doing it wrong. If I'm right, what I just felt was a Conjuration effect. Conjuration isn't what we need here. A composite effect with Tutation and Transmutation will…never mind; just get me down there."

"Gavin, you're in no condition to go to the front line," Terris said. "I'm not about to risk your life," he leaned close now to whisper, "or my daughter never speaking to me again."

"Terris," Gavin said, his voice a tired sigh and his form of address drawing shocked expressions from everyone but Roth, "I can't even manifest an orb of power right now. I'm not stupid enough to try an invocation in my current state, but I can tell them what they're doing wrong and how to do it right. Young man, how long will it take Ivarson to assault the gap in the wall?"

"His lines weren't ready fer an assault, yer lordship…sloppy work on th' part of 'is officers. It'll take him at least an hour to get everything in position."

"Plenty of time to fix this, Terris," Gavin said, "if I go now."

Terris looked to Roth for his opinion.

"I'll take him myself, Your Majesty, and make sure he behaves."

Terris nodded and turned back to the messenger. "What's your name, son?"

"Thaddeus Cooper, sire, Corporal Thaddeus Cooper."

"Son, you feel up to some dangerous duty?" Terris asked.

The young soldier beamed. "Yes, sir! I was top of my class in swordsmanship."

"Well, I can't have a mere corporal guarding one of my closest friends," Terris said, watching the young man's expression sink, "so I guess that means you just made Sergeant. Don't leave this man's side anytime he's outside the palace complex," pointing to Gavin, "and tell one of the door guards which unit was yours. I'll send a runner with your new orders and details of your promotion."

* * *

GAVIN COULDN'T REMEMBER the last time he'd felt such fear and anxiety permeating a place. Everyone Gavin saw as he, Roth, and Thaddeus rode through the city spoke in hushed tones and cautious glances. A short distance from the palace, they reached what looked like a small street market, and they had to stop for a large crowd to disburse.

A young woman walked up to Gavin, wringing her hands and said, "Please, sir, they say the walls fell. Is it true?"

Gavin weighed the options of how to respond. Out of the many options available, Gavin said, "Yes, it's true."

The woman blanched, eyes wide. "Oh, no! We're all lost!"

"Don't despair, miss," Gavin said. "There is one asset this city has that the army out there does not."

"What could that be?"

"I am Kirloth, and I've not traveled from Tel Mivar to see this city fall while I draw breath. Tell everyone who asks: The Great Houses of Tel stand with King Terris Muran."

For once, Gavin saw no fear upon recognition of his House. For that woman, Kirloth meant hope.

The crowd ahead dispersed enough for them to resume their travel, and had Gavin been looking, he might have seen an old man with wildly unkempt white hair wearing a gray robe with a tattered hem standing on the edge of the crowd. If Gavin had noticed the old man, Gavin would've seen him smiling and nodding with admiration.

GAVIN SAW his friends standing not too far away from the piles of dirt that had once been massive stone blocks making up a section of the city's wall. The Cavaliers were serving as officers among the regular army and town guard, and it was clear they were massing to defend the breach at all costs.

It surprised Gavin just a bit that his friends were so wrapped up in talking among themselves that they didn't see him arrive. He was also glad they hadn't seen him, for Roth had to help him dismount.

"I don't know what we're going to do," Gavin heard Lillian say as he approached. "I don't know how to put the wall back together, and Mariana is only one of us with any true combat experience."

"Then, I guess it's good I'm here," Gavin said, and everyone spun to face him.

"Gavin? What are you doing out of bed?" Lillian asked.

"How-are-you-feeling?" Wynn asked.

Gavin smiled. "I'm not fully recovered yet, but you don't need my power right now. What you need is my knowledge. Roth, I need a stick with a point."

Roth turned and snapped a branch off a nearby tree and carved a point on it before handing it to Gavin.

"I felt you guys attempt a Conjuration effect," Gavin said. "Let me guess. It didn't last very long?"

"Perhaps a minute," Mariana replied, "and it was dreadful to do."

Gavin nodded and scratched out the runes symbolizing two Words of Power on the dirt. "You need a composite effect; well, honestly, invoking a Word of Transmutation would do, but I want to set a section of the wall as an anchor-point to embed protections throughout the entire wall. This Word here invokes a Transmutation effect, and its associate on the right is a Word of Tutation. Today, you're going to get a small feeling of what it was like for our ancestors to create the city we know today as Tel Mivar."

"Uhm, Gavin?" Braden said.

"Yes, Braden?"

"Our ancestors were way more powerful wizards than we are. There's no way we can duplicate what they did."

Gavin smiled. "That's not necessarily true. As far as I'm concerned, you just lack experience. So, now, I'm going to tell you how you're going to do it. It's deceptively simple, and it's related to the test Marcus had me do when we first met. First, each of you, memorize the Words we're going to use. Then, close your eyes and concentrate on the seed of power within you. It's going to be close to what feels like the pit of your soul."

Gavin watched each of them close their eyes and waited a few moments.

"Now," Gavin said, "reach out and take each other's hands."

"They're dressing lines for a charge," Roth said. "It looks like light cavalry."

Gavin looked at Roth and frowned. "Shush. That's not important now." Gavin turned back to his friends. "Okay, people, you should be feeling each other's presence, both physically and through the Art. Form a picture in your mind of a solid stone wall, long enough to fill the gap and matching the dimensions for the rest of the wall. Don't try pulling the stone from the earth; we already have enough dirt here to do the job. Concentrate on it, and envision the new wall immune to the Art. When I say 'three,' speak the Words you memorized."

Out in the field, about a thousand light cavalry were charging the breach in the wall. They were about two hundred yards away and closing.

"One…two…three!"

Four voices spoke in chorus, blending the two Words together into one syllable, "*Rhyskaal-Sykhurhos*." Gavin felt the power take hold, and he watched the dirt rise up to fill the space and solidify. Within a heartbeat, the breach in the wall had become solid stone again, and he felt a faint resonance of Tutation emanating from the solid stone.

SOMETIMES, horses are smarter than people. A rider can run a horse until it founders, but no horse will willingly charge a stone wall, especially when that wall just appeared in a space that used to be air. The front rank of the cavalry charge outside stopped cold, the riders flying head-first into the wall. This sudden stop produced a chain reaction through the successive ranks until fully one-third of the cavalry-riders lay on the ground in some form of injury.

.   .   .

GAVIN NOTICED everyone still had their eyes closed. Lillian was the first to open her eyes, but she did so slowly.

"Well?" Lillian asked, as the others opened their eyes. "How'd we do?"

"In my eyes, you've more than earned the rank of *Magus*. That wall is as perfect as we could make it. How did it feel to invoke your first composite effect all by yourselves?"

"By the gods, it hurt," Braden said. "I've never felt that kind of pain when working the Art before."

The others nodded to agree.

"The more of them you do, the easier it will become," Gavin said. "Trust me; I know."

CHAPTER 23

As with any news or gossip, word of what 'the Apprentices' achieved spread through the capital like fire in dry grass. Knowledge that the king did indeed have a counter to Ivarson's wizards bolstered morale better than an extra thousand troops supporting the king ever could have. For the first time since the siege began, the people started to believe that they just might survive and that the turmoil might just end well after all.

GAVIN, Lillian, Mariana, Wynn, and Braden occupied various seats along with Kiri and Terris in a sitting room off the royal apartment. Refreshments sat on a cart, wheeled into the room by a member of the kitchen staff, and the furnishings and decorations around the room were tasteful and elegant.

"Lady Mivar," Terris said, "I want to thank you for the kindness you showed my daughter. While we were getting reacquainted, she spent no small amount of time discussing the friendship you two have developed."

"Please, Your Majesty," Lillian said, "feel free to address me as

'Lillian,' and you're welcome. Still, befriending your daughter was no great effort, I assure you. She helped me through a bad time, and I feel I owe her more than mere friendship."

Terris sat silent for several moments before looking to each of Gavin's friends in turn as he said, "It has been a matter of royal decree for many centuries that there is one who may address the King—or Queen—of Vushaar as a friend and by first name in any circumstance. That one was the black-robed wizard known as Marcus. When Kiri was just a newborn, I amended that decree to include Q'Orval as a kind of reward for all his years of steadfast service, and yesterday, I amended that decree again…to include the five of you. I'm sure there are those at court who would prefer I be addressed in all circumstances as 'Your Majesty,' but you've shown such kindness and friendship to my daughter, addressing me as such shall be *your* choice. Know that I do not expect it."

When it seemed Gavin and his friends didn't know what to say, Kiri smiled, saying, "Thank you, Father. They're almost family to me, and I would never have expected them to address me as 'Your Highness,' no matter the situation."

Terris nodded his response to Kiri's gratitude and shifted his attention to Gavin. "So, Roth tells me you have something to discuss with me about the city's outer wall."

"Yes, Terris, I do," Gavin said. "I want to embed a protection against magic in your city's outer wall to prevent what happened a few days ago from ever happening again. Matter of fact, if we do it right, it will stop all magical effects that originate outside the wall from affecting the city."

Terris blinked. "You can do that?"

"Oh, yes. We'll have to use a composite effect of both Transmutation *and* Tutation to make it work. If we didn't make the walls a solid piece of stone, we'd have to embed the protection in each, individual block, you see."

"What of the redoubts and gatehouses?"

"We'll include those as well. After all, it wouldn't make much sense to leave them unprotected. It would be rather embarrassing if someone disintegrated a gatehouse or redoubt, somewhere down the line. I doubt I'd *ever* live that one down."

Terris looked as though he were still wrapping his mind around the idea of the walls being immune to magic. "How long would it take?"

Gavin shrugged. "A few weeks, at least. I'm still not back to my former strength yet, and I think reconstituting the wall almost put my friends on their backs. There will be a certain recovery period after each invocation, but the good news is that we won't have to destroy any fortifications to make this happen. We'll just transmute the existing structures to solid stone and embed the protection against magic at that time. If we weren't staring at a hostile army on the north approaches to the city, I'd consider discussing the addition of a few other effects as well, but I'd say the protection against magic is by far the most important at this point. It'll also keep Ivarson's wizards from lobbing fireballs and such over the walls to terrorize people."

Gavin fell silent as he rubbed his chin and stared at the wall, lost in thought.

"Now that I think about it, I think one of us should be on the wall facing Ivarson's encampment at all times. If his wizards try something, we're sorely out of position to counter it until we complete the protection, and there are enough of us that we can rotate out in shifts to keep the strain manageable."

Terris waved his left hand in a gesture of agreement. "Whatever you think is best, Gavin. I know next to nothing about magic, and my court wizard, Fallon, has never seen combat. No slight to him, either; he has simply directed his studies down other avenues."

"And he's probably a product of the College's curriculum," Gavin said. "They don't allow for the fundamental differences between wizards and mages, so any wizards who graduate are little more than empowered mages. If I ever have the opportunity, I'll take steps to correct that."

"Oh, I'm sorry," Terris said. "The post's title is 'Court Wizard.' Fallon is a mage."

"Ah," Gavin said, his expression looking like he'd just put his foot in his mouth. "My apologies, then." Just then, Gavin's eyes widened just a bit, as he remembered something. "By any chance, do you know to whom I should speak to purchase property in the city?"

"I've no idea, I'm afraid, but Q'Orval should be able to direct you to someone. May I ask why?"

Gavin's eyes shifted to Kiri's left shoulder. "I have some research I've put off for far too long, and it will give me something to do between the work on the wall and taking my turn waiting for Ivarson's wizards to try something else."

* * *

It was the evening of the day a week after Gavin told Terris of his plan to improve the city's outer wall. Kiri and Lillian sat in Kiri's private dining room, candles around the room creating a comfortable, friendly ambiance.

"Thank you so much for accepting my invitation to dinner," Kiri said. "I've really missed our late-night conversations."

"I know! I've missed them, too. It's been very busy lately, and I welcome the chance to unwind and visit with you."

"Have you started work on the outer wall yet?"

Lillian nodded. "Oh, yes. We're moving west along the wall from that section Ivarson's wizards disintegrated. We did the north gate and portcullis first, and honestly, that was worse than the wall."

"Oh? That surprises me. Since it's smaller than the wall sections between redoubts, I would've thought it would be easier."

"You're forgetting the portcullis and all the reinforced doors throughout the gatehouse. We can't turn them into a solid piece of stone, like we're doing with the walls themselves. At least there are only three left. We are *very* glad your city planners didn't make more gates!"

"Oh, my. I hadn't considered the portcullis and all the reinforced doors. That would make things a bit more complicated."

Lillian responded with a fervent nod. "So...how are things with you? Are you getting settled back in and reintegrated into things around here?"

"It still feels a little surreal. Just the other morning, for the first few moments when I woke up in my room, I had to stop and think about where I was. Father hasn't made a general announcement about my return, either. He says he doesn't want to share me with the court yet."

"You are happy to be home, though, right?"

"You have no idea, Lillian. I feel like the luckiest woman in the world." The smile faded from Kiri's face as her eyes shifted away from Lillian.

"That thought right there," Lillian said. "What is it?"

"Oh, it's nothing. It's not important, really."

"Come on...give. You'll feel better if you talk about it."

Kiri sighed and shook her head. "No, Lillian, I'm not sure I will."

"You told me about the prophecy of the Slave Queen. You told me about what you endured before Gavin found you. How could that thought be any worse than either of those?"

"It's...well...it's still a little disconcerting when I wake up and I don't see a bed made of folded blankets on the floor. I'm home. I'm safe. My father is safe. It seems like I have everything I've wanted these last few years, and yet..."

"And yet?"

Kiri lifted her head to look Lillian in her eyes, knowing Lillian would see the conflict swirling within her. "And yet, I miss him, Lillian. I haven't seen Gavin since the sitting room with Father, and I miss him...more than I ever expected I would. I mean, I hoped we'd remain friends and all that, once I made it home. But now that I'm back and slowly easing into my old life? It's starting to feel like something's missing, and that something is Gavin."

"I'd say that's normal, Kiri," Lillian said, offering her friend an encouraging smile. "Gavin's been such a fundamental part of your life for so long. I'm not surprised you feel a void now that you're moving in separate directions."

Kiri nodded. "Maybe that's all it is. Maybe I'm just feeling insecure with all the changes in my life right now. Does he...does he ever speak of me, ask of me?"

"No, Kiri, he hasn't," Lillian said, unsure of whether she should add 'I'm sorry.'

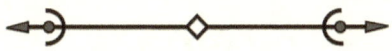

CHAPTER 24

The house occupied a street-corner a short distance from the palace complex. As such, it was made of brick and looked to be well-maintained down through the years. The agent selling the property spent quite some time extolling its virtues, revisiting time and again how close it was to the palace complex. After all, a man of Gavin's stature should appreciate such proximity to the crown.

Several times during the unctuous fop's diatribe, Gavin came rather close to informing him exactly how close he actually was to the crown of Vushaar; the agent wasn't on the list of those expected to address the King by name, after all. Each time, though, Gavin stayed his tongue. He had no desire to be any more memorable to this man than absolutely necessary.

"You said this place has a wine cellar?" Gavin asked, interrupting the man's spiel as he wound up for another go.

"Oh my, yes! One of the finest wine cellars outside of the palace, and make no mistake about that. Would you like to see it?"

Gavin nodded. "I would indeed."

The agent pivoted on his left heel and led Gavin to a door just off the kitchen. It opened on silent hinges, and the agent led Gavin down a set of stone steps to the space below. While windows lit the rest of the house, the agent—or someone—had lit the sconces of the cellar in preparation for just such an inspection. The wine cellar extended almost the full footprint of the house and looked more like a basement than a simple wine cellar. Tall, wooden racks that sat empty created aisles throughout the space, while large casks with spigots lined the brick walls.

"Yes," Gavin said, eyeing the space, "this will be perfect. I think it's time we discussed price."

"Very good, milord," the agent said. "Forgive me, but I must first address certain distasteful matters. You're obviously a man of breeding; I mean your interest in this property alone tells me that, but the owners have insisted that I verify any prospective buyer's… ahem…funds before any offer is communicated."

"Ah, yes. That's an excellent point. I have a goodly sum in the Bank of Tel back home, but it never occurred to me that I might require more than the traveling funds I brought with me."

"Milord, you should have no problem, then. Most banks have agreements in place to extend lines of credit for their more well-to-do patrons. I'm sure the Royal Bank of Vushaar has such an agreement with the Bank of Tel already in place."

Gavin's eyebrows lifted just a bit. "That is rather handy, and I'm sure you'd have no problem directing me to the local branch of the Royal Bank of Vushaar?"

"Local branch?" the agent asked, amusement curling his lips as he pointed to one wall without hesitation. "Milord, the *headquarters* for the Royal Bank is three blocks that way."

* * *

THE ELVEN EMBASSY to Vushaar occupied an entire city block five streets north of the entrance to the palace complex, and anyone other than an elf who saw it would've sworn it was one of the city's parks. Tall hedges formed what would've been walls on any other property, and the gates were archways of woven hedge and vines.

Scores of trees filled the space within the hedge-walls whose canopies somehow failed to restrict the sunlight from streaming in.

The actual embassy building itself was much smaller than a corresponding structure built by humans would be and showcased the elves' commitment to living in harmony with nature, rather than bending her to their will. It was a small structure, formed from a large, still-living tree. In addition to office space, the structure provided living quarters for the ambassador and four staff.

"Yes? How may I help you?" the elf inside the entrance asked as Elayna led Sarres into the embassy.

"Is the ambassador in?" Elayna asked. "I know she travels back and forth to Arundel."

"Ambassador Telanna is indeed in residence at the moment," the elf said. "Who may I say is calling?"

"Her sister, Elayna, and Sarres of the Sentinels of Nature."

A SHORT TIME LATER, Telanna received Elayna and Sarres in her residence. Telanna was on the tall side for an Elven female, her build lithe even for an elf, and her wavy brown hair cascaded past her shoulders. She wore robes of the finest silk the elves produced without any jewelry or other adornments.

"Elayna, dear sister, it has been too long," Telanna said, sweeping Elayna into her arms. Upon releasing her sister from the embrace, Telanna directed her attention to Sarres and nodded once in respectful acknowledgement. "Sarres, it is good to see you again. Please, both of you, sit and be welcome. Refreshments are already on the way."

"Our gratitude, sister," Elayna said, as she assumed a seat near Telanna and Sarres sat in a chair across from her. "How is it with you?"

"I must confess that life has been a bit boring since Ivarson began his siege. No one seems too interested in pursuing trade or entry permits for the High Forest at the present."

"I can't imagine why," Elayna said.

"Well, it certainly seems like you made good time reaching the city. I honestly didn't expect you for another couple of weeks, at best."

Elayna and Sarres looked at one another before Elayna said, "Yes…well, we really didn't have much choice in the matter. We were standing around the remains of a slaver camp, which Gavin had just laid waste, with the outriders of a conscription army from Ivarson minutes away, and Gavin apparently decided to bring us straight here, though how he did it still boggles my mind. I would've sworn he'd never been to the capital before."

"I don't think he has," Sarres said. "If you recall, he had Kiri focus all her thoughts on home and someplace large enough to receive all of us. Somehow, he tapped into that to direct the teleportation."

"That," Telanna said, "is impressive. I've not heard of any wizards capable of that for several thousand years."

"Well," Sarres said, "he was trained by Kirloth himself. I'm sure that counts for quite a bit."

"And what of your primary task?" Telanna asked. "Do you think he would be amenable to assisting us with our…problem?"

"Problem?" Elayna said, her lips almost curling into a grin. "I'd call having a dark elf on the throne of the High Forest a bit more than a problem, sister. You never did tell me how the Sylvan Synod allowed *that* to happen."

"Yes," Telanna said, drawing out the word almost to a hiss. "Not one of our finer moments, I'll admit, and the worst part of it is, he's so popular that it would spark a civil war if we moved against him directly. None of the Synod has managed to put forth a proposal for removing him that the rest of us didn't think would lead to civil war. That's why I asked you find Gavin Cross when I learned of him; I fear it will require an outsider to provoke the dark elf into revealing himself."

"I still say the simplest solution is just to have someone put an arrow in him," Sarres said. "There are so many of us who could make the shot from outside the palace compound that it would be almost impossible to determine who was responsible. Oh, yes…

there would be a bit of an uproar for a time, but nothing even remotely close to the upheaval we'd have with a civil war."

"And what would you have us do when it finally came out that the Synod had him killed, Sarres?" Telanna asked. "Don't think that possibility wasn't discussed, and there wasn't a one of us who wanted to see what kind of storm *that* action would precipitate."

"Getting back to your original question, sister," Elayna said, "I do believe Gavin would be agreeable to assisting us...if we approached him in the right way. There isn't any point to approaching him until he's dealt with everything that brought him to Vushaar, but it shouldn't be a problem to introduce you once he's nearing preparations to leave."

"That's good," Telanna replied. "I've had the sense there's a great storm brewing for quite some time now, and the thought of a dark elf ruling the High Forest when that storm arrives gives me nightmares."

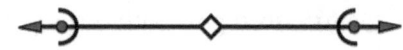

CHAPTER 25

G avin watched the work crew break down the wine racks and casks in the basement of his new property. In all truth, Gavin knew he didn't need to be here for this part of it, but the fact was that he didn't know where else to be. Elayna and Sarres disappeared into the Elven embassy the day before, and Lillian was spending most of her time not on rotation with Kiri. Wynn and Braden seemed to be enjoying their first time outside of Tel; during their off-rotation times, they traveled the capital city, visiting taprooms and markets, savoring everything the city offered.

"You're welcome to visit her, too," a voice said just behind Gavin's left shoulder.

Gavin glanced and half-smiled at Declan in greeting. "I suppose so, but I don't see how I could be anything other than a reminder of these last few years. Yes, I've tried to ensure her time with me was better than...well...*before*, but I don't want to do anything that jeopardizes settling back into her old life."

Declan scoffed. "For all your knowledge and learning, you can be such a damn fool sometimes. The only constant is that everything changes. Nothing—and I mean *nothing*—ever remains the same. Besides, I don't think this has anything to do with you thinking you'll just remind her of all she endured. I think this has everything to do with you being afraid."

"Is that so? If you're right, just for the sake of conversation, what has me so afraid?"

"It could be a few different things. In other circumstances, I would include inexperience on the list, but the fact you have a daughter somewhere eliminates that one. No…out of everything it could be, I'd say it's fear, fear of everything you don't know about yourself. If you have a daughter, does that mean you're married? What happens if you allow yourself to build something here, only to regain everything and you were to learn you were a happy family man with someone else?"

Gavin turned to regard Declan in silence as the bard looked out over the basement from their position on the outsized landing, midway down the stairs. Gavin had no intention of letting Declan know just how close he'd come, but at the same time, Gavin suspected he knew already.

"Yes, well…whatever the reason, I have many things to do, Declan, and only so much time. I have to prioritize."

Declan nodded and turned away from the workmen to look Gavin right in his eyes. "Yes, we all must prioritize our time, but are you certain your priorities are right?"

"You know what I plan to do here, Declan. Yes, I feel it's right for this to be my focus." Gavin turned and snapped his fingers. One wouldn't think the snap of a man's fingers—no matter how loud—would carry across the brick-enclosed space filled with noise of hammers, prybars, and cracking wood…but it did.

The foreman pivoted on his heel and approached the staircase from the floor, saying, "Yes, sir?"

"You and your people are making excellent progress," Gavin said. "Once you clear out the space, have someone remove and empty the sconces as your final task. You can leave them on the counter upstairs, and I'll see to them later. Close the outer door behind you when you leave."

"Do you want me to put a locking latch on the outer doors? I noticed they had only the basic latch when we arrived."

Gavin shook his head. "There's nothing in here worth anyone's time, and by the time there is, I'll have dealt with the doors myself. Good day, sir!"

* * *

IN MANY WAYS, the position of Court Wizard for the Vushaari Throne was an artifact of a much earlier age, almost an anachronism really, and Fallon suspected the only reason it still existed to provide him a job was Terris didn't want to break with tradition. Fallon didn't really see why he had a job in all truth. Oh, he didn't mind the income or his quarters, but the most contribution he'd ever made was to stand a few steps behind the King's left shoulder during his time holding court. And his inability to protect his employer's city from Ivarson's arcanists left a sour taste in his mouth. He knew *exactly* who these 'Apprentices' were, and what's more, he had no doubts as to their mentor. Members of the Society of the Arcane rarely ascribed to such banalities as hero worship, but if arcanists at large had anything approaching celebrities or figurative demigods, people who carried such names as Mivar, Roshan, Wygoth, Cothos or...Kirloth...certainly deserved the status, especially when there were many witnesses to Kirloth reducing the stone mansion at the Sivas estate to a puddle of molten rock.

The quarters and workspace for the Court Wizard of Vushaar occupied the upper two floors of the tower on the opposite side of the palace complex from the ancient keep that had been renovated and refurbished many times down through the millennia...and with good reason. It wasn't outside the realm of possibility that one of his experiments could rather explosively fail; goodness knows, the annals recording the tenures of the Court Wizard chronicled more than one case where the position was suddenly *vacated* without warning...or much in the way of earthly remains. All that remained of one poor sod who held the post about fifteen hundred years ago was a small splotch of red goo on the north wall that no cleaner yet devised could remove, not even a disintegration spell.

. . .

THE CURRENT WORK occupying Fallon's attention was the construction of a baton that would put a target to sleep with one touch. The major impediment to his success was finding some way to key it to the town guard and Cavaliers, so that when they inevitably fell into the wrong hands, the batons would just be simple sticks.

"Master Fallon!" Fallon recognized the voice of his assistant, pulling him from his concentration. *That's odd; he only usually used that tone for a royal summons*, Fallon thought as he marked his place in the grimoire and swiveled his stool to face the laboratory's door.

"Yes, Jasper?"

"You have a...a...you have a visitor!" Jasper's pallor was not *quite* as white as talc, and his eyes looked wide enough to drive a wagon through, while all the sweat was starting to make him look as if he'd been slow-dancing in a torrential downpour.

Fallon couldn't remember ever seeing the lad so keyed up. Oh, certainly; Jasper was a bit excitable, and that incident with the fireballs last month hadn't helped at all...but not even the arrival of Roth Thatcherson produced *this*.

"Honestly, Jasper," Fallon said with a sigh as he pushed himself off his stool and the seat swiveled back to its home position, "you have to learn to get control of your nerves. Do you think initiates at the College allow their nerves to run away with them? Now, who is this visitor, and what does he or she want?"

"Master...it's K-Kirloth!"

Claws of ice surrounded Fallon's heart, and he licked his lips, trying for all the world to understand why his mouth was full of parched sand all of a sudden.

What could he possibly want with me? A small voice quailed in the dark recesses of Fallon's mind, as his consciousness realized how long they had been standing there. "Oh, by the gods...is he still *waiting*? Move, damn you; move!"

Jasper just managed to step aside as he watched his mentor charge through the doorway faster than he'd ever seen him move before.

.   .   .

FALLON MANAGED to slow both his gait and his heart somewhere between dashing out of his office and approaching the sitting room that doubled as a reception area. His living quarters occupied most of the first of his two floors, with his laboratory and library occupying the second. This Kirloth was just a man, the same as he, and it wasn't like he didn't deserve his own share of respect. After all, he was a graduate with honors from the College of the Arcane and one of the youngest in history to achieve *Magus* within the Society for his scholarly works. And let's not forget he was the Court Wizard of the oldest, most respected dynasty in the world...

The man turned as Fallon entered the room, and Fallon couldn't believe how young he was. True, actual wizards tended to age slower than 'normal' people, but this man looked to be barely out of his teens! And then, Fallon looked into his eyes and just...stopped. Every piece of his mental pep talk the last few moments evaporated at the sight of those eyes. This young man possessed the knowledge and power to level the city if he so chose, and what's more, he *knew* it. The act might very well kill him, but one more corpse in whatever remained of the capital wouldn't make much difference at that point. As Fallon gazed into those bright, green eyes, he knew he stood before a soul that bore more than its share of *choices*.

"I apologize for my unannounced arrival, Master Fallon," the young man said, and Fallon was surprised yet again by the kindness and respect in his voice. "My name is Gavin Cross, and I'm glad to make your acquaintance. I have no wish to take you away from anything; perhaps, we could discuss making an appointment?"

Fallon saw a number of paths stretching out from him in that instant. He could be the insecure mage and feel threatened by the man who had brought the Council of Magisters to heel on not one but at least two separate occasions. He could be the pompous mage, the man Terris Muran asked to serve as Court Wizard. He knew one of those would be the choice of far too many of his counterparts throughout the Society, especially if they—like Fallon—were born the youngest child of a subsistence farmer in the hinterlands of Roshan Province. In the end, Fallon chose a different path.

"Think nothing of it," Fallon said, striding across the room and extending his hand. "It's a pleasure to meet you as well. I have no idea why you visited today, but the more I consider it, I have a puzzle upstairs you might enjoy."

Gavin smiled as he shook Fallon's hand. "I never could resist a puzzle."

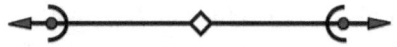

CHAPTER 26

A few moments later, Gavin and Fallon stood in a room on the second floor that served many roles. A large, round table made of centuries-old oak occupied the center of the room, and chairs of equal age surrounded it. Windows looked out onto the palace compound and the city. In its time, the room had served as everything from a dining room, meeting room, even a sleeping room…and several roles in between. Jasper had just finished laying out all of his master's notes for his current project on the table and retreated to a corner of the room, not wanting to draw attention but not about to miss the conversation that would soon occur.

"Thank you, Jasper, for moving all this over from the lab," Fallon said as he led Gavin to the table. "When the unrest in the kingdom started taking a nasty edge to it, His Majesty came to me and asked if there was any way to put a violent someone to sleep that did not require any magical ability to use. In and of itself, constructing an item to deliver a sleep effect isn't a significant challenge. It was when I decided to find a way to make it so that only Town Guardsmen or Cavaliers in good standing could use these items that I encountered problems."

Gavin nodded. "Yes, of course. Even though it's not especially destructive or powerful, the world doesn't need a rash of rogue sleep items. Imagine the field day the Guild of Shadows would have with something like this."

"Yes, of course…or killers or really anyone of ill intent. Everything on the table represents all my work, and I was hoping you might be able to point out something I've missed."

Gavin turned to the table and leaned over it, studying the notes and diagrams before him. The diagram of the Enchantment effect —the sleep spell being part of the Enchantment School—was well drawn and annotated, as well as all of Fallon's work to tie the item to the Town Guard and Cavaliers.

"If I'm reading these notes correctly," Gavin said, "you're trying to tie the working state of the item to the people themselves."

"Yes, that's correct. It didn't take me long to realize, though, that each of these items would have to be crafted for a specific person, and if they left the Guard or Cavaliers, the item would still work for them."

"Everyone who works for the Town Guard and the Cavaliers takes an oath when they join, right?" Gavin asked.

Fallon nodded. "Yes. It's one of my duties to administer the oath to the Cavaliers."

"Well, in that case, I'd tie the item to the oath and not the person. You could create the items in bulk, then, and be assured that any oath-breakers would no longer have access to them. They'd just be a rod or stick or whatever you decide to make the physical form. If you really want to lock the items down, obtain a drop or two of the King's blood and use it when you bind the effect to the oaths these people take."

Fallon stood in silence, staring at Gavin. He was silent for so long that Gavin started wondering if he'd offended the man somehow.

"I haven't felt like this since I was a student," Fallon said at last.

"Oh? How so?"

"Watching someone make something I've struggled with for

some time seem so simple. I feel like a fool for not thinking of the oath."

"Please, don't. This work is one of the finest examples of imbued item creation that I've ever seen. I feel like I should have Braden study with you for a year to learn what you know."

"I'm sorry. Braden?"

Gavin nodded, one side of his mouth curling in a half-smile. "Braden Wygoth—one of my apprentices—dreams of creating imbued items capable of rivaling the artifacts of old, and you sir are a true craftsman. Would it be possible to obtain copies of this and a couple others? I have no background with imbued item creation, myself, and this would be excellent teaching material."

Gavin was focused on the pages occupying the table, so he wasn't able to see when Fallon's eyes for a moment.

"Forgive me," Fallon said, "but I need to make sure I understand. You're asking me for copies of these notes and other similar projects to help teach one of your apprentices who wants to create imbued items?"

Gavin lifted his attention from the table and saw how close to overwhelmed Fallon was. He nodded once, saying, "Yes, that's exactly what I'm asking."

Fallon broke into a grin that looked fit to split his face. "You have no idea what an honor that is! Of course, you're welcome to copies! Was that why you visited today?"

"No, actually. I wanted to ask you something else." Fallon gestured for him to continue, and Gavin said, "I'm in the process of establishing my own laboratory to pursue a research project of my own. I just have one, small problem."

"Oh? What's that?"

Gavin shrugged. "I've never used a laboratory. I have no idea what I'd need in terms of supplies and equipment. Oh, some stuff is just common sense, like protective wards to keep any catastrophic failures from leaving the lab, but that's about the extent of it. My mentor hadn't gotten around to the magical research portion of his curriculum before he died."

"Ah, I see," Fallon said. "Just out of curiosity, what was in the curriculum he did cover?"

"Words of Power and composite effects," Gavin said and took a certain silent pleasure out of watching Fallon blanch when he caught up to what Gavin had just said.

"Yes, well…I imagine that *would* take some time," Fallon said, his voice small and quiet.

"By the by," Gavin said, "please forgive me if I'm speaking out of turn, but did you know your assistant over there is a latent wizard?"

Fallon's eyes went wide as he spun to look at Jasper, and Jasper looked like he wanted to hide somewhere with all the scrutiny directed at him.

"I don't know how old he is, but if he doesn't start learning to use it soon, it'll fade on him. From what I've read and a few things my mentor said, the ideal time to start training a wizard is their late teens."

"He's sixteen," Fallon said. "I'm teaching him the basics in preparation for his application to the College as a favor for…well… for a friend of the family."

Gavin nodded his understanding. "Nothing wrong with that. My mentor took me on as a favor for one of his friends, or so I've been told. Think it over, and if you'd like me to write up some exercises to start him on the path he deserves, let me know."

A silence descended on the room for a few moments before Gavin put his hand on his face. "Oh goodness, Fallon, I am sorry. That didn't come out like it sounded in my head."

"Think nothing of it," Fallon said. "I've felt for a long time now that we do those few wizards who are left a grave disservice by putting them through the same curriculum as our mage initiates. The only problem is that we have no wizards to train them." He gave Gavin a sidelong glance. "Perhaps, someone should change that."

Gavin grinned and chuckled. "I'm not sure the Council wants me *anywhere near* a group of young, impressionable minds…especially young, impressionable wizards."

"One does hear things, even in Vushaar," Fallon said, "but I would argue that's beside the point. You are the first wizard trained by a wizard since I don't know when. If they had any sense at all, they'd offer you your choice of classrooms without a second thought. Oh, and while I'm thinking about it, it would be my honor to assist you with setting up your laboratory. Just tell me where and when."

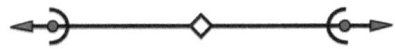

CHAPTER 27

Gavin and Declan once again stood at the landing halfway down the steps into the basement of the property Gavin purchased. The space below them did not resemble its previous incarnation as a wine cellar in even the slightest way. Several bookshelves lined the walls where the large casks once sat. A table with several chairs occupied the space directly under the stairs, and three slate-boards on wheeled frames stood near the table. A large circle inset into the floor occupied the far corner to Gavin's right, and a lectern for a book or papers stood beside it. The sconces hanging from their fixtures along the walls filled the room with light while not consuming any fuel or radiating heat, much like the sconces Gavin had seen in every building he'd visited across Tel Mivar.

"Fallon does impressive work," Declan said.

Gavin nodded. "Indeed. I shall have to find some way to reward him. The time has come, Declan. I've allowed myself to be distracted for far too long. I need a slave branding iron, a slave, and a slaver. I imagine you'll be able to hire someone from the group we delivered from the slaver camp, and I want the person *hired*, not conscripted. I'm not all that concerned where you locate a slaver or a slave brand."

"Should I hire the slaver as well?"

Gavin shrugged. "I don't really care. He or she won't be leaving this project alive, so it makes no difference to me."

"May I ask what you're planning?"

"The time has come to remove Kiri's slave mark. I will start by examining the effect of the mark on a slave and the embedded power in a slave brand. I may need a slaver to use said brand on another person somewhere down the line to observe the embedded effects in action, so I'd rather not have to scour the countryside looking for a slaver when I need one…well, have the Wraiths scour the countryside, anyway. We both know I will be relying heavily on you and your associates for various aspects of this."

"Have you considered that you could probably use the brand yourself and get a better understanding of how it does what it does?"

"Perhaps," Gavin said, "but suppose whatever protects me from being branded ruins any brand I try to use? I don't know how often those things are made, but I'm sure we'd eventually run through the supply of them."

"There aren't any more being made. Those arcanists responsible for their creation made one hundred fifty brands and refused to make any more, after destroying all their notes and records. I don't know exact numbers, but I do know several have been lost or destroyed down through the centuries. There may be sixty still in use, at most."

Gavin turned and leaned against the bannister, crossing his arms across his chest. "How difficult do you think it will be to acquire one?"

"Several slaver groups are operating throughout Vushaar during all this unpleasantness. It shouldn't be too difficult to retrieve one or two."

"Once you have one or two branding irons and a slaver, I'm not concerned what befalls any other slavers nearby at the time. Do with them as you will."

At Declan's nod, Gavin turned and strode up the stairs. It was almost time for his turn on the wall.

* * *

A SLIGHT BREEZE blew north toward the sea when Gavin stepped out onto the wall. Sergeant Khelson turned and smiled at seeing Gavin.

"Afternoon, Sergeant," Gavin said as he approached and shook hands with the veteran. "How goes the siege?"

"Pretty well for us," Khelson said, "but not so well for them. We slipped a few scouts into their perimeter last night, and they just reported back. You see those encampments way off by themselves to the east of their main army?"

"I do."

"Those are their sick camps. When someone starts showing signs of illness, they get shipped over there, and those camps have been steadily growing over the past few days." Khelson shrugged. "If you're not almost vicious about enforcing proper latrine discipline, there's not really anyway to avoid mass sickness during a siege. Even then, your soldiers are still going to fall sick to some degree, and the jungle terrain to the north is a hotbed of disease. If the druids hadn't created jungle-free swaths of land for us after the Godswar, we wouldn't have the roads connecting our northern cities and settlements. Plus, Ivarson's starting to get a bit short on rations. Loyal units of the army have been raiding supply trains headed for this army, and skirmishers have been picking off foraging parties. Before too long, he'll be forced to make a major push to gain the city just to get our granaries if nothing else."

"It sounds like it won't be too long before his army starts falling apart, then. Between starvation and mass sickness, his men are going to start re-thinking their commitment to whatever Ivarson's promising."

"Whatever happened to that sergeant His Majesty had following you around?"

Gavin shrugged. "Poor fellow wasn't equipped to handle being around me. Come to find out, workings of the Art unsettled him quite a bit. I had a quiet word with the king, and he took over a squad when that sergeant transferred to another unit."

"He must be rather sensitive, then. I've not seen you do anything unsettling."

Now, Gavin grinned, saying, "That just means you haven't known me long enough."

Movement off to his left drew Gavin's attention, and he shifted his attention to see Elayna, Sarres, and a female elf Gavin didn't recognize step out of the gatehouse and approach. Elayna wore her scale-mail armor and carried her kite shield and flanged mace. Sarres wore his studded leathers; he carried his bow in his left hand with his twin swords hanging from either side and a large quiver of arrows peeking up over his right shoulder. The elf Gavin didn't know carried a simple wooden staff, looking very much like it had once been a felled limb from a tree, and wore studded leather armor as well.

"Ambassador," Sergeant Khelson said, addressing the elf Gavin didn't know, "this isn't really the place for civilians. You should probably return to your embassy."

"I appreciate your concern for my well-being, Sergeant," the ambassador said, "but we are here to assist with the defense. We have discussed the matter and feel we should stand with Vushaar, just as the Great Houses of Tel do."

"That's very nice and all," Sergeant Khelson said, "but without approval from the chain of command, starting with His Majesty, I can't really allow you up here."

Just then, one of the soldiers ran up to Khelson and took his arm, pointing to the north and saying, "Sergeant, they're moving to charge the walls!"

Gavin looked in the direction the soldier was pointing and saw a large mass of Ivarson's army marching toward the wall under the cover of shields, making the mass look like a giant armadillo.

"Those shields may provide some measure of protection against your archers," Gavin said, "but let's see how well they protect against *me*."

"Gavin," Elayna said, moving to stand at his side, "I would introduce you to Telanna, the ambassador from my people to Vushaar and my sister. She also happens to be a *very* accomplished druid in her own right."

"It's nice to meet you," Gavin said, "though I suppose the circumstances could be better. I've not heard of druids before."

Telanna angled her head to the side, as if to shrug. "Think of us as priests and priestesses of nature. We strengthen and care for the land, which in turn strengthens and cares for us."

"How close do they have to be for your magic?" Sergeant Khelson asked, glancing at Gavin.

Gavin started to speak but stopped. He frowned and scratched his jaw a moment. After a few moments more, he shrugged. "To be honest, I'm not really sure. I could probably do something to them where they are now, but the closer they are, the less power I'll need. If you want to see the kind of thing that made poor Thaddeus want to faint, I should probably wait until they're one hundred—maybe two hundred—yards away. I've been waiting for them to build catapults; I have a couple ideas I'd like to try."

Khelson frowned and turned his head to look at Gavin. "Do I even want to know?"

"I wouldn't tell you, even if you asked. I don't know that the ideas would work in the first place, so I'm not about to get everyone's hopes up."

OVER THE COURSE of the next several minutes, the mundane defenders prepared to meet the assault on the wall while Gavin and the elves calmly watched its approach. The on-rushing force reached the point where Gavin decided they were close enough, and he sighed.

"I really hate this part," he said to no one in particular.

"You hate wielding the Art?" Telanna asked, her right eyebrow quirking upward.

Gavin shook his head. "No, of course not. I hate using it to kill."

Without further ado, Gavin lifted his hands and outstretched his fingers toward the oncoming force. He didn't understand why, but he felt some physical gesture was appropriate. Then, having focused his mind on the effect he wanted to produce, he invoked a Word of Evocation, "*Idluhn.*"

As no one else present was a wizard, no one felt the eruption of Gavin's power as he bent reality to his will. Sparks of electricity suddenly crackled between his fingers and thumbs for a heartbeat or two, growing louder and more intense until everyone within fifty feet of Gavin could feel any hair on their bodies standing on end. That feeling abruptly ended as ten bolts of lightning shot from Gavin's outstretched fingers with such auditory ferocity those closest were struck temporarily deaf…but that wasn't the worst. Oh, no. After all, with lightning, there is almost always *thunder*.

The lightning crossed the short distance to the onrushing force in less time than the eye could follow, and as it was not natural lightning, it followed the intent Gavin invoked. Each of those ten bolts of lightning struck a rebel soldier about six soldiers away from the next bolt of lightning. The accumulated charge then proceeded to hop from person to person four ranks deep into the formation and over seventy percent across the front rank. Those within the field of effect died instantly, standing rigid—every joint locked—while the massive amount of electrical current surged through them only to collapse like puppets with their strings cut in less time than it takes a person to snap his or her fingers. What had been a charging assault force of almost a thousand souls mere moments before now ground to a halt and recoiled from the hemisphere of death where their comrades used to be.

The lightning was crackling through the enemy when the loudest thunder ever heard in recent memory exploded from Gavin's position. The six feet centered around Gavin seemed to be an eye in the storm, with the elves and a couple soldiers largely unaffected beyond the immense thunderclap pummeling their ears. Beyond that, the shockwave sent every person for seventy-five feet in any direction rolling like bowling pins away from Gavin and shattered windows on the far side of the city to the south. Not one single piece of glass or crystal survived within fifteen city blocks of Gavin's location on the walls.

The elves looked around them in undisguised disbelief as Sergeant Khelson pulled himself back to his feet and ambled over to Gavin. He looked out toward the assault force to see them pulling back toward Ivarson's lines as he held his left hand to that ear.

Gavin thought he heard the sergeant mutter, "I wonder if the king would let *me* transfer…"

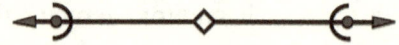

CHAPTER 28

Two days after Gavin's 'defense' of the walls, Kiri entered her father's study and found him sitting with Q'Orval. Terris's study was a comfortable room, the walls lined with bookcases outside of two floor-to-ceiling windows. The furniture was upholstered in the Muran family colors.

"You wanted to see me, Father?" Kiri asked.

Terris smiled as he looked at the woman his little girl had become, saying, "Yes, I did. Please, be comfortable."

Kiri moved to a sofa across from her father and Q'Orval and sat. So many questions raged within her, but she remembered the training from her youth and folded her hands in her lap until one of others felt ready to speak. Never be the first to speak.

"With Kaila's death, there's a growing sentiment that I take another wife to re-establish the royal line, and I wanted to discuss with you about returning to your position as Crown Princess."

Memories of so many conversations flitted through Kiri's mind, but one phrase stood out among all others, *The Slave Queen of Vushaar*. Kiri worked her lower lip between her teeth as she lifted her hand to the slave mark on her shoulder.

"What of this? Would you have the people accept a slave as queen?"

Terris shook his head. "No. I would have them accept my daughter and rightful heir as queen. Kiri, I should never have sent you away, and I am sorrier than you will ever know that I did."

All the time between when she departed Birsha aboard the *Sprite* and when she stood once more in her family's palace flitted through Kiri's mind. Yes, a considerable amount of that time was a fate none should ever experience, but a name smothered those terrors. She didn't understand how that name could smother those terrors, nor did she understand all the reactions that name produced throughout herself. Still yet, she knew in that moment that she was *precisely* where she was supposed to be precisely *when* she was supposed to be there. No one deserved all that she had endured, but at the same time, every experience of her life made her who she was.

Kiri took a breath and shrugged, saying, "What's past is past, Father. There's no need to dwell on it, but I would be dishonest if I didn't explain how anxious the idea of resuming my responsibilities makes me. I'm not sure it's my place anymore."

"Nonsense," Terris scoffed. "It has always been your place."

"What does the Privy Council say?"

"I've not asked. At this time, only Q'Orval, myself, and those Cavaliers who work the Residence know you're alive, let alone returned to us."

Kiri took a deep breath and nodded. "Please call a meeting, then, Father. We should start with them, and I would ask that Gavin and Lillian be there as well."

* * *

The Privy Council served as an advisory body to the king and was as close to a cross-section of the kingdom's population as could be achieved. There were thirteen members: four from the working-class citizens, four from the merchant middle class, and four from the traditional aristocracy. Q'Orval served as the final member.

The Privy Council met in a small conference room just down

the hall from the large meeting space that currently served as a war room. A large, circular table occupied the center of the room, and said table had two seats—both ornately carved and inlaid—that awaited the final attendees. For almost four years, one of those chairs sat empty.

The members were seated around the table, and everyone—aside from Q'Orval—kept glancing at the corner of the room. Two, rather plush chairs occupied a corner near the door, and they were not normal furniture for the room. What attracted even more surreptitious attention was that the occupants of those seats were not even Vushaari. Gavin and Lillian sat in those chairs, and more than one councilmember regarded Gavin with unease, bordering on outright fear.

The meeting room's door opened, and a Cavalier stepped into the room and stepped to the right side of the door before snapping to attention and announcing, "Ladies and gentlemen, His Majesty Terris Muran, King of Vushaar!"

Gavin, Lillian, Q'Orval, and those members of the Privy Council not of the aristocracy were on their feet by the time the Cavalier reached 'Majesty' in his annunciation. The members of the aristocracy were on their feet by the time Terris entered the room, with the Cavalier closing the door after Terris's passage.

Terris walked to the table and stood behind his customary seat, nodding to each person in turn as he said, "I want to thank you all for coming on such short notice. I asked for this meeting to discuss a situation many have broached these past few weeks, specifically my heir. Please, be seated."

Everyone assumed their seats.

"Almost four years ago now," Terris continued, "the courier *Sprite* went down in a storm while crossing the Inner Sea from Birsha to Tel Mivar. At the time, we believed there were no survivors. We were wrong." Terris nodded to the Cavalier.

The Cavalier opened the door once again and stepped to the customary position, snapping to attention once more and saying, "Your Majesty, ladies and gentlemen, Her Highness Kiri Muran!"

Terris, Q'Orval, Gavin, and Lillian stood, leading the room

amidst a chorus of astonished gasps. Even as they rose, the members of the Privy Council spun to face the door as Kiri strode into the room. Gavin saw one man's eyes narrow at the sight of Kiri, and Gavin had the feeling that man deserved further attention.

Kiri walked to the unoccupied chair at her father's right side and nodded to the council, saying, "Thank you." Her voice was strong and, as far as Gavin was concerned, beautiful as always. As Terris sat, everyone else did as well.

"Your Majesty," a man said, and Gavin thought it was the man he wanted to know more about, "while we are all overjoyed to see Her Highness returned to us, we must consider that returning Her Highness to the position of Crown Princess would only serve to delay the dynastic crisis what I'm sure we all hope would be a great many years. Everyone knows those who have been branded cannot bear or sire children."

"You are correct, Count Varkas," Terris said. "However, efforts are already underway to remove the slave mark from my daughter."

Kiri's eyes shot to her father, her expression making it clear she knew of no such efforts.

"While we all know of Fallon's prowess with the Art, Your Majesty," Count Varkas responded, "no records—or even rumors—exist of anyone ever successfully removing a slave mark. Do we really want to risk Her Highness's life on a fool's errand?"

"I couldn't be more pleased with Fallon's service as Court Wizard, but he isn't conducting the research into the slave marks," Terris said.

"If I may, Your Majesty, may we know who is?"

Gavin stood and took two steps toward the table, saying, "That would be me."

"And just who are...you," Count Varkas's voice trailed off to a whisper as his eyes locked on Gavin's medallion. Gavin could've been wrong, but he thought he saw some color leave the man's face. The silence that descended upon the room quickly approached the level of awkward.

"If you would, please introduce yourself for anyone who may not be familiar with the House Glyphs," Terris said.

Gavin nodded once. "My name is Gavin Cross; I am Kirloth. My associate is Lillian, heir to House Mivar and one of my apprentices."

The silence in the room was so thorough and pervasive as the members of the Privy Council stared at Gavin with wide eyes, a pin striking the stone floor in the hall outside would have been an ear-splitting cacophony...much like Gavin's thunderclap a few days before.

A middle-aged man with many laugh lines around his eyes and mouth was the first to break the silence. He was one of those representing the merchants and middle class. "Sir, if I may, I would very much like to shake your hand after the meeting. I am Cyril, a proud member of the Glaziers' Association for many years, and I was told that you are to thank for the cornucopia of work we now have. It had been a bit of a drought, what with the siege and all."

Gavin pushed himself as far into the 'Kirloth' mindset as he could to stave off the acute embarrassment he felt trying to color his cheeks and ears. He nodded once and returned to his seat.

"While it is impossible to gauge a timeframe for such things, Count Varkas," Terris said, resuming the meeting, "I have no doubt at all my daughter will not suffer that mark forever."

Gavin made certain to memorize the man's name for a conversation he planned to have with Declan after the meeting.

"Your Majesty," one of worker-class representatives said at the conclusion of a few moments of whispers between them, "Her Highness's compassion, honor, and dedication to the people of Vushaar are almost legendary, and we see no reason to continue the dynastic discussion at this time, as the Crown Princess never died."

Those representing the merchants and middle class whispered among themselves for a few moments before Cyril spoke, "We of the merchants and middle class would like to add our support to that, Your Majesty, and furthermore, we believe it would do the people some good if Her Highness's return were announced as soon as practically possible."

"Your Majesty," Count Varkas said, "forgive me, but I would like to take a moment to address a complaint one of my constituents made not too long ago."

"Oh? What is this complaint?" Terris asked.

"Some weeks ago, Janson Roensil, his daughter, and thirteen of their most loyal retainers were murdered in cold blood, and I must regretfully inform you that the man responsible for their deaths is none other than the man you're relying on to be Her Highness's savior from the slave mark. I demand Gavin Cross be charged with mass murder."

"This is a very grave charge indeed," Terris said. "Gavin, what have you to say in response?"

Gavin stood and approached the table.

"I do not deny in the least that I killed those people, but I dispute the characterization that it was murder," Gavin said, drawing a gasp from certain members of the council. "What he's not telling you is that I killed them only *after* they refused to surrender, having led a force upwards of twelve hundred mercenaries to murder everyone at the Claymark estate and take their lands. Janson Roensil died not fifty yards from Claymark's front gate." Gavin paused and frowned. "I'm sorry, Terris; it's been so long I can't speak to the statement that my blood was cold when I killed them. I simply don't remember my emotional state at the time."

"Roensil attacked the Claymarks?" Terris asked. "I thought my father settled that years ago."

Gavin shrugged. "Apparently, Roensil decided to bet on Ivarson and move against your father-in-law. There were some rumors that he was selling grain to Ivarson's army, but I've not had the opportunity to investigate further."

"This is sovereign Vushaari soil," Count Varkas said, his voice a growl. "What gives you the right to investigate anything?"

"You make a very good point; however, forgive me for being crass, but who's going to stop me? Those people were clear and present threats to individuals under my protection, and I will respond to all such threats. I don't care where I am. I don't intend anyone offense, but I will not stand by and allow my people to be threatened."

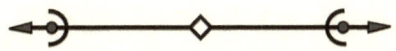

CHAPTER 29

K iri pulled Lillian into an embrace as they left the dining room for the sitting room in Kiri's suite and held that embrace for several moments. Upon separating, Kiri indicated the various sitting possibilities around the room as she sat in a loveseat beneath a window and folded her legs to one side, leaning against the loveseat's arm.

"It's so good to see you again, Lillian," Kiri said as Lillian duplicated Kiri's pose in the sofa across from her. "There have been quite a few 'Crown Princess' moments lately, and I find myself looking back to the days when I was just Kiri."

"It's good to see you again, too. I'm sure Gavin wouldn't mind you leaving with us when we go, if all this is so unpleasant."

Kiri shook her head. "It's a nice fantasy, but I'm a Muran and the last of my line as of this moment. I owe it to the people of Vushaar to be their Crown Princess and—one day—their Queen."

Silence descended on the sitting room for several moments before Lillian lifted her eyes to meet Kiri's. She took a breath and said, "Kiri, I'm very grateful for the hospitality your father has shown me and my friends, but you don't owe the people of Vushaar anything...not one single thing. I've watched Gavin these past few weeks, and I have seen unguarded moments when his shoulders slump and he looks every inch to be a man shouldering a burden greater than any twelve people should ever have to bear. It won't be tomorrow or next week or maybe even two years from now, but one day, we'll wake up to find Gavin Cross is no more. All we'll have left is Kirloth."

Kiri nodded. "I haven't forgotten the last thing he said in the Privy Council meeting the other day. We are so alike; both of us must assume a role we wouldn't choose for ourselves." Silence reigned for a few moments before Kiri spoke once more. "People are still talking about what he did on the wall the other day. Could you or any of the others have done that?"

Lillian shrugged. "I…don't know. I'm not…I don't…this is going to sound bad. I don't have the capacity for sheer, unbridled destruction that Gavin does. None of us do. You have to be able to envision the effect you want to create, and none of us—not Mariana, Wynn, or Braden—could have ever envisioned that web of lightning bolts or what he did to that slaver camp. I still remember the sound of that barn roof's spine snapping as whatever Gavin created sucked the barn in on itself."

"Has he said anything to you about studying the slave marks?"

Lillian shook her head. "No, but I'm certain it's why he built that lab. He hasn't been working with us very much lately. He has spent time with Braden in Fallon's tower, but Wynn, Mariana, and I have pretty much been left to our own devices. We did most of the work, protecting the wall from magic; he was there, but it was more in a supervisory role."

Kiri looked down at the floor for a few moments before saying, "I miss him, Lillian. A part of me almost doesn't want the siege to end. The thought of choosing between being Crown Princess of Vushaar and leaving with you…and Gavin…tears me up inside."

"Well, I know where you live now. You're only a teleportation effect away. It's not like you'll never see me again."

* * *

THE NEXT MORNING, Lillian sat down at the table where Gavin was eating breakfast. He nodded his greetings with a smile as he lifted a cup of tea to his lips. For the next few minutes, they each ate in silence, and even though she finished her meal well before Gavin, Lillian pushed her dishes aside and waited.

Soon, Gavin pushed his dishes aside as well and regarded his apprentice. "Something tells me you have more on your mind than just sharing the morning meal with me."

Lillian took a breath, as she steadied her nerves and said, "Gavin, Kiri asked for my help back in Tel Mivar. It was during the time you were away after Marcus's death."

"Okay." Gavin shrugged. "That isn't a problem, Lillian, and I don't understand why you mention it now."

Lillian withdrew several folded pieces of parchment from within her robe. "She asked me to accompany her to the Restricted Section of the Library, and she showed me a book that detailed the creation of the slave marks. She asked for my help in deciphering a diagram of the composite effect that created the slave brand."

"Is that so?"

Lillian nodded and unfolded the pages, pushing them across to Gavin. "I knew enough to identify the pieces of the effect, but I couldn't begin to fathom how to unravel it. I made a tracing of the diagram and several notes on the description of the diagram in the book. I meant to discuss this with you…"

"But we haven't exactly been idle since then, have we?"

"No, we haven't." Lillian fell silent for a few moments. "Gavin, have we offended you somehow?"

Gavin frowned. "What in the world could make you think that?"

"Well, it's just that we haven't seen a lot of you lately. In all truth, we didn't *think* we had offended you, but I just thought I'd ask."

"Lillian, I've been wrestling with something in the back of my mind while we've worked on everything here, and I was very glad to see you sit with me. It saved me from having to locate one of you. Do you know the house I bought just outside the palace gates?" Lillian nodded. "I would like for you to gather Mariana, Wynn, and

Braden and meet me there as soon as you can. There is a matter we must discuss."

IT WASN'T VERY MUCH LATER AT all when Lillian led her fellow apprentices into the house Gavin purchased. Aside from five chairs in the main room, no other furniture existed. Gavin occupied one chair, and the other four were arranged in a rough semicircle facing him.

"Thank you for coming," Gavin said, "and please, be seated." Once everyone was seated, Gavin continued. "I've never made it a secret that I don't consider myself a master of arcane lore, but you asked me to teach you what I know; I've tried to do that.

"The mentor/apprentice arrangement is an artifact of a time when the Society of the Arcane didn't exist. There are no evaluation criteria, no rubrics setting forth guidelines to know when your apprenticeship is complete. In fact, my own research into the matter suggests that apprenticeships back then only ended when the mentor said they ended."

Gavin fell silent and lowered his gaze to the floor, and his friends glanced to one another as if trying to determine what was happening or what they should do. After several moments, Gavin lifted his head.

"Lillian met me in the dining room this morning and asked if you had offended me in some way. I didn't tell her so at the time, but nothing could be further from the truth. I am incredibly proud of each of you. You handled the composite effect to protect the city's outer wall against magic with skill and professionalism. You have each taken multiple turns on the wall, standing guard against Ivarson's arcanists, and impressed those soldiers around you while you did so. I've heard more than one officer discuss pushing a request up the chain of command for the king to consider employing arcanists in the Army of Vushaar, based on your example alone."

"Do you think you might have had a hand in that, too, Gavin?" Lillian asked, a slight grin forming.

Gavin shook his head. "Look around you sometime when we walk among the soldiers together, Lillian. No one wants a contingent of arcanists like me. They respect me, respect my abilities and knowledge, and appreciate my service on their behalf...but that respect is built upon a foundation of fear. Not one of them would ever invite me to sit with them in their favorite taproom and swap stories.

"Now, as I was saying...I have been giving the matter a great deal of thought, and I have reached an inescapable conclusion. There is nothing further I can teach you. By the authority vested in me under Article 23 of the Arcanists' Code, I declare your apprenticeships complete and grant you the rank of *Magus* within the Society of the Arcane."

Silence reigned as Gavin's friends looked to one another, their expressions ranging from shock to disbelief.

"But...but we're not ready!" Mariana said.

"Is that so? Tell me what Word you would use to invoke a fireball to use against a group attacking the city's wall."

"Well, I personally would use *Luhrhym*, but I know you used *Idluhn* the other day for that lightning effect."

Gavin shifted his attention. "Wynn, how would you remove a harmful effect from someone?"

"I'd-use-the-Word-of-Tutation-*Rhosed*."

"Lillian, can you diagram a composite effect that creates a sky in an underground environment and provides the full experience of being outside under the sun, moon, and stars?"

"No," Lillian said. "I don't have parchment, ink, or a stylus... but otherwise, yes."

Gavin smiled, and his gaze shifted to Braden. "Explain how magical effects are embedded in objects."

"The easiest method is to add a drop of a wizard's blood during the item's construction, if the method permits. Such materials as metal, though, don't absorb it, so you must stamp or engrave runes into the metal as you fill the item with power."

"Now, this last question is for any of you. Name four other

arcanists who possess even a quarter of your knowledge about, and experience with, the Words of Power."

They all looked to one another again, and at last, they turned their attention back to Gavin as Lillian said, "I'm not sure there are any…not within the Society, anyway."

"I don't believe that apprenticeships were ever intended to instill all the knowledge an arcanist would ever need. Marcus certainly didn't treat them that way. Apprenticeships provide the basics, a foundation from which the arcanist can pursue whatever studies of the Art she or he desires, and that time has come for you.

"Only one thing remains. In perusing Marcus's journals while trying to decide where to take your training next, I found his description of a ritual in which every new arcanist would participate upon completion of their apprenticeship. As part of this ritual, you will examine your heart and mind and decide your philosophy toward the Art."

Gavin reached down to the floor beside his seat and retrieved a sheaf of parchment none of his friends had noticed. He stood and handed one piece of parchment to each of his friends. As Gavin returned to his seat holding the final piece of parchment for himself, they turned the parchment over and looked at the writing. The handwriting was obviously Gavin's, and the words were written out in the language of magic, not using any of the Words of Power they knew but almost like a spell.

Gavin watched his friends frown as they looked at what he'd handed them, smiling just a bit.

"Gavin," Mariana said, "what is this?"

"The simple answer is ink on parchment, but the truth of the matter is that I don't know what it is, beyond being the words to the ritual your ancestors participated in at the completion of their apprenticeships."

Gavin watched his friends look to one another, and they all nodded. Then, they looked to Gavin once more, and Mariana said, "Let's do it, then."

They recited the words to the ritual, and from Gavin's perspective, nothing seemed to happen right away. After several moments, though, halos of light particles formed over each person's head and swirled for a heartbeat or three before cascading down over their bodies. In the wake of the light particles, their robes were no longer the student robes they had worn into the house. Mariana's robe turned red, and the *Magus* rank runes on the cuffs of her sleeves were black. Braden's robe became green, his rank runes black as well. Lillian's robe was now white, not surprising Gavin at all, and her rank runes were black. What made Gavin stare in awe, though, was Wynn's blue robe; Gavin never would've expected Wynn to be a scholar.

When the light particles disappeared at last, Gavin watched his friends collapse against the back of their chairs as if tired.

"That was…intense," Braden said.

"Nothing happened to me," Gavin said. "What did it feel like to you guys?"

"It felt like something crawling through every part of who I am, looking for something so small it required intense scrutiny to find it," Lillian said.

The others nodded.

"It-felt-exactly-like-that," Wynn said.

"So, what happens now?" Mariana asked.

Gavin shrugged. "What do you want to happen now? Each of you knows the Word of Transmutation that will create a gateway to wherever you want to go."

"What if we want to stay with you?" Lillian asked. "Work with you on your projects?"

"It's up to you. The important thing, to me, is that each of you understand you're free to make your own decisions. Discuss the matter, and let me know what you decide."

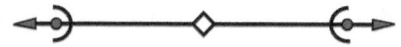

CHAPTER 30

Gavin stood before one of the slate chalkboards in his lab. He just finished drawing out the diagram Lillian had given him, sized to fit the chalkboard, and he sat on one of the table's chairs, angled to face the chalkboard as he flipped through the notes Lillian had made.

"Why would Marcus have created this?" Gavin said. "Oh, sure...I can understand him not wanting any more arcanists to die trying to make this themselves, especially since the ones working on it were probably mages, but still...there's something involved with all this I'm not seeing."

Footfalls on the stairs behind him drew Gavin's attention, and he turned to see Declan leading a woman into the basement. She wore a simple linen shift, and while her expression was nonexistent, her eyes made Gavin think of a prey animal ready to bolt.

Gavin stood and met them just a short distance in from the base of the stairs.

"Gavin," Declan said by way of greeting.

Gavin gave the woman his best neutral, encouraging smile and extended his right hand, saying, "Hi. I'm Gavin Cross."

The woman shied away from Gavin as she stared at the floor.

"This is your home now," Gavin continued. "Please, pick out a bedroom upstairs, and I'll see to it that it's furnished. Come to think of it…"

Gavin pulled back his robe and withdrew the coin purse hanging off his belt. He opened it and withdrew a handful of coins. Holding them out in his hands, he showed Declan.

"Is that enough for clothes, food, and bedroom furniture?"

Declan looked at the gold coins with an emerald and ruby laying among them and nodded. "I think I can make it work."

"Okay. Use whatever coin you had left over from…well…" Gavin nodded his head toward the woman. "…the market, too."

Declan chuckled. "You really have no idea what things cost, do you?"

Gavin shook his head and shrugged. "I bought that stuff at Hakamri's when Jasmine and I went for that ride after Marcus's death, but otherwise, no…not really."

"What you're holding would outfit three houses this size," Declan said, "if not outright buy those three houses, considering the gems."

"Oh, okay. See that she has good clothes and that we have good food, here in the house." Gavin turned his attention back to the woman. "Did he tell you why I asked him to hire you?"

The woman shook her head just enough for Gavin to see without looking up.

Gavin sighed. He reached out with his right hand slowly, making an obvious motion with his palm up and hand open. He watched as the woman went rigid at the sight of his hand, and Gavin hooked the edge of his index finger under her chin and lifted her face to look at him.

"We just met; I understand. I don't know how long you've been a slave, but there's something you need to understand. Just because the law says you're a slave, doesn't mean I think you are. This is something we'll have to work at, but don't ever fear for a moment that I'll harm you in any way. When you return from shopping with Declan, I'll have an amulet for you that will indicate you're under my protection, and if you're ever away from the house and someone harms you, I want to know about it. Oh, Declan…we'll probably need kitchen stuff, too. Pots, pans, knives, forks…all that stuff."

Declan nodded, his expression hinting at mild amusement. "I thought so, myself. How goes the work?"

Gavin looked over his shoulder to the chalkboard, saying, "It's fiendishly complex…and clever. I'm still picking it apart, but the entire effect hangs on the Tutation construct at the core."

"So, we just find a way to break that construct?"

"No, I don't think so," Gavin said. "I think that's where everyone else went wrong. There's enough energy bound up in the matrix that breaking the core construct could easily kill the person bound by it. Heh…I'd be surprised if the backlash didn't harm the arcanist who broke it, too. We need to find a way to bleed off the energy, I think, and let the matrix fade on its own. But I've only been looking at it this morning. I'm still working on understanding exactly what Marcus did to make it."

"Well, we'll leave you to it. Some of my associates are watching the house."

Gavin nodded and wandered back over to the notes and chalkboard. "Thank you, Declan."

* * *

GAVIN WAS NOT aware of how much time had passed when he heard Lillian calling his name. He looked up from a tabletop now littered with notes and diagrams to see Lillian standing on the last step of the staircase.

"Hi, Lillian. What did you need?"

"The banquet announcing Kiri's return? Did you want to attend?"

Gavin turned his head, his eyes flitting across the notes covering the table and the chalkboards. "I don't know. I think I'm finally starting to make some progress deciphering what Marcus did. I'm not sure I can afford the time."

Gavin felt Lillian place a hand on his shoulder, and he turned to face her once more. She held out an envelope.

"What's this?" he asked.

Lillian said nothing, just held the envelope out to him.

Gavin took the envelope and opened it. It contained two items: a folded note on fine stationary and an invitation. Gavin unfolded the note to read:

Dear Gavin,

I would be honored if you were to attend the banquet this evening. There is no doubt in my mind that I am safe in my family's home, but knowing I'm safe and feeling I'm safe are two very different things.

The last time I felt safe, I was by your side. Besides, I would very much like to see you.

Warmest Regards,
Kiri

Gavin stood in silence, staring at the note. His eyes never left the stationary, but his mind went over everything he had to do, all the time he felt he needed. There was no way he'd ever complete his research if he kept allowing interruptions, but at the same time, she said she felt safe around him.

"It looks like I'm going to a banquet," Gavin said.

That evening, Gavin stood with his friends in the Grand Ballroom of the palace, among a mass of people in their finest attire. A quintet of musicians provided an understated ambiance to the event, the music just loud and strong enough to be an undercurrent without dominating. Gavin smiled at seeing Declan acting as the lutist for the quintet.

A door at the far side of the ballroom opened, and Gavin saw Varne, the Royal Herald, enter. He nodded once, and the music faded.

"My lords and ladies," Varne said, his strong voice filling the hall, "it is my honor and privilege to present His Majesty Terris Muran, King of Vushaar, and Her Highness Kiri Muran, Crown Princess."

Gavin listened to the gasps moving through the attendees like a wave. The gasps didn't last long enough to give him an appreciation of any reaction other than surprise. Gavin saw Terris and Kiri forming a receiving line just as he noticed someone at his side; it was Varne.

"Good evening, sir. His Majesty and Her Highness have requested you and your...associates...lead the guests as they receive you."

Gavin nodded once and passed off his drink to a server with a silver tray roving through the crowd. Lillian, Mariana, Wynn, and Braden did likewise, and the five of them followed Varne through the crowd to take their place at the head of the receiving line.

Once Gavin and his friends were delivered, Varne took his place off to Terris's left and slightly behind him, where he proceeded to announce each guest in his hall-filling voice.

"Gavin Cross of House Kirloth!"

Gavin stepped up to Terris and nodded once. Terris extended his hand—a rare honor—which Gavin accepted.

As he shook Gavin's hand, Terris smiled, saying, "Thank you for coming this evening, Gavin. I don't know if I'll ever feel I've repaid you for bringing my daughter back to me."

Gavin shrugged. "I wasn't aware we were keeping score, Terris."

Terris nodded once, and Gavin took the step necessary to stand in front of Kiri.

"It's been a while, Gavin," Kiri said.

"It has, yes."

"I'm glad you came."

Gavin remained silent for a few heartbeats as he gazed into her eyes. At last, he said, "I wouldn't be anywhere else."

CHAPTER 31

The sun streamed down through a cloudless sky, warming everything it touched. A light breeze blew through the south gate from the Sarnath Hills, carrying a hint of the snow on the not-too-distant peaks. The traffic entering the capital that morning was light, and all in all, it was a good day to be one of the soldiers manning the gate.

Covax and his squaddie Wren turned back to face south after searching and passing one of the few wagons that could travel the path through the Sarnath Hills. The next in line was a tall figure, easily topping Covax in height and wearing a hooded, gray, woolen robe.

"State your name and business," Covax said, as Wren moved to stand to the figure's left and slightly behind.

"I am Xythe," the figure said, pronouncing the name 'zith' in an eerily feminine voice, "and I seek the one known as Gavin Cross."

Covax and Wren knew that name. How could they not?

"And what business do you have with Master Cross?" Covax asked. "Does he expect you?"

"Doubtful," Xythe said. "I am not certain he even remembers me. I have traveled from my homeland to beg instruction in the Art;

I would become one of the Apprentices of Kirloth, if he'll have me."

Covax and Wren shared another glance, and Covax said, "I'm afraid I'll have to ask you to open your robe."

Without acknowledging Covax's statement, Xythe pulled open the robe and jerked her head to throw the hood back. Covax, Wren, and several others nearby were startled to see a dracon standing before them, and what's more, Covax counted no less than thirteen different weapons strapped to various places on the leather harness the dracon wore.

"Uh…" Covax said, drawing out the syllable as he stared at the implements of violence. This dracon was a walking arsenal. "Do you know how to use all of those?"

Xythe nodded once. "I have spent the last twenty years serving in my people's Guard, and my trainer indicated I have some small skill."

"Have you ever been to the capital before? Do you know your way around?"

"I am only two hundred. My people had already withdrawn from the world when I hatched, so this is my first time out among the naturals."

"Right then. I'll send one of our runners with you as far as the palace gate. I imagine that's where you'll find Master Cross."

Xythe gave a partial bow as she closed her robe, saying, "My gratitude."

* * *

THE SOUND of footfalls drew Gavin's attention, and he turned to see Fallon and Jasper halfway down the steps into the basement. Jasper looked worried.

"We knocked several times," Fallon said.

Gavin motioned for them to come the rest of the way into the basement and indicated the chairs around the table. "Please, make yourselves comfortable, and I apologize for not noticing the knocking. I can't swear that I even heard it."

Fallon and Jasper sat a few chairs down from Gavin, and Gavin noticed how uneasy Jasper still looked.

"Thank you," Fallon said. "I was hoping you had a few moments to discuss something."

"Of course," Gavin said. He turned a chair out from the table so that it faced Fallon and Jasper and sat, leaning forward and giving his guests his full attention. "Please, proceed."

Fallon glanced at Jasper before saying, "Jasper and I have been talking. I feel I have given him a solid grounding in the basics of the Art, but the fact of the matter is that I'm a mage. That won't ever change. Jasper is also my nephew by my younger sister, and when she came to me about Jasper's continued interest in the Art, I wasn't aware any wizards trained by wizards still existed."

Gavin chuckled. "Depending on *when* she came to you, there may not have been any wizards trained by wizards...well, beyond my mentor of course. I woke up in the southwestern warrens of Tel Mivar with no knowledge beyond my name a little over a year ago."

Gavin watched Fallon's jaw slacken, and after a few moments, Fallon said, "You mean you've only been active for a *year*?"

"A little over a year, if my math is right...maybe a year and a half or a little over now," Gavin said with a shrug. "I'm still a little fuzzy on your calendar; I can't quite get past the whole 'ten months with thirty days per month' thing. I keep wanting to say the year is twelve months long."

Fallon and Jasper stared at Gavin in silence. After a short time, Fallon said, frowning, "I can't think of any calendar known that has twelve months per year."

Gavin nodded and shrugged. "That's merely one of the oddities about me, but I believe I've diverted us from your topic."

"Yes, of course. Ever since you offered to provide study materials for Jasper, I haven't gotten the thought out of my mind that keeping him with me is doing him a vast disservice. Jasper, his mother, and I sat down and discussed the matter, and we want to discuss what would be required for you to take Jasper on as an apprentice as was in the old ways. Jasper would like very much to be a wizard trained by a wizard."

"I understand," Gavin said. "My first question…why doesn't Jasper speak for himself?"

"I…well…" Fallon said.

"You scare me, sir," Jasper said, speaking for the first time. "I've learned a great many things under my uncle's tutelage, and I'm grateful beyond words that he'd take me on. But then, I look at what you can do—what your other apprentices can do—and I'm both awed and afraid. There's no spell I've ever heard of—or that my uncle has ever heard of, either—that could duplicate that lightning web you created. I don't know if lightning web is the proper name, but that was so impressive. I want to know how to do that."

Gavin nodded as he scratched at his chin. "So…you seek power."

Jasper was quick to shake his head side to side, saying, "Oh, no, sir! I seek knowledge. I don't know if I'll ever know why I was born with this power and my sister or my mother wasn't; from everything I've read, no one knows why wizards are wizards, but I want to explore this and understand it as best I can."

"Tell me about your family, Jasper," Gavin said.

"I'm the oldest, and it's just my mother, my sister, and me. My father…well, I never really knew him. Mother told me he was a leatherworker, and we were traveling to the capital where he was going to open a shop. My sister was still a babe. I wasn't much older. Mother said they came on us out of the forest while we camped. Father fought them off, but he was so wounded he didn't make it. We made it to the capital, and Uncle Fallon has been helping us ever since. Mother doesn't really like it, but she's been so busy raising my sister it's been difficult to find paying work."

Gavin nodded. "I'm sorry you never had the chance to know your father really well, Jasper. Do you know what happened to the bandits who attacked your family?"

"They ran into a mounted patrol as they fled my father. The patrol brought them back to our camp to verify the truth of the story the bandits told them, and a week later, they were hung for banditry in Thartan."

"Well," Gavin said, "that saves me from having to track them down, then."

Astonishment dominated Jasper's expression as he looked at Gavin, saying, "You'd track them down...even after all this time? I mean, I was barely walking when it happened."

"I can't promise I would've been successful, but oh yes. I would certainly have spent effort and resources to learn if any of them still lived yet and correct that if they did." A silence descended on the table for several moments before Gavin resumed speaking. "Very well. You should be aware that I no longer have any apprentices. Those the people of the city at large know as 'the Apprentices' completed their apprenticeships a few days ago. Are you certain you want to become my apprentice?"

Jasper nodded.

"So be it. Under the authority vested in me by Article 23 of the Arcanists' Code, I hereby name you, Jasper, to be my apprentice as was in the old ways. As I expect you to devote your full time to the tasks and studies I assign you, I will pay you a monthly stipend to ensure your needs are met. Any surplus is yours to do with as you choose."

"Did you pay your former apprentices a stipend, sir?" Jasper asked.

"I did not."

"Then, I won't-"

"Jasper, my mentor paid me a monthly stipend during my time with him, and my former apprentices are the Heirs to the Great Houses of Tel. The stipend my mentor paid me—and I will pay you—would have been little more than a rounding error to their finances."

"Oh."

"You'll start tomorrow. I'll have Wynn work with you to get an understanding of what you already know, and we'll work out a study plan from there. Oh, that's something else. You won't be working with me exclusively; for a while, at least, you'll split your study time between myself and my former apprentices. I want them to have some experience teaching others. Is this a problem?"

"Oh, no, sir…but if they're not your apprentices anymore?"

Gavin smiled. "Just because there's nothing else *I* have to teach them doesn't mean there's nothing else for them to learn."

Just then, the door to the basement flew open and slammed against its stop. Heavy footfalls heralded the arrival of a Wraith in plain clothes who had been watching the house.

"Milord, come quickly," the Wraith said. "There are fighters assaulting the palace gates!"

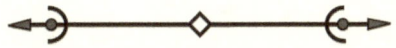

CHAPTER 32

Gavin stared at the woman for no more than a heartbeat. He was out of his chair faster than someone could snap their fingers and striding toward the staircase.

"What information do you have?"

The woman shrugged. "Not much. A group of people dressed like a mix of refugees, itinerant traders, and such charged the gates. The Cavaliers are trying to beat them back far enough to lower the portcullis, but the last I saw, it was a stalemate."

By now, Gavin was taking the stairs two at a time, and Fallon and Jasper were just starting to stand.

"What should we do?" Fallon asked.

Gavin stopped at the landing in the middle of the stairs and looked at his two guests. For a heartbeat, he was silent but then said, "Wait here, or maybe visit a bakery for a pastry. My people and I will handle this."

* * *

XYTHE FOLLOWED the message runner through the streets of the Vushaari capital. In many ways, it felt very odd to be outside and around people after all the years of her youth, but her parents had told her she needed to follow her heart and dreams…which meant finding Kirloth and begging him to teach her. Myriad scents assaulted her as they entered the markets, and Xythe smiled as they passed a particularly fragrant bakery; she had always loved the scents of fresh bread and pastries.

"The street leading to the palace is just up here," the runner said.

"I appreciate you helping me find my way," Xythe said. "This place is both like and unlike my home. I fear I would've been lost beyond hope, were it not for you."

The young man blushed. "You're welcome. It's what I do. I want to start my own courier business when I get older…if I can find the coin for it."

"Before we part, give me your name and details on how to find you. I shall speak of your kindness and goals to my mentor…if he will have me."

The young man stopped short and stared at her. "You would mention me t-to Kirloth?"

"Is it unwise? What little I interacted with him in my homeland, he seemed to be a very kind soul. Was I wrong?"

"Oh, no! It isn't that at all. It's just he has the ears of the King and Crown Princess. I never thought I would come to the attention of someone like that. That's a greater kindness than I could ever hope to repay." A commotion drew the young man's attention, and he moved to stop a town guardsman. "Jeth, is something wrong? Why are all these people-"

"Apologies, Brant," the guardsman said. "A mass of people have assaulted the palace gates, and they're calling in anyone available. You shouldn't be anywhere near here."

"Okay. Thank you." Brant turned back to Xythe. "I don't think we'll reach the palace gates."

"Yes, I heard. Tell me how to reach the palace gates. I shall help with the defense, but I would not have you endangered."

"Uh…I'm not sure. You're my responsibility."

Xythe smiled, which given the rows of flesh-rending teeth might not have been the best choice. "Child, I have more years with my blades than your defenders have been alive...and my people were created for battle. Tell me how to reach the palace gate."

* * *

"Have your people set up on the roofs and high locations around the fighting with bows and crossbows," Gavin said, as he and the female Wraith exited the house. "I don't want you to be noticed, but if targets of opportunity present themselves, there's no reason not to take advantage."

The woman nodded and moved off to collect her fellows.

Gavin turned left and headed for the palace. It wasn't long at all before he heard the sounds of fighting, and he soon turned a corner and found himself looking at the back of a mass of people fighting with the Cavaliers to breach the palace gates. There were more fighters than could conveniently attack the gates, and those toward the rear served as a guard to protect against being flanked. Several noticed Gavin as he moved to the center of the street and maintained a steady pace toward the gates. The fighters started to gather, watching Gavin.

"Well, I suppose they should know who they face...at the very least," Gavin whispered. He squared his shoulders, focused his mind on his intent, and invoked the Word, "*Thyphos*." Thirty feet above Gavin's head, the fifteen-feet-wide battle standard of Kirloth flashed into being, bright enough to stand out well against the morning sun.

The men stopped, staring at the glowing standard. They glanced at one another, and more than one glanced around as if trying to find a side street that would allow him or her to slip away. Gavin's eyes scanned the crowd as he waited for them to make a move, and he heard footfalls at his side. Glancing to his side, Gavin saw a tall figure in a brown traveling robe.

"Master Kirloth," the figure said, the voice eerily feminine, "I have traveled from my homeland to beg you to teach me. I am Xythe; I do not know if you remember me."

"I'm afraid I'm not in a position to discuss much right now,"

Gavin said, the most of his attention on the would-be fighters watching him. "I have this little problem to deal with."

"I would assist you, if you'll permit it." Xythe said and removed her robe.

Gavin spared her a quick glance, his eyes flitting across the various weapons he could see. "Ah...why not. I wouldn't want you to be bored."

Xythe drew two short swords that would've been full-length longswords for anyone Gavin's size, and her lips drew back in an almost-feral grin. "When do we commence hostilities?"

Gavin started to speak, but more noise behind him drew his attention. He looked over his shoulder and saw a sizeable force of Cavaliers and town guard turn the corner. "Xythe, we need to step aside to make room for our friends. I'm sure they wouldn't like it if we didn't share."

Now, the fighters ahead of them looked even more unsure. In a gradual progression from the center of the group to the outer edge, the fighters laid down their arms one-by-one and knelt, lacing their fingers behind their heads.

The Cavaliers leading the town guard arrived, and Gavin looked to the officer in charge. She wasn't someone Gavin recognized.

"Not my preferred method of starting a day," Gavin said, his tone conversational.

"No, not at all," the Cavalier said. "Is this dracon with you?"

"Yes. Her name is Xythe, and she has traveled to seek apprenticeship with me."

"I've never known wizards to be much fighters," the Cavalier said, "no offense."

Gavin smiled. "By and large, we're not...but I have a feeling Xythe will surprise you. After all, the dracons were created to be shock troops during the Godswar, and they haven't let their training slip."

"Sergeant," the Cavalier said, "have the town guard take charge of those surrendered combatants. I want them treated well and with honor; we'll want to interrogate them later."

Several town guard started moving toward the kneeling fighters when several in the back ranks of those trying to break through the gate turned and saw them. Gavin recognized the threat they posed to their surprise flank attack and knew moments counted. He snapped his fingers, saying, "Go, Xythe!"

Xythe went straight to a sprint, running all out. As she neared the kneeling fighters, she pushed off with her legs and vaulted over them, resuming her sprint as she touched the ground once more. In less than a minute, she reached those fighters who had turned and started cutting them down to keep them from alerting their fellows.

Xythe's blades danced through blocks and strikes, and the rear-most ranks of the fighters fell like wheat at harvest before her. When a fighter in front of her spun and drew back his blade, Xythe didn't hesitate. She leaned down, turning her head to one side and used her razor-sharp teeth to rip out the man's throat in a geyser of blood all while cutting down another fighter with each sword. She spat out the remains of the man's throat as she lifted her right foot and kicked the corpse into the back of the next fighter.

"By the gods…" the Cavalier at Gavin's side whispered. Gavin glanced her way and saw she was a little pale.

"Yup…just think what it would be like if we had twenty of her people."

"It would be a slaughter," the Cavalier said, her voice barely above a whisper.

Xythe was now well into the fourth rank from the rear and those at the extreme sides around her were gathering to surround her. **TWANG**s of crossbows and bows erupted from the roofs of the buildings all around them, and quarrels and arrows cut down many of those who were moving to surround Xythe.

Gavin saw several still standing, and he focused on the fighters assaulting the gate as a whole, invoking the Word, "*Thraxys.*"

Those few remaining from the four, rear-most ranks collapsed to the ground dead, and some thirty more ahead of Xythe joined them. By now, no more than three ranks of fighters remained between Xythe and the gate, and they realized in short order they had been flanked.

"I think it's about time for you," Gavin said. "They look about ready to rout."

The Cavalier nodded and drew her sword. She held it high, shouting, "For Vushaar and the King!" Those Cavaliers behind her took up the cry, and the entire group of them charged the gates.

Faced with a bloody demon of claws, teeth, scales, and blades in their midst—soon to be joined by upwards of a hundred Cavaliers—the fighters began shouting their surrender. Of the three hundred fighters that began the assault on the palace gates, a little less than seventy-five surrendered…and not even half of those were uninjured.

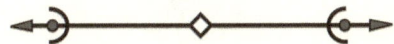

CHAPTER 33

A whirlwind of activity subsumed the palace complex in the days following the attack. While the quick response of Gavin and Xythe ensured the attack was short-lived, the attack still wounded or killed Cavaliers. Several artisans collaborated to repair what little damage to the gates existed, and several cleaning crews expended a great amount of effort swabbing the blood off the paving stones right outside the palace gates.

About a week after the attack, the king held a ceremony and banquet to honor all those who rushed to defend the palace gates... including Gavin, Xythe, and Gavin's former apprentices. The ceremony was a brief affair, with all due gravitas and gratitude from the King, and the banquet was a pleasant and stately affair for the necessary mingling such an event almost demanded.

"Oh, my," Kiri said in a hushed tone as she leaned close to Lillian. "Gavin is not pleased *at all* with my father calling him out in front of everyone, is he?"

Lillian chuckled. "You don't know the half of it. The only reason—the only reason whatsoever—Gavin agreed to appear and accept the award your father presented is that he didn't want us—Mariana, Wynn, Braden, and Xythe—to be passed over as well or feel like we had to refuse. I was there when the royal courier arrived with Gavin's invitation, you know."

"You never told me that! What did he do?"

"When he opened the envelope and read the invitation, I swear I saw his eyes flash—literally flash—and the invitation erupted in flame. I never heard or saw him invoke a Word. He just suddenly held a pile of ash in his hand. I thought the courier was going to pass out or soil himself. I guess Gavin realized what he'd done, because *then*, he invoked a Word that reconstituted the invitation in its pristine condition. Let me tell you; the courier looked beyond terrified at that point. Gavin looked at the courier, took a deep breath, and said, 'Tell him I accept.' The courier bolted out of the basement like he feared for his life."

"Oh, that poor boy," Kiri replied, failing to contain her mirth. "I'll have Father give him a bonus; I'd say he earned it."

"I really love the string quartet. Do they host concerts or anything? I could sit and listen to them play for hours."

ON THE OPPOSITE side of the banquet hall from Kiri and Lillian, Count Varkas held court with a number of sycophants and toadies, a crystal glass in his hand and oft refilled.

"What's your take on the state of Vushaar, Varkas?" Joric Torgunson, Baron of Torstead, asked as he lifted his own glass to his lips.

"I tell you, Joric, I cannot see as how anything other than base sentimentality guided the King to re-affirming his daughter as the Crown Princess…especially now that she's a slave of all things. There's no hope of continuing the dynasty, unless he takes a new wife and disinherits Kiri, and we've never held to that silly nonsense of adoption. Blood is all that matters, as it should."

"I thought you voted to support her re-affirmation as Crown Princess in that Privy Council meeting."

"Ha," Varkas barked. "I only did so because the peasants and the merchants forced my hand by speaking before me. I don't know how anyone could *ever* conceive she'll have what it takes to lead this country. Why, the only place that wench deserves to be is in my bedchamber, begging for mercy."

A hush radiated outward from Count Varkas and Baron Torstead, and those around them started drawing back until they were singled out by a ring of empty floorspace bounded by offended expressions all around.

"Look at these sheep, Torstead," Varkas said, his voice still a bit raised as he gestured around him with his glass. "Every one of them acts like Terris Muran is still a man to be feared. How long do you think it will be before they finally see his time is ending?"

"Not everyone here is a sheep, Varkas," Baron Torstead countered, his eyes looking over Varkas's right shoulder.

"Oh? Surely, *you* don't think I should fear the King?"

"Everyone with any sense fears the King," Torstead said, "but no. There's someone about whom you should have far more immediate concerns."

"Really? Who?"

Baron Torstead jerked his chin to point over Varkas's right shoulder, saying, "Him."

Varkas turned, swaying a bit and sloshing his glass. He found one face not expressing surprise or offense. That face was granite for all it expressed anything, and the cold, passionless glare carried a far more effective doom than any of those surprised or offended.

Gavin Cross lifted his left hand, only his index finger and thumb extended, and a server faded out of the crowd. He turned his head just enough to direct his words to the server, but the angle was sufficient that neither Baron Torstead nor Varkas could read his lips.

The server, however, was in plain view; they read her response, "Yes, Milord; it shall be done."

Gavin held his gaze on Varkas's eyes for a few moments more, before he turned and disappeared into the crowd. Watching the back of the black-robed wizard fade into the finery of those invited to the royal event, Varkas realized he was covered in a cold sweat.

* * *

THAT NIGHT, Count Varkas and his party vanished as they traveled to the Count's home in the city. He had an estate and lands in the southeastern portion of the kingdom, but he maintained a residence in the capital to assist with his duties as a member of the King's Privy Council.

The next night, a nobleman known to maintain various business interests with Count Varkas vanished as well. The man's wife woke up the following morning to find herself alone in bed, with no indication when or if her husband departed.

Over the next week, twenty-five more people vanished without a trace. They ranged from minor merchants and two influential people within the Vushaar's Guild of Drovers to several high officers in Vushaar's Royal Bank and three officers on the Vushaari Army's General Staff, who routinely attended the War Council meetings.

* * *

GAVIN SAT at the table in his lab. The diagrams of the composite effect to create the slave brands held his entire focus and full attention. As he examined the diagrams, he would write notes on the top sheet of a stack of parchment at his right; when that sheet was full of notes, it would join its many fellows facedown on a pile further to the right. Now and then, Gavin would make some whispered statement that was clearly a vocalization of his primary thought at the time, which often puzzled—or outright confused—Braden who stood over Gavin's left shoulder.

Declan sat at the far end of the table, working on his own stack of notes. As one of the world's most renowned bards, he felt it his duty to chronicle history as it unfolded before him, and he was writing down his notes, thoughts, and experiences to join all the pages he had compiled since meeting Gavin. When the man who dueled Milthas takes an apprentice for the first time in six thousand years and *then* names that man his heir...well...history was about to become a runaway freight wagon, and Declan wanted to record as much of it as he could.

. . .

Declan looked up at the sound of footfalls on the steps behind him that came around his left side. He saw the slave he'd hired at Gavin's request. She wrung her hands as her nerves compelled her to stop just a short distance away from Declan and not all that close to Gavin.

"Excuse me," she said. Her voice was so soft and tentative, Declan almost didn't catch what she said.

Declan smiled and laid aside his stylus, slipping out of his chair. He approached the woman from behind and saw her flinch and almost jump when he brushed his fingers across her left shoulder.

"I'm sorry; forgive me," she said. "I would never disturb, but there's someone to see him."

"You'll never break through his focus if you keep trying as you were. Be loud and assertive. Force him to take notice of you, or he never will. It's not rudeness on his part; he simply is so focused and consumed by his thoughts that none of us or this place exist to him right now."

The poor woman looked like Declan had just ordered her death.

"He will *never* harm you; I promise you that."

The woman turned and approached Gavin, who still betrayed no reaction to her presence. Declan watched the woman lift her left hand, lower it back to her side, and then lift it again before she placed it on Gavin's shoulder.

"You have a visitor," she said in a strong, clear voice.

Gavin turned to her, saying, "Huh?"

"I said there's someone here to see you."

Gavin frowned and looked at Declan over the woman's shoulder. Declan shrugged. Gavin turned to Braden, and Braden shrugged.

Gavin turned back to face the woman and said, "Okay. Who is it?"

"He introduced himself as Varne, the Royal Herald."

Gavin sat in silence for several moments as his eyes flicked back and forth as if he were reading several pages. At last, he spoke. "Hmmm...I have no idea why he's here. Let's go ask."

Gavin indicated for the woman to lead the way, and Declan chose to follow as well, with Braden falling in behind him. They trooped up the stairs and found Varne standing in the vacant space that would've been a parlor if the house were actually furnished and used as a house.

"Good day to you, Varne," Gavin said as he entered the room. "What brings you so far from the palace?"

"Good day to you as well, Gavin. His Majesty asked me to enquire if you might have some time to speak with him in the somewhat near future. He stressed to me that I should not interrupt your research in any way or intimate that this is some kind of royal command if you were at a critical juncture with your work."

Gavin turned to look behind him and, seeing Braden, said, "Braden, are we at a critical juncture?"

"How should I know? I'm still trying to catch up to your understanding of the work."

"Ah," Gavin said, turning back to Varne. "Well, there you have it. Is the King free now?"

"I...uh...well, I don't know really, but I'm sure you wouldn't have to wait long if he isn't free."

Gavin turned to the woman. "Are Mariana, Lillian, and Wynn still upstairs with Jasper and Xythe?"

"Yes, sir."

"When they finally take a break, please tell them I've gone to answer the King's request for a few moments of my time."

"Yes, sir."

"All right, Varne. Let's head out."

* * *

GAVIN LOOKED up from his seat in the King's private study when he heard the door open. When he saw Terris and Q'Orval enter, he stood and nodded his greeting, extending his hand.

Terris and Q'Orval both shook his hand warmly and proceeded to seats of their own, Terris gesturing for Gavin to resume his.

"Thank you for coming on such short notice," Terris said. "I hope Varne didn't interrupt anything sensitive."

"Oh, not at all. I'm still deconstructing the composite effect that created the slave brands. Compared to that, what we did for your city's wall was child's play. I tell you...if I'm ever half the arcanist my mentor was, I'll be amazed."

"I see. Gavin, I find myself in a bit of a situation, and I'm hoping you can help."

"Of course, Terris. If it is within my power to help, you need only make me aware."

"We've had a number of disappearances lately, and some of them...well...some of them had access to sensitive information about our city's defenses and financial institutions. Even if I win the civil war, the knowledge some of these people possess could cripple the country."

"Disappearances, you say?"

"Yes."

"Were they officers on your General Staff, a few high-level bankers, and assorted others by chance? Maybe a nobleman on your Privy Council?"

"Yes..."

"You don't need to worry about them *ever* presenting a threat to the country, Terris."

Terris and Q'Orval shared a glance before Terris directed his attention back to Gavin. "Gavin...I've heard some things that may have occurred at the banquet a week ago. Forgive me for being so blunt, but what did you do?"

Gavin sat in silence for several moments before answering, "What did I do? Not all that much. I just gave an order."

"You gave an order."

"Yes, Terris, I did. I don't know your opinion of Count Varkas, but I assure you that he was no friend. I heard him clearly say the only place Kiri deserved to be was in his bedchamber, begging for mercy."

"By the gods," Q'Orval said, his tone hushed. "It's a wonder you didn't burn him to ash right there."

"I won't lie by telling you the thought didn't cross my mind, but in the end, I decided it was past time I devoted some attention to learning as much about Count Varkas as I could. The order I gave was to have him interrogated by individuals who are supreme masters of their craft. During those conversations, Count Varkas volunteered several people who were working with him toward preparing to move against whoever wins this civil war, using the chaos and weakness of the immediate aftermath to gain power. Even if he hadn't had the designs for Kiri that he did, that information right there sealed his fate."

"It'll cause all kinds of problems when those bodies finally surface."

"Terris," Gavin said, "I'm Kirloth. Do you honestly expect *any* bodies will ever surface?"

"Well, what if one of these interrogators announce what they did to the world?"

Gavin pushed himself to his feet, shaking his head. "The sun will rise in the west before one of my people *ever* considers betraying me. They hold their service to me in too high regard and consider it an incredible honor. Good day, Terris."

Gavin left, with Declan trailing close behind. Terris and Q'Orval watched them leave before Terris turned to his close friend.

"Thoughts?"

Q'Orval leaned further back in the chair and sighed, saying, "I'm remembering a section from Volume II of Mivar's Histories."

"Which one?"

"The section where Mivar chronicles the creation and formation of the Wraiths of Kirloth."

"What's a military unit of the Godswar have to do with this?"

Q'Orval lifted his gaze to meet his king's eyes. "I know how much you study history. Have you ever seen any accounts of them being disbanded?"

"Oh."

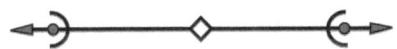

CHAPTER 34

Days passed. Gavin spent almost every waking minute in the basement lab, devoting his full effort and intellect to deciphering the diagrams of Marcus's ritualized composite effect. Braden assisted where he could, but by and large, he spent more time learning from Gavin's work. In the end, Gavin covered the tabletop with notes, breaking down the diagrammed composite effect into its constituent parts, and separate pages showing how those parts interconnected.

From there, Gavin summoned the slave Declan had hired for him. Over the course of several days, he examined the slave brand through his *skathos*, using Divination invocations to highlight all the tendrils of magic woven through the woman's body from the brand. Braden took notes as Gavin relayed what he learned.

Gavin sat—almost flopped—in one of the chairs surrounding the parchment-strewn table in his basement lab. He took a deep breath and released it as a slow, heavy sigh.

"I think we've made as much progress as we're going to make."

He scratched at his chin a few moments. "We need...a new perspective."

"How do we get that?" Braden asked, his rumbling voice almost echoing off the basement walls.

"No way I'm proud of," Gavin said. "I'm going to prey on someone's desperation."

"What?"

"You'll see."

Gavin pushed himself to his feet and crossed the room to the stairs. He took the stairs two at a time and searched the house for Declan, who was nowhere to be found. Instead, he stepped outside the house and approached one of Declan's associates who watched the house. This particular associate was a woman who bore a rather faint resemblance to Kiri, with her dark hair and olive complexion.

"Yes, Milord?"

"I have a request. I'm not...I don't...this is not a request I would make under normal circumstances, but I find myself with few choices that are dwindling fast. I need a woman with children who is close to desperation...maybe a refugee. Well, it doesn't have to be a woman, but to my mind, a woman would be far more disposed to make the kind of sacrifice I plan to ask of her to save her children than a man. Besides, as much as I would prefer otherwise, men seem to have more options in society than women."

"Milord, if I may, you sound more than a little conflicted about this."

Gavin chuckled. "That's good, I suppose...because I am. The problem is that I don't see any other way to obtain the knowledge I need. If I'm successful, this will ultimately lead to removing Kiri's slave mark." Gavin fell silent for several moments before he lifted his eyes to meet those of the woman he faced. "Are you willing to find me that woman?"

The woman nodded once at long last.

"Thank you."

.   .   .

A SHORT TIME LATER, the woman returned. She ushered a woman into the main room of the house and departed. Gavin sat on a simple chair with no arms, looking over his new guest from head to toe, but his expression bore no lust or leer. The woman was tanned but not dark enough to be the olive complexion so prevalent among Vushaari. Her stringy, blond hair clung to her head, matted and unwashed. Her hands and forearms were dirty, her fingernails almost black from all the dirt and grime under them. A simple cotton shift covered her body; Gavin thought it might have once been white or perhaps an off-white but no longer. She wore no shoes.

"That lady said you might have a job for me," she said, her voice almost tentative.

Gavin nodded. "I do. Please, sit. I want to explain the situation, what I'm asking, and what I'm offering. I do not want a blanket acceptance; this should be an informed choice on your part."

The woman wrung her hands for a moment. "Is that nice lady really feeding my children?"

Gavin shrugged. "Is that what she said she would do while we talked?"

"Yes."

"Then, you have no need to worry or fear. They will be fed well and be safer than you could imagine."

Tension left the woman, and she sat across from Gavin, folding her hands in her lap.

"Forgive me if I tell you anything you already know. I don't know your background, so I'm going to tell you all I can think of that will be pertinent." Gavin indicated his attire and medallion with his left hand. "As you can see, I am an arcanist, specifically a wizard of House Kirloth. What you may not know is that I am the head of my House."

"Oh, no, sir. Everyone's talking about Kirloth and his Apprentices. It's all over the city how the walls would've been breached, and the siege lost, without their work."

"I see. Well, then. For some time, I have been devoting all my available time to researching the slave marks and a method to remove them. I understand the effect that creates the slave brands, but I can't shake the feeling I'm missing crucial pieces of information. I have devised a method to record what happens magically when someone is branded, and I have a slave brand. What I am proposing is that you allow yourself to be branded by a slaver we've...well...acquired. If you agree, I'll pay you a stipend and provide quarters here in this house for you and your children. The time will come when I'm ready to try removing the slave mark, and there is the chance that will fail and result in your death. If my test does indeed fail and result in your death, I give you my word that I will see to your children's care and ensure they receive the finest education and opportunities to be found anywhere in the world."

"Let me be sure I understand. You want to have your pet slaver brand me and then try to remove the brand. If you fail and I die, you'll see to my children's care and education. What happens if you succeed?"

"Well, for one thing, it'll be like you were never branded in the first place, but I see no reason for you not to be rewarded for taking this risk. I'll see to it that you have the funds necessary to set yourself and your children up in whatever life you desire."

"Why not have someone brand you?"

Gavin chuckled. "A slaver tried already. There's a protection built into the effect that created the slave brands that protects wizards from being branded. Depending on the strength of wizard the slaver tries to brand, the result is anything from being marked themselves to the most agonizing death you can imagine. I witnessed the agonizing death."

"Oh."

Silence descended on the room and maintained for quite a while. The situation was reaching the point where Gavin was going to ask for a response when the woman lifted her head and looked Gavin right in his eyes.

"Ivarson's army killed my husband and burned our farm and everything we had when we wouldn't give our crops to them. I don't know why they didn't take us. This city is overrun with refugees, and every one of them has a story similar to mine. Very few of them will ever have any opportunities offered them. Starvation or worse are all my children have to look forward to, and I can't remember the last time I ate, for giving them every scrap of food I get. I accept."

"Well, let's start with some food and a bath for you. Then, we'll get you and your children some clothes. It's already late afternoon, and I'll need to find out what my associate did with our pet slaver. Let's pick a room for you upstairs, and we'll make a list of any furniture it needs and whatever else you or your children need. We'll proceed as soon as I've located the pet slaver."

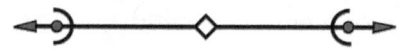

CHAPTER 35

"Gavin, may I speak with you?"

Gavin pulled his attention away from his notes and looked to his right. He saw Lillian standing a short distance away, her fists on her hips. Her facial expression didn't communicate happiness, either.

"Of course, Lillian. What do you need?"

"Are you really going to have a slaver brand some refugee woman?"

Gavin nodded. "Yes, I am. We've entered into an agreement for her to assist me with my research."

"Did you tell her what the cost of failure is…for her?"

"Yes, I did."

Lillian's eyes narrowed as she worked her jaw. "Gavin, I'm not happy with this. This is a new low for you. That you could casually set up some poor woman as a sacrifice…it's…well…it's something Marcus would've done. It's not who you are, Gavin."

"What makes you think I decided upon that path *casually*, Lillian? Do you think I just plucked some desperate soul off the street and threw wealth and food at her without explaining the full extent of what I was trying to do?" Gavin pushed himself to his feet and took a few steps away from the table, pivoting to gesture at all the note-pages that hid the tabletop. "I've gone as far as I can go, Lillian. Yes, I've broken down and deciphered the entire effect, but that doesn't mean I have a solution. There's no part of those diagrams anywhere—*anywhere*—that is designed to cause the death of the slave if the brand is removed, so it's an unintended consequence. Matter of fact, everything I've seen in those diagrams almost *screams* that Marcus intended the marks to be removable, but damned if I can see how.

"Oh, sure...I could invoke a dispelling effect on a slave, but I'm not so indifferent to life that I'll risk someone like that. I am literally working with people's lives, Lillian...your friend included. You think Kiri *wants* to spend the rest of her life branded a slave?"

"She's your friend, too, Gavin."

"I have to see the branding effect take hold," Gavin said, continuing on as if Lillian hadn't spoken. "I've already examined the slave Declan hired for me to a far greater degree than probably even she realizes. I've seen the tendrils of power radiating out from that brand throughout her entire being. I've seen how it blocks her from having children. Did you know that every slave's brand is linked to every other brand?"

Lillian's eyes went wide. "What? I've never heard anything about that."

Gavin chuckled. "I doubt even the slavers know. It's buried deep in the effect. There is a link between every slave brand through the world's ambient magic, almost like some gigantic invisible web. I have no idea how the old man did it, but it is breathtaking in its artistry. Matter of fact, there are tendrils of power like the links between brands I haven't even identified yet; maybe they link the slaves to the brands that marked them...or maybe the slavers somehow. I don't know, because I've never watched a brand in action with all the knowledge I now have. But that's the solution, don't you see? If I can successfully remove one slave brand, I can remove them *all*."

"And what if I told you I cannot support you using some innocent as a glorified laboratory tool? What if I told you it's wrong and you need to choose between our friendship and continuing in this?"

Gavin turned and locked gazes with Lillian. He stood silent for quite a while, with the rising and falling of his chest as he breathed the only indication he was alive.

"If that is truly how you feel, Lillian, I respect your opinion and your values...but I do not share them. You know the Word of Transmutation to teleport yourself home. You may do so whenever it suits you, but I have work to do."

* * *

"He really *said* that?" Kiri asked as she leaned forward from her relaxed pose on the sofa.

Kiri and Lillian faced each other across Kiri's private sitting room, once again having shared a meal. They mirrored each other in their poses, leaning against the arm of the sofa with their legs folded beneath them. They each held a crystal glass containing one of the finest vintages of wine produced in recent years, a post-prandial refreshment.

Lillian nodded. "I've never seen him like this, Kiri. Well...no, that's not quite right. I've seen him aloof and unyielding toward others but never *us*."

"Did you mention it to Braden or Wynn?"

"Oh, no. I never considered it. Wynn is thoroughly enjoying his role as lead instructor for Gavin's new apprentices; I've never seen him so happy. And Braden? Well, Braden is just as happy I think. He's watching and learning how to deconstruct an artifact no one today understands. I've seen him sitting off by himself, doodling ideas for imbued items using designs based on what he's learning at Gavin's side. If I asked them to leave, they'd probably leave...but I can't help but feel they'd always resent me for asking."

"What of Mariana? I haven't seen much of her lately...or the elves, come to think of it."

Lillian smiled. "Mariana's happily ensconced in the barracks and practice spaces for your Cavaliers, and from a few whispers I've overheard, she's making a name for herself. I think there's a part of Mariana that has always regretted being born a Wizard of the Great Houses and Heir to Cothos to boot. I've never seen her happier than when she's training with arms among like-minded souls." Silence descended on the room for several moments, before Lillian lifted her eyes to meet Kiri's. "Are you considering approaching Gavin about his plans?"

Kiri worked her lower lip between her teeth for several moments before she shook her head. "No. I've thought on it during our visit, and I can't bring myself to do it. Like Wynn and Braden, I can't help but feel he'd stop if I asked him…but I'd also be lying if I said there wasn't a part of me that's afraid he'd turn his back on me and keep following his course. We are from such different worlds, Lillian, but I can't stop thinking about him. I keep hoping…well, it's silly I suppose."

"Kiri Muran, we've shared so much, silly and otherwise. You never need to censor your thoughts with me."

Kiri lowered her eyes to gaze at the floor. "I…I keep hoping he'll visit and tell me how much he has missed me and never wants to leave me again. I never thought being so close to someone could feel like I'm so far away."

"You could always go to him. I know it isn't usually done that way, but there's nothing saying you can't."

Kiri shook her head. "It'll never work, Lillian. I'm a—*the* Crown Princess. I will be Queen of Vushaar someday, and it's always been discussed and assumed that my marriage would be one of state to ensure the best future for Vushaar."

"I can see that," Lillian said, "but was your parents' marriage a marriage of state?"

Kiri lifted her gaze to a portrait hanging on the wall over Lillian's left shoulder. It depicted her parents standing somewhere on the Claymark Estate, after their wedding but before Kiri. They stood close together, her father's arms around her mother's shoulders, and they looked so…happy.

A wistful smile curled Kiri's lips as she shook her head. "No. It wasn't. Grandfather was—and still is—the major grain supplier in the country, so a lot of people tried to say it was a kind of dynastic marriage between the royal family and the family of the country's greatest merchant prince. But that wasn't it at all. I asked Father once when I was thirteen or so and had overheard someone saying something to that effect, and Father said that he'd never met anyone who felt more *right* to him...someone who accepted him as Terris Muran and not the Crown Prince of Vushaar. He told me Mother was the only woman he ever met who didn't seem to care he was the second most powerful person in the land and later the King."

"So...it's not like there isn't precedent for a non-dynastic marriage. Besides, Gavin being Kirloth is probably prestigious enough that no one would gainsay you setting your sights on him, if he's truly who you want."

Kiri shook herself. "We need to change the subject. You have me thinking thoughts I shouldn't be...especially since Gavin has never cared to share his thoughts or feelings."

"What should we discuss then? The weather?"

"It *has* been rather hot lately."

THE CAVALIER PATROLLING the halls of the Crown Princess's personal wing stopped for the briefest moment at the sound of almost-adolescent giggling echoing into the hall.

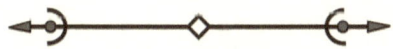

CHAPTER 36

A tense ambiance filled the basement laboratory. The refugee woman Gavin hired stared at the slaver who stood a short distance away and held a slave branding iron. The slaver looked rather tense himself, sweat coating his brow and eyes jerking from point to point all around him. Declan—standing behind the slaver—seemed untouched by the tension in the room, while Braden stood off to one side as if not sure where to stand, and Gavin? He stood between the refugee and slaver, with his back to the staircase and out of their direct line...and his frustration was building.

"You keep me caged up like an animal for weeks," the slaver said, "and you have the nerve to expect me to bark when you say 'speak?' What are you? Insane? Why should I do anything for you?"

The woman flinched away from the slaver's harsh tone, asking, "Will this hurt?"

Gavin directed his attention to the woman. "I don't know if it hurts; I'm sorry." Then, Gavin turned to the slaver, and when he spoke, his voice was slightly deeper and unyielding...the voice his friends had come to associate with 'Kirloth.' "You should do whatever I tell you to do in the hope that you will enjoy a quick and pain-less death, and right this moment, it's looking like it'll be slower and rather agonizing. The age of the slavers is finished and shall not come again. You can help me see to that, or I need to acquire another slaver, someone more agreeable to being useful."

The slaver stared at Gavin for several moments before he swallowed hard and turned to the woman. "Hold your hand up like you're catching an apple. It seems to hurt less that way."

"Hold," Gavin said. He stepped to a small end table off to his right and retrieved one of two specially prepared crystals. He returned to his position and invoked a composite effect, blending Words of Divination, Transmutation, and Illusion, "*Stynohs-Zyrhaek-Zaethyx.*"

Any wizard within a block and a half of the house felt the resonance of Gavin's power, and the crystal in Gavin's hand took on a kaleidoscopic radiance as the effect took hold.

Gavin nodded in satisfaction, looking at the crystal through his *skathos* before lifting his attention to the slaver and saying, "Proceed."

The slaver lifted the hand holding the branding iron and pressed it against the palm of the woman's hand. Gavin closed his eyes and concentrated with his *skathos* just in time to 'watch' the effect take hold. He saw the power embedded in the brand snake outward through the woman's arm and suffuse her entire being, manifesting as the brand everyone knew so well on her left shoulder. It was over in an instant, and the woman collapsed to her knees as she gasped for air. Still concentrating on his *skathos*, Gavin saw two tendrils extend from those suffusing the woman: one reached out and merged with the brand and the other the slaver.

"Oh, my," Gavin whispered. "Now, isn't *that* interesting…"

GAVIN SAT at the table in his lab. Even though the composite effect he invoked recorded everything he witnessed through his *skathos* to the crystal he held, Gavin still felt it important to write down his first-hand observations, and he was re-reading those observations in preparation for calling on the Illusion portion of the crystal to watch the woman's branding a second time at a much slower speed. After all, he didn't want to miss anything about how the branding effect worked.

"Gavin?"

Gavin turned and saw Lillian standing at the base of the stairs. He quirked his eyebrows in a silent question as he gestured at a nearby chair. Lillian crossed the space between her and the chair, taking a seat.

"Am I still welcome here?"

Gavin chuckled. "Lillian, you were never unwelcome. Just because we have different values and opinions on one, specific matter doesn't mean we're suddenly at odds in all things." A faint memory of a conversation between two friends—more of an impression, really—floated up to the forefront of his mind from the gray mists surrounding his consciousness. "I *always* will be your friend."

"Is there any way I can help?"

"Is that what you really want to do? Or do you feel as though you should help to prove yourself?"

"You're working to remove Kiri's slave brand. I suppose it's naïve to think something that's caused such pain and suffering could be removed without inflicting pain and suffering in the process."

Gavin shook his head. "No, Lillian. That's not naïve at all. In fact, I would prefer to remove Kiri's brand without anyone suffering, but I don't have that luxury. I need to understand how the brand affects people, because the diagrams of how to make the brands doesn't explain that. There's no way they could...beyond a bird's-eye view anyway."

"So...Gavin...how can I help?"

"Well, there is something. I was going to ask Braden to do it, but perhaps, it would be more instructive for him to watch through his *skathos* instead."

"Why do I get the impression whatever this is won't be that much fun for me?"

"Well, I certainly didn't enjoy it when it happened to me," Gavin said. "I want my pet slaver to brand you, and I don't want you wearing your medallion in plain sight when he does it."

Lillian frowned. "Won't that…kill him?"

"Lillian, he was never going to leave this project alive anyway, and at no point have I promised he would. Besides, it may not kill him outright; there's always the chance that it'll leave him with your House Glyph burned into his forehead or palm but still alive. I've watched a commoner get branded through my *skathos*, and it was far more instructive than I could've imagined. Now, the only thing left is to see how the protection against wizards being branded activates."

Lillian sat in silence for several moments, her eyes and face angled down. After several moments, she lifted her face to Gavin once more and took a deep breath. She grasped her medallion by its chain and pulled the neck of her dress out from her shoulders far enough to drop the medallion inside and said, "When do we start?"

A SHORT TIME LATER, the slaver once again stood in Gavin's laboratory holding the branding iron and facing Lillian. Declan stood behind him, a dagger at the ready, and Braden stood off to one side.

"So, I'm supposed to brand some other poor girl?" the slaver said. "You creating yourself a personal harem or something?"

Gavin shifted his attention to the slaver and lifted one eyebrow. It seemed the ambient temperature dropped just a bit under that gaze.

"Uhm…yes, well…girlie, I want you to hold your hand out like you're catching an apple."

Lillian lifted her right arm and curled her fingers as requested. Gavin held the second crystal and invoked the composite effect to record the proceedings once more before saying, "Proceed."

The slaver started lifting the brand, and Gavin closed his eyes to concentrate on his *skathos*. To his *skathos*, he saw Declan and the slaver as people-shaped forms of energy that pulsed in time with their heartbeats. Lillian, Braden, or any wizard looked to be roiling, seething masses of kaleidoscopic power just barely contained within their physical forms. Gavin could approximate their individual strengths as arcanists by how turbulent the power's motion within them was and how bright it glowed. His former apprentices were bright, but if he focused on himself, the radiance of his power *hurt*.

The moment the slave brand touched Lillian's palm, Gavin saw the embedded power reach out to her as a series of snake-like tendrils, just as before. This time, though, Gavin watched as Lillian's power latched onto those tendrils like a predatory beast and sucked them into her very core, swirling like a torrent or whirlpool.

With no warning whatsoever, Lillian's power destroyed the tendrils in a flash and surged into the brand. Gavin felt and watched Lillian's power twist and blacken the brand as her power surged through it and into the slaver. The slaver screamed.

Gavin watched through his *skathos* as Lillian's power subsumed every facet and section of the slaver's being drowning out the man's life force with the overflow erupting out the man's eyes and mouth as he screamed. Gavin had no doubt he'd see familiar eldritch flames leaping toward the ceiling if he opened his eyes. At long last, Lillian's power stopped cascading into the slaver, and what was left concentrated in the man's forehead, burning the Glyph of Mivar into the man's flesh...just before the corpse collapsed to the floor.

Gavin released his grip on the crystal to stop the effect's recording of the happenings and opened his eyes. He saw what he expected to see, the corpse of a slaver laying on the floor. When he turned his attention to Lillian, he saw a reaction he remembered all too well: she herself looked ready to drop.

"*Pharhyk*," Gavin invoked, causing a nearby chair to slide across the floor to stop just behind Lillian. He extended his left hand to her, and she grasped his forearm with both her hands as he helped her ease onto the chair.

"Did it make you feel like you were going to pass out?" Lillian asked.

Gavin nodded. "If we hadn't been faced with half a dozen slavers, I probably would've slid right down into the alley's muck and had myself a pleasant nap."

"I think...I think I'm just going to sit here for a little bit. Did you see what you needed to see?"

Gavin's mind flashed back to watching through his *skathos* as Lillian's power destroyed the brand's tendrils and smiled. "Yes, I think I did."

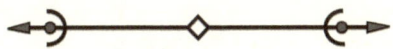

CHAPTER 37

Gavin looked up from the notes in front of him at the sound of footsteps on the stairs. He saw the refugee woman tentatively walking down the stairs. She seemed afraid, and Gavin didn't know whether she was afraid of him or what he was going to say. She reached the basement floor and approached, stopping a respectful distance away from Gavin.

"You wanted to see me?"

Gavin nodded. "It's time. I have everything prepared and am ready to attempt removing the mark. Are you ready?"

The woman nodded and visibly forced herself not to wring her hands. "I suspected that's why you wanted to see me. Before I came downstairs, I told my children I loved them very much...in...in case...it doesn't go as planned."

"Well, let's see what we can do to ensure events follow the plan. Shall we?"

The woman gave Gavin what looked to be a rather cautious smile. "I like that idea. What do I need to do?"

"Follow me over here."

Gavin turned and led the woman across the basement to the ring set into the floor. It seemed to sparkle just a bit, regardless of whether it was within direct light, and it was a smaller twin to the ring in the floor of the arena back in Tel Mivar. Gavin entered the ring, and the ambient power seemed to vanish. The woman followed him into the ring and frowned.

"What is it?" Gavin asked.

"I'm not sure. I can't describe it, really, but my shoulder where the mark is feels…weird."

"Ah. The inside of this ring makes me feel weird, too. It's much more peaceful for me in here."

"It is? Why?"

"The ring acts as an anchor for an anti-magic field. Any magical effects occurring inside the ring cannot affect anything outside, and likewise, any magical effects that occur outside the ring cannot pass across the ring to affect anything inside."

"Oh…that's kind of impressive."

"I know, right? I never dreamed the kind of things I can do now were possible." Gavin squared his shoulders and schooled his face into what he once would've called a poker face. "Are you ready?"

"Will it hurt?"

Gavin lifted his hands as he shrugged. "I honestly have no idea. I've never done this before, and I've not found any records that anyone else has *ever* tried this either. We're charting new waters, here."

"Well, we might as well find out. There's no reason to wait."

Gavin smiled. "Atta-girl."

The woman frowned as she cocked her head to one side, expressing confusion. Before she could say anything, though, Gavin continued.

"This will probably seem a bit icky, but I'm going to prick my thumb and swab the mark on your shoulder with a drop of my blood. I have no diseases that I know of, and this is crucial to the attempt.

The woman nodded.

Gavin withdrew a needle from inside his robe and pricked his left thumb just enough for blood to well up, and he squeezed his thumb with his left index finger and thumb to help the process along once he'd put away the needle. Once Gavin had a respectable amount of blood that was trying to run down his thumb to his palm, Gavin shifted his right hand to swab his blood across the slave mark adorning the woman's left shoulder. The moment his blood touched the mark, the woman let out a little gasp, and Gavin felt a crackling sensation through his *skathos*. Not waiting another moment, Gavin focused his mind on his intent, pressed his left palm into the woman's shoulder, and invoked a composite effect, "*Idluhn-Rhyskaal.*"

Gavin felt his invocation take hold as an extension of his power slammed into the slave mark and its tendrils suffused throughout the woman. The Word of Evocation that began his composite effect drenched the slave mark's embedded effect with his own power, and the Word of Transmutation altered his power pouring into the woman in such a way Gavin hoped the protection against wizards being branded would take hold and forcibly eject the mark and its tendrils from the woman. Not knowing how the previous failures had been attempted, he just didn't know if doing so would the kill the woman in the process.

Gavin used his *skathos* to watch his composite effect hammer through the slave mark's power and spread out across the woman's entire being very much resembling a mesh or net or spiderweb, and he couldn't hold back his triumphant grin when that composite effect began mimicking the roiling, seething power he lived with every day…just to a much smaller degree.

The protections for wizards Marcus had built into the slave brands flared, like an eruption of flame, and Gavin heard the woman scream as he felt heat begin radiating from her like smith's forge. What Gavin was not prepared for was his composite effect and the protection for wizards flowing together and begin feeding off of each other almost like catalysts in a runaway reaction. That seething cataract of power swirled and intensified, saturating the woman's entire being in moments. Through his *skathos*, Gavin could actually sense the tendrils of the slave mark separating from the woman, and all at once, the binding that the slave mark represented shattered. The power released as an eldritch inferno erupting from the woman's mouth as she screamed.

After an agonizing eternity that was a few heartbeats at most, all trace of both the slave mark and Gavin's composite effect was gone from the woman's body, and she collapsed to her knees, gasping for breath and drenched in sweat.

But she was alive and whole.

* * *

TWO MEN SAT on a wide stoop not too far from the house Gavin was using for his laboratory and school. One looked to be an old man with wild, unkempt snow-white hair and a beard to match; he wore a gray robe that was tattered and frayed around its hem, and he held a block of wood in his right hand that he was shaping into a bird with the knife in his left. His associate looked to be a young man with sandy blond hair and a Van Dyke beard; he wore plain, traveling clothes made of resilient canvas and leather to survive the rigors of the road.

"Huh...I wouldn't have done it that way," the old man said as he paid extra attention to shaping the wooden bird's left eye. "Bit of a battering-ram approach, that was."

"Yes, well," the young man said, "when you're strong enough to drive a nail with one strike of the hammer, why bother with the finesse required to use a screw? Besides, he did it, didn't he?"

"Heh...he did indeed."

"We should be going. Staying here too long could give others...ideas."

The old man sighed and pushed himself to his feet. "I suppose you're right."

The young man vanished in the blink of an eye as the old man tossed the knife over his shoulder, where it disappeared into nothingness. He tossed the bird carving into the air, watching the final unneeded chips of wood break off and rain down to the street. The wren chirped as it flapped its wings and flew away. By the time the world's newest bird flew over Gavin's house, the old man had faded away as if he'd never been.

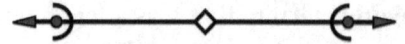

CHAPTER 38

It was mid-morning, and sun shone down on the city from a cloudless sky. In the basement laboratory, Gavin leaned back against the wall, looking at the woman standing before him. She was the slave Declan had hired all those weeks before, and she wrung her hands at her waist, her expression a mixture of anxiety and hope.

"Neela said you removed the slave mark from her. Is that true?"

Gavin nodded. "How long have you been a slave?"

"A little over a year and a half, but it *seems* so much longer. You have no idea how people act when they consider you property."

"Oh, I might have a better idea than you think, but I'll never know the day-to-day experiences you've survived. I'm sure they were fairly horrific at times."

The woman held her silence, but her expression spoke volumes.

"Are you ready to be a slave no more?"

"I would give *anything* not to be a slave anymore…even my life."

Gavin sighed. "Well, I won't lie to you. There is that chance. I'm not going to follow the exact same procedure I did with Neela. We won't be inside the anti-magic ring when I do this, and I've decided I'm going to pour enough power into this that every slave *everywhere* will have their mark removed. And if I'm right, this will have the side effect of death for anyone who's ever used a slave brand."

The woman's anxiety left her expression, replaced by a cold satisfaction. "I hope you're right. Let's do this."

"I have to prick my thumb and swab my blood on your slave mark. Does that bother you?"

"I've washed off worse than your blood…many times."

Gavin didn't really have a reply for that, so he withdrew a needle from his robe and held his hand poised to prick his thumb. A thought working its way through his consciousness stopped him.

"Hmmm…I may need a better conduit than one drop of blood, given the scope of what I hope to achieve. This is probably going to be a bit icky." Gavin turned and stabbed the needle into the wooden support of the staircase's handrail. Then, he turned back to the woman, lifted his right hand, and invoked a Word of Conjuration, "*Nythraex.*"

A gray mist formed in the air above Gavin's right hand and formed a knife that looked beyond razor-sharp. Gavin wrapped his fingers around the knife's hilt and drew the conjured blade across the palm of his left hand, leaving a red line in its wake. Gavin tossed the bloody knife into the air, where it vanished into nothingness, and he pressed his left palm against the woman's slave mark. Once again, he experienced that crackling sensation as the power within his blood started reacting to the magic of slave mark.

Gavin took a deep breath and cleared his mind of everything but his desired effect. Then, he once more invoked the composite effect he'd used just the day before, "*Idluhn-Rhyskaal.*"

Gavin felt his power slam into the woman's slave mark and begin unraveling its effects across her entire being…but this time, he also felt his power traverse the tendrils linking her slave mark to all the others. It was then that Gavin felt his strength start draining like bathwater from a tub once the drain's stopper is removed.

* * *

IT WAS court day once again. Kiri sat on the throne beside her father that had once belonged to her mother, and she forced her expression to remain neutral as a representative from the Jewelers' Guild droned on about how his guild needed a subsidy from the Royal Treasury. After all, no one was spending much money on jewelry...what with the siege and all. Kiri was counting the moments until the man would be quiet, so her father could tell him what a fool he was; well, her father would probably phrase it better than that. Maybe she'd spent too much time around Gavin; he was much more abrupt with people at times.

Kiri's carefully crafted non-expression vanished when she felt a spike of heat in her left shoulder, focused in her slave mark. She never noticed the jeweler fall silent himself, his face betraying an uncertain expression of his own. The spike of heat in her shoulder flared out to invade her entire being, and every muscle she possessed contracted, forcing her to launch to her feet with her back arched and head back and mouth open. Eldritch flames erupted from her mouth as sweat inundated every surface of her body.

By now, the jeweler mimicked her pose, back arched with his head back. An eldritch bonfire erupting from his open mouth, the flames almost licked the throne room's ceiling while he screamed in the ghastliest agony anyone present had ever heard. By now, quite a few other members of the crowd had joined the jeweler in his pose, their screaming a macabre accompaniment to the whole affair.

As suddenly as the screaming began, it ended, and everyone collapsed to the floor. Kiri gasped for breath, her court clothes soaked with sweat and clinging to her body...her left shoulder devoid of any slave mark. The jeweler and the others dispersed throughout the crowd breathed no more, the Glyph of Kirloth burned into their foreheads.

ALL ACROSS THE city and in the siege camp beyond, every former slave lay on the ground gasping for breath, their shoulders marked no more. It would be several days before word reached the capital that no slave marks existed anywhere in Vushaar.

* * *

ALL ACROSS THE Kingdom of Tel, those with slave marks found themselves gasping in the wake of excruciating pain and free once again. Along with them, almost one in a hundred lay dead wherever they had stood, the Glyph of Kirloth burned into their foreheads as if they themselves had tried to brand Gavin…the entire Royal Family of Tel—Leuwyn, his two sons, and his wife—and several members of the Royal Guard among them.

* * *

THE WOMAN PUSHED herself up to her hands and knees when she'd finally regained enough strength to do so. She was free. Her shoulder bore no mark, and it was all because of…him. She let out a little cry as she hurriedly moved to Gavin's side. He lay unconscious on the floor of the laboratory. He still breathed, but it was incredibly faint.

She jerked her head up as the door slammed against the wall, the footfalls a thunderous cascade as Gavin's apprentices—even those he called 'apprentice' no longer—rushed down the stairs.

"I didn't…I didn't do anything! I didn't hurt him!" She said, her voice laden with anxiety and fear.

Lillian knelt and pulled the woman to her feet as Mariana, Braden, and Xythe knelt around Gavin's insensate form. Lillian drew her away from Gavin and held her in a tight embrace.

"We know you didn't harm him," Lillian said, her voice soft and soothing. "You're safe."

More footfalls sounded on the stairs, and everyone looked up. Declan stopped on the landing in the middle of the stairs, his breathing ragged.

"What happened?" Declan asked between gasps. "A session of court was just interrupted by several nobles in the crowd dying like they'd tried to brand Gavin."

"We don't know," Mariana said. "We felt an incredible surge of power and came here to find Gavin like this."

"He removed my slave mark," the woman said, her voice barely loud enough to carry up to Declan. "He said he was going to try to remove them all."

"By the gods..." Braden whispered, his rumbling voice drenched with awe.

"Let's take him to his room in the palace," Lillian said. "Declan, find Elayna and bring her to Gavin's room in the palace. She's probably in the Elven Embassy."

"Wynn," Braden said as he moved to Gavin's head, "you get his feet, and I'll get his shoulders."

"Never mind that," Xythe said, pushing everyone between her and Gavin aside. "I'll carry him myself. Hold the doors for me."

"Doors?" Lillian said, her voice incredulous. She took a deep breath and invoked a Word of Transmutation, "*Paedryx*."

A sapphire arch almost as wide as the laboratory table rose up out of the basement's floor. Once it was half-again as tall as Xythe, it stopped rising and flashed, becoming a doorway to the palace courtyard. Xythe—holding Gavin in her arms—led the Apprentices through the gateway with Lillian bringing up the rear, as the gateway would close when she passed through it.

A NUMBER of Cavaliers moved their hands to their swords when the gateway first appeared in the palace courtyard. Even so many days after the assault on the palace, everyone entrusted with the safety of the palace complex still had a bit of hyper-vigilance about them. None of them recognized Gavin cradled in Xythe's arms, and the dracon stopped when she processed how many soldiers were ready to draw steel. Lillian, Mariana, Wynn, and Braden fanned out around Xythe, eyeing the Cavaliers, and their expressions were not friendly at all. Jasper was almost invisible behind Xythe.

"The first one to draw steel *dies*," Mariana said as she lifted her right hand and manifested an orb of power. "I suggest everyone remove their hands from their sword hilts to lessen the temptation."

Soon, Lillian, Wynn, and Braden held their own orbs of power, and all four scanned the assembled Cavaliers for any hint of movement. After several moments of no motion whatsoever from the Cavaliers, Lillian turned and led the group into the palace; she'd only seen Gavin leave his room once, and she hoped she remembered the way.

LILLIAN TOOK ONLY two wrong turns before they encountered one of the palace's servants. The servant was kind enough to lead them to the room that had been set aside for Gavin on the fourth floor of the residential wing. They had just arrived in Gavin's room, Xythe gently laying him on the bed and Mariana and Wynn removing his shoes when footfalls that sounded like a charging brigade of soldiers echoed down the halls. Braden stepped to the door and glanced outside. He stepped back from the door and almost whispered, "Oh, damn…"

"What is it, Braden?" Lillian asked.

Braden didn't have a chance to answer before Kiri came into the room, the squad of Cavaliers that served as her personal protection detail taking up positions in the hall outside.

At the sight of Gavin laying on the bed, by all indications dead, she froze mid-step with her hand half-way to covering her mouth in shock.

"Is…is he dead?" Kiri asked.

Lillian rushed to her friend's side, taking in her left shoulder now free of a slave mark, and pulled Kiri into an embrace. "No, Kiri, not yet. I've sent Declan to find Elayna."

Kiri's eyes filled with moisture, and outwardly, she didn't respond to Lillian's embrace. Everyone who cared to look could see her self-control warring with her emotions as she stared at Gavin laying on the bed.

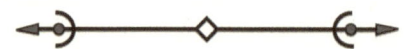

CHAPTER 39

No one was really aware of how much time passed after Kiri's arrival when a commotion in the hall outside drew the attention of everyone in Gavin's room. Kiri turned toward the door, and Lillian motioned for everyone else to stay with Gavin as she followed her friend outside.

Outside, two Cavaliers stood in the middle of the hall, blocking Declan's path with Elayna behind him. The bard didn't possess any *visible* weapons, but there was no denying the sheer malice and threat he radiated.

"Step aside if you want to live," Declan said.

"There's four of us and one of you," one of the two Cavaliers said. "Besides, what are you going to do, sing us to death?"

"If he doesn't kill you," Kiri said, drawing blades hidden within her court attire, "I will. Last warning...stand aside and let them pass."

The shocked expressions of the two Cavaliers closest to Kiri betrayed their lack of knowledge that she carried blades, and their fellows joined them in that shocked state of affairs when they glanced behind them and saw the Crown Princess holding those blades with more than passing familiarity. The two Cavaliers blocking Declan and Elayna stepped aside, angling themselves to put their backs to either wall.

Elayna pushed past Declan and strode to enter Gavin's room. Kiri turned to follow her, returning her blades to their hiding places as Declan moved to her side.

"Was it really necessary to draw steel on your own guards?" he asked.

Kiri shrugged. "I don't know how much time Gavin has, and I didn't want him to die while they postured and dithered. Besides, how far away from drawing steel were you?"

Declan chose not to answer that question, and the Cavaliers in the hall glanced to one another, all wondering what steel Declan had to draw.

"How is he, Elayna?" Kiri asked as she watched her friend lean over Gavin.

"I can just barely feel his life-beat," Elayna said. "It's faint, very faint."

"Whatever you need," Kiri said, "name it."

Elayna took a deep breath and released it as a slow sigh. "I fear he is beyond the hope of herbs and apothecaries. I shall pray."

Elayna squared her shoulders and closed her eyes, concentrating on that connection to her ancestor she had felt all her life...the elven woman the world knew as Xanta. She slowly rubbed her hands together as she recited the words to the prayer that would call upon her faith and channel Xanta's power for healing. Within a moment of completing the prayer, a healthy green glow the color of nature—vibrant and alive in the newness of Spring—surrounded her right hand. Elayna reached out and took Gavin's hand in hers as she closed her eyes to concentrate on channeling as much of Grand-mother's power as She would allow.

But Elayna rocked back on her heels as a solid wall of shim-mering golden power unfolded across her senses, cutting her off from channeling any power into Gavin. A voice spoke with such power and strength within her mind it rattled her consciousness like thunder rattles windows.

YOU SHALL NOT INTERFERE

ELAYNA RELEASED GAVIN'S HAND, allowing it to fall back to rest upon the mattress as she weaved to regain her balance.

"What happened?" Kiri asked. "What's wrong?"

Elayna blinked her eyes and moved her head like she was trying to shake her thoughts clear. Finally, she looked up to meet Kiri's gaze and said, "I can do nothing for him."

"So, he's beyond all hope then?" Kiri asked, her voice catching. "He's dying?"

"No, child, that's not what I meant. Grandmother and I are not *allowed* to intervene. I was blocked from channeling Her healing power into Gavin."

"Blocked?" Braden asked. "Blocked by whom?"

"I don't know," Elayna said, but she suspected. Only another god could block a god's influence, and only one god chose gold for a primary color.

Kiri looked for all the world like she was about to collapse in a torrent of tears, but suddenly, her expression hardened as her eyes shifted from wet with moisture to a glare. She pivoted on her heel and strode from the room, confused Cavaliers trailing in her wake.

* * *

KIRI APPROACHED HER OBJECTIVE, and by now, her glare was such no one who met her dared say a word. She reached the doors to the palace's shrine to Valthon and turned to the two Cavaliers who'd been with her since she left the throne room.

"You will wait out here, no matter what you hear in there," Kiri said, her voice the personification of death. "I'll have the head of anyone who enters."

Without waiting for a response, Kiri opened the doors, stepped inside, and slammed the doors closed. The guards heard the latches slam into place moments thereafter.

THE SHRINE WAS devoid of life, except for her. Kiri scanned the room, her eyes finally settling on the statue at the front of the room. Windows on one wall allowed sunlight to light the room, and the remembrance candles burning beside the doors filled the shrine with the pleasant scent of lavender and citrus.

Kiri strode down the center aisle, her arms rigid at her side and her hands balled into fists. She stopped about ten feet from the altar, about fifteen feet from the pedestal upon which the statue stood, and her glare felt sufficient to reduce the statue to lava right there.

"You damned bastard," Kiri said, spitting out the words through clenched teeth. "This is all your fault. I swear the day after I inherit the throne this shrine will be destroyed, even if I have to swing the hammer myself!"

For several moments, silence reigned.

"That's a very strong oath, young lady," a voice worn with age said from behind Kiri. "Be sure you mean it."

Kiri looked over her shoulder and saw an old man sitting on the front pew. His snow-white hair was in wild disarray, and he wore a gray robe that was tattered and frayed around the hem at his ankles. Kiri recognized him in an instant, but this time, he exuded none of the grandfatherly rascal of her past encounters.

"You told me all I had to do to save my father and my people was to find a man named Gavin Cross," Kiri said, turning fully to face the old man.

"So I did," the old man said, "and are your people not saved? Ivarson's siege is broken, whether he realizes it yet or not. The wizards sent by the Necromancer of Skullkeep to support him are blocked, and now, he has an uprising of former slaves on his hands. Not even Lornithar's hosts could breach this city's walls, Kiri; the force that remains out there is no match for the loyal elements of the Vushaari army, not to mention the Cavaliers. I fail to see the problem."

Kiri couldn't maintain the rage any longer. She seemed to collapse in upon herself as she staggered backward into the altar and slid down it to sit on the floor. Her grief was back full force now, and then some.

"You never told me I'd...I...that he'd become such a close friend! He has saved me and others so many times, and the one time he needs someone to save him, I can't."

The old man rose to his feet and walked over to sit by Kiri. He wrapped his left arm around her and pulled her close.

"I know, child," he said, "but consider this. We're not all-knowing, despite what the priests are determined to believe. But suppose that we were. Suppose that we knew everything that would happen to people, and then, suppose that we told you. What point would life have?"

Sobs wracked Kiri's torso. "What am I supposed to do now?"

The old man shrugged. "What everyone does, Kiri; live your life. Don't let grief consume you, and one day—perhaps soon, find happiness where you can."

"He never even told me goodbye."

"How could he?" the old man asked. "He knew he didn't have the strength to walk away from you. Now, I'm sorry, but I have to go. A number of people are rather worried about you."

"DID SHE HAVE A DAGGER OR A KNIFE?" Roth asked, his voice a harsh growl.

Roth Thatcherson stood outside the sealed shrine of Valthon, and the object of his ire was the former lieutenant—now a sergeant —of Kiri's personal guard.

The man glanced at the king standing over Roth's shoulder and stammered incoherence.

Roth's glare intensified, and he grabbed the soldier by his uniform tunic. "Did you even think to look?"

Before the man could respond in any way, the doors of the shrine swung open on their squeaky hinges. Roth, Terris, and the Cavaliers present—well, minus the former lieutenant—turned to look into the shrine.

Kiri sat on the far side of the shrine at the foot of the altar, her arms wrapped around her shins and pulling her knees to her chest while she cried. Terris's hurried stride carried him to her in short order. Roth turned his attention back to the man he was assaulting and pushed him away.

"Get out of here," he said. "We'll talk later."

Roth turned his attention to the sole remaining Cavalier from Kiri's protective detail. "Go to the barracks, and send four of Her Highness's personal detachment here. They can stand duty with His Majesty's men and I."

Roth turned to pull the doors closed once more, watching a father cradling his grieving daughter in his arms.

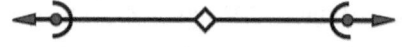

CHAPTER 40

In the days following Kiri's visit to the Shrine of Valthon, she slipped further and further away, withdrawing into herself. She wasn't truly catatonic, but neither did she seem all that interested in the world around her. No one—not even her father or Lillian—could break through Kiri's all-consuming grief, and as the passing days became weeks, she began losing weight, given her infrequent meals, and soon was little more than a shadow of her former self.

* * *

It was so surreal. Gavin was standing in a void. There was no sound, no smells. He was surrounded by nothingness, and yet he could see himself as well as if he were standing in the noon-time sun. The most unsettling yet was that it felt like he was standing on something solid. And then…Gavin was not alone.

Bellos stood in front of him. No poof of smoke, no fanfare, nothing…he was just *there*. He was about Gavin's height with sandy-blond hair and deep blue eyes, and he seemed no more than a few years Gavin's senior. He wore a Van Dyke beard, not unlike Gavin's mentor, though this man's goatee ended in a point. He wore gold robes, and a gold dragon-head amulet rested atop his sternum.

"Forgive me, Gavin, for making you wait so long," Bellos said as he approached and extended his right hand.

Gavin accepted the man's hand almost out of reflex, and as he shook hands, he asked, "Am I dead?"

The man smiled just a bit. "No, not yet. Oh, make no mistake; without intervention, your odds are not good. But I brought you here to make an offer."

Gavin sighed and rubbed his face with his left hand. "If my suspicions are correct, what you offer is something I'm not sure I want."

Bellos made an offering gesture with his left hand, and armchairs appeared beside them. "Let's sit and discuss the matter. Perhaps, you see something I do not, and just maybe, I see something you do not."

* * *

VALERA STOOD in the corridor outside the Chamber of the Council, having just walked out on a particularly fierce argument between several of her fellow magisters. Her limited authority as Eldest of the Council, more a position of respect than any true authority, was no longer sufficient to keep the factions on the Council in line. She was just about to offer a prayer for guidance to Bellos when she heard a whoosh of fire above her head.

Valera frowned as she started to lift her gaze; the only things above her head were…the sconces. The elderly wizard gaped open-mouthed as the sconces mounted high on the walls erupted sequentially in golden flame and continued to burn as they had not for almost six hundred years.

Tears of joy filling her eyes, Valera spun around and looked at the gold hand-plate that rested just beside the door to the Chamber of the Council. No longer did it look dull and tarnished…oh, no. It now shone a bright, vibrant gold that sparkled and reflected the light. Once all the sconces within the Tower were burning a golden flame, the braziers evenly spaced around the College's walls erupted with golden fire.

Soon thereafter, the street lamps throughout the city that had been dormant for over half a millennium erupted with golden fire, startling every citizen who saw them and re-kindling a hope that many had long ago dismissed as folly. Finally, the braziers atop the guard towers that were spaced around the city's massive walls erupted as well. All the sconces and braziers of the city having finally lit, the final golden flame erupted above the Tower of the Council itself. With the spires of the Tower formed so much like the fingers and thumb of a person's hand, a new generation finally saw the complement to that design: a massive orb of golden fire that dwarfed the puny flame burning atop the harbor's lighthouse.

* * *

Terris sat on a stone bench at the edge of his great-grandmother's garden. The sun had just set. He still remembered how much he enjoyed helping his wife, Rionne, tend the garden, even though he wasn't much use for growing things, and it was here that he came to seek solace when he could find it nowhere else.

"I'm losing her, Rionne," the king said as he gazed at the small pond in the garden's center, "and I don't know what to do. It's worse than after you died. She stopped eating yesterday. I can't bear to see her like this. I want to make it better, but I don't know how."

The gravel crunched behind him, and Terris looked over his shoulder. Roth approached with Lillian at his side.

"How is she?" Terris asked.

Lillian sighed and lowered her head. "I tried, Your Majesty, but she still won't eat. She drank a little bit, but not a lot."

Terris inhaled to speak, but before he could, bright light drew his attention. He turned and looked up at the tower that served as the royal residence. Golden radiance almost brighter than the sun shone from a corner room on the fourth floor, but before anyone could speak, a column of fire that did not burn nor radiate heat erupted from the flagstones in front of him. The column deposited a man-shaped figure in a purple robe with gold runes on the sleeve-cuffs and cowl of the robe's hood. The robe's hood was pulled up over the figure's head, and deep, impenetrable shadow hid the figure's face, a pair of eyes the color of flame all that could be seen.

Lillian gasped as she recognized the new arrival.

"I am Nathrac," the figure said, his voice so deep everyone present felt it resonate against their bones, "Chief of the Citadel Guard and commander of the garrison at Tel Mivar. You three bear witness: the Archmagister is named."

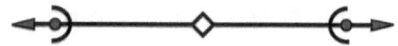

WHAT'S NEXT?

The story continues in "Archmagister," and the paperback will be available soon.

Visit your favorite retailer and search for ISBN:
9781733473569

* * *

Want to keep up-to-date and receive exclusive content?

Sign-up for my newsletter:
kfplink.com/g8i

RATE THIS BOOK

Did you enjoy this story? If you did, please consider leaving a review.

Reviews are the lifeblood of visibility for independent authors, especially on the eBook retailers. The more reviews a book has, the more visible it will be on the retailers' sites.

I appreciate all reviews…good, bad, or indifferent.

If you would like to leave a review, visit this book's review page (http://kfplink.com/596).

AUTHOR'S NOTE
7 FEBRUARY 2019

First and foremost, thank you for reading…both the novel and these notes! I hope you enjoyed *Into Vushaar*!

Please, consider leaving a review where you acquired this novel. Reviews are crucial to independent authors (like myself and many, many others). I appreciate all reviews…good, bad, or indifferent.

If you're so inclined, here are the best ways to contact me:

- The Contact Page of my site (valthon.net/contact)
- Facebook
- Of course, you can also send me an email: sendrobmail@knightsfallpress.com.

If you're still reading this, thanks for the dedication…or perhaps the curiosity. :) As I said above, I hope you enjoyed reading *Into Vushaar*. Thank you.

TYPOS

Typos and little slips in grammar are the bane of any author. Unfortunately, they are almost impossible to eradicate completely. I can show you many traditionally published books—twenty years old and more—that have a 'whoopsie' here and there.

That being said, if you find a typo or something that seems to be an error in grammar, please do not hesitate to contact me at typos@knightsfallpress.com.

I will periodically collate any emails and produce an updated PDF and eBook files, and I'll make an announcement in my monthly newsletter when the updates have been published.

ACKNOWLEDGMENTS

There's an old saying: it takes a village to raise a child. I don't know if that's true or not, but it certainly seems true where publishing a novel is concerned. You would not be reading this were it not for contributions from several people.

This work would not be what it is without the editing efforts of Keri Karandrakis.

Did you like the cover? The background image was created by Jakub Skop (https://www.behance.net/JakubSkop).

A special THANK YOU goes out to Lori Carrender who spotted a glaring problem in Chapter 39 (a duplicated section). Thank you, Lori!

Without my grandparents, Bob & Janice Miller, I honestly don't know where I'd be today; my grandfather taught me to read and love reading, and my grandmother taught me to develop and exercise my imagination. This novel (not to mention my life in general) certainly would not have happened without my parents, Vernon & Judy Kerns.

ADDITIONAL ACKNOWLEDGMENTS

I've been working on this Fantasy story since the vicinity of 2000, and during that time, many people have provided feedback, thoughts, inspiration, or education in varying amounts. I greatly appreciate their time and contribution, and if you think your name should be on this list but don't see it, I truly apologize for the oversight. If you're curious, the list is alphabetical by last name.

Shanalyse Barnett
Naomi Haines
Jon Hartmann

THE NOVELS OF ROBERT M. KERNS

For a complete and accurate listing of all publications, both currently available and forthcoming, please visit Knightsfall Press.

Knightsfall Press - Books

https://knightsfall.press/books

SO...WHO'S THE AUTHOR?

Robert M. Kerns (or Rob if you ever meet him in person) is a geek, and he claims that label proudly. Most of his geekiness revolves around Information Technology (IT), having over fifteen years in the industry; within IT, he especially prefers Servers and Networks, and he often makes the claim that his residence has a better data infrastructure than some businesses.

Beyond IT, Rob enjoys Science Fiction and Fantasy of (almost) all stripes. He is a voracious reader, with his favorite books too numerous to list.

Rob has been writing for over 20 years, and *Awakening* is his debut novel.

Connect with Rob at knightsfall.press.

facebook.com/RobertMKerns

amazon.com/author/robertmkerns

bookbub.com/authors/robert-m-kerns